# MAN LAW

## PRIVATE PROTECTORS SERIES

## ADRIENNE GIORDANO

ALG PUBLISHING

Edited by Gina Bernal

Copyedited by Elizabeth Neal

Cover Design by Lewellen Designs

Author Photo by Debora Giordano

Print Edition ISBN: 978-1-942504-57-3

Digital Edition ISBN: 978-1-942504-56-6

*For Dad, who taught me what it means to never give up. I miss you every day.*

# MAN LAW

## PRIVATE PROTECTORS SERIES

### ADRIENNE GIORDANO

ALG PUBLISHING

# 1

*Man Law: Never mess with your best friend's sister.*

"AH, SHIT." VIC ANDREWS, BUTTHEAD SUPREME, LISTENED TO the churn of the ocean's waves. Or was it his life skittering off its axis?

Gina laughed that belly laugh of hers and he couldn't help smiling. He extracted himself from her lush little body and rolled off. The St. Barth sand stuck to his back. Yep, they'd worked up a sweat. Salty sea air invaded his nostrils and he inhaled, letting the moisture flood his system.

*Jesus Hotel Christ.*

What had he been thinking? He'd been heading back to his room after closing down the resort's bar and there she was, the girl—er, woman—of his dreams, crying on the beach. No condition for her to be in after witnessing her brother's marriage to the love of his life.

Vic didn't mention the fact it was 3:00 a.m. and she was

alone on a secluded beach where any drunken asshole, like him, could have at her. Although technically he wasn't drunk. Buzzed maybe. Big difference. Besides, they'd been at a wedding. Buzzed was allowed.

Gina moved and he finally turned toward her. "I'm—"

"No, absolutely not," she said. She swiped at her curly mane of dark hair. Her face gave away nothing, but that meant squat. Gina knew how to hide bad moods.

The whoosh of the ocean lapping against the shore distracted him and he stared into the blackness.

"What did I say?" he asked.

"You were going to apologize. I don't want to hear it."

Apologize? Him? "I'm not sorry." He touched her arm. "Are you?"

*Please don't say you're sorry. Please.*

That would be all he needed. He'd just freakin' obliterated the sister rule Mike had invoked nearly a million—maybe two million—times. The sister rule was Man Law, and Man Laws were about the only rules Vic followed.

He only wanted to check on her, and before he knew it, voila, the clothes were off, the condom was on and they were humping like bunnies right there on the beach. At least no one saw them. All the well-meaning people were asleep.

Gina brushed sand from her legs and stood to straighten the slip like dress he'd shoved up over her hips. The silky fabric glided over her curves, and the activity in Vic's lower region made him groan. A thirty-five-year-old mother of three, and she was killing him. He should be ashamed.

Screw that.

She was right there. Right there. And, because he'd probably never get the opportunity again, he should grab her and—

"I'm not sorry," Gina said. "Not about the sex. I'm sorry about other things, but this, I loved."

Vic retrieved his pants and stood. Gina and her honesty. Good or bad, she just put it out there and didn't worry about the repercussions. He guessed it came from losing her husband at the age of thirty-one. She had nothing to lose.

"I need to go," she said, watching him with her big brown eyes as the moonlight drenched her face. He put his shirt on. Did she have to look at him that way? Particularly when he wanted a replay.

"Aren't the kids bunking with your folks?"

"They are, but you know how Matthew is. He might search for me."

Fifteen-year-old Matt, her eldest son, took his job as man of the family seriously.

"Right. Okay." Vic motioned toward the resort. "I'll walk you."

Gina held up a hand. "I'll be fine."

Nuh-uh. No way. "I *am* going to walk you. It's late and you shouldn't go by yourself."

Hell, she shouldn't have been out here alone in the first place, but he knew she'd tear him a few new ones if he said it.

She stood there, peering up at him and—*God*—she was fantastic. She had a classic oval face with high cheekbones and a nose he knew she hated. For over two years now he'd imagined running his finger over the little bump in it, but never dared. Every inch of her seemed perfectly imperfect.

*Blown sister rule.*

Gina shoved her fingers through her curls. "We screwed up. I can't believe it. We've been so good."

"We didn't screw up. We had a simultaneous brain fart. Again."

She laughed and shook her head.

"Anyway, walk me to the edge of the beach. You can see my room from there and can watch me go up."

"Gina, what's the big deal? Nobody will know we just—" he waved his hand, "—you know."

"It'll be better if you don't walk me. With his mental radar, Michael is probably waiting by the door. On his damned wedding night. I swear he's a freak. He should stay out of it."

Oh, boy. She was getting fired up. *Maintenance mode.* His friend needed protection. They were both ex-special ops, but they didn't stand a chance against all five foot three of Gina.

"Mike loves you. He's trying to protect you."

"From you? You're his best friend."

Vic ran his hands over her shoulders. "Yeah, but I'm not right for you."

"The circumstances aren't right. That's true, but he doesn't have to keep reminding me."

"He does it to me too."

They strolled to the edge of the beach, and he squeezed her hand. *Don't go. Just stay for a while.* All he wanted was more time with her. Not a lot to ask.

On tiptoes, she brushed a kiss over his lips. A little hum escaped his throat. What the hell was that?

"I had a great time," she said. "You were just what I needed."

"I think a 'but' is coming."

"We can't do this again."

Yep. Not good. "I know."

She pulled her hand from his and hauled ass toward her room. Away from him.

He waited while she went up the stairs and she stopped in front of the window of the room next to hers. A minute later the door opened and Matt came out. He turned and, apparently using his Spidey sense, looked straight at Vic.

*And we're busted.*

## 2

---

*Man Law: Never get caught.*

*Six Weeks Later*

"You got me," Vic said when Lynx picked up the phone.

Whose number had he just called? Knowing Lynx, he probably talked some unsuspecting blonde into letting him use her phone. His old army buddy now worked for the State Department and was completely paranoid about their calls being traced. When Lynx wanted to speak with Vic regarding sensitive matters, he sent a fax—a *fax* for God's sake—from the FedEx store down the street from his D.C. office. Vic would call him back from a secure line—in this case a prepaid cell phone.

"You're in a jackpot."

Vic sat straighter in his desk chair. "Translate." Lynx had

a flair for drama, and being in a jackpot could mean a whole lot of bullshit things.

"The job you did for us last month."

A car horn honked from Lynx's end. He must be outdoors. "The Israel thing?"

"Yeah. The brother is pissed at you."

"There's a shocker. The sheikh should be pissed at someone."

Namely Vic, who'd been hired by a secret U.S. government agency to take out the sheikh's little brother, an Osama wannabe. Mike, the CEO of Taylor Security, liked to call them off-the-books jobs.

"No," Lynx said. "He's pissed at *you*. Your cover is blown."

Vic's shoulders went rock hard. He'd need a sledgehammer to get them loose again.

"What the fuck, Lynx?"

"Hey, I'm just giving you rumor mill here, but it's coming from a good source. My contact at the agency accidentally let me find out. The sheikh threw money at someone who threw money at someone, and now he's got your name."

He shot out of his chair, every muscle in his body seizing. "Son of a bitch. Who gave me up? There can't be six people who knew about that op."

"Please. With the kind of money this guy can toss around, anyone can be bought."

Vic grabbed a pencil from the desk, snapped it in half. "Did I get set up?"

"No. Someone got greedy."

"My ass is in the wind?"

"Yeah. Watch your six. Gotta go."

Vic punched the button to end the call. He'd wipe the phone clean and destroy it later. No harm in being careful.

He stared out his corner office window. Just a businessman enjoying the June sun while the Chicago lunch-hour crowd swarmed the lakefront path. People everywhere.

*Deep breath. Work the problem.* When he'd taken the Israel job, the agency told him it was a solo mission. He'd sneak into the country as a tourist using a fake passport, and if he got into trouble, no one would pull him out.

He didn't get into trouble.

He'd completed his mission.

For his country.

And now his cover was blown. Sure sounded like a setup.

The hammering in his ears started, and he stacked his hands on top of his head. This could be crap. Lynx said it was a rumor.

Vic hustled down the hall to Mike's office and found him at his desk. Early in Vic's army career, he and Mike were Rangers together and they had a history of saving each other's asses.

"I got a problem," Vic said as he stormed into the office and shut the door behind him. He took three deep breaths. *Focus.*

Mike snapped his head from his computer and stared. His dark eyes had an intensity that drove the ladies wild, but these days he was a one-woman man.

"You heard me right. I got a problem."

Vic had maybe uttered those words three times in the fifteen years he'd known Mike. Each time, someone had been injured or dead. Mike leaned back in his swanky leather chair. Felix Unger's contemporary twin could have decorated this place. Everything in chrome, with sharp angles and fancy art. One lone stack of paper sat neatly bundled to the left. Mike didn't go for mess.

"What's up?"

"Remember the job I did last month? Lynx just called. My cover is blown. The sheikh spent big bucks to find out who I was."

Mike squinted. "Those fuckers gave you up?"

"One of them, yeah."

"Do you know who?"

"Hell no. And it's too damned bad, because I'd like to break his fucking kneecaps."

Pain shot through Vic's jaw and he lightened up on the teeth grinding.

"Okay," Mike said. "We can assume they're gonna come after you."

Vic stalked the office. *Crap.* Sweat beaded down the sides of his face and he swiped at it. He was losing it. Fear was not something he allowed himself, but this rattled him. When was the last time that happened? How about never? The last few months had been this way, though. Something gnawed at him, eating away his insides.

Five years with Delta Force ensured he could take care of this problem, but he didn't want to do it in a city that had welcomed him when he left the military.

"We got a whole army of guys here ready to cowboy up," Mike said. "We could even bring a few back from overseas."

They had at least five hundred men in the Middle East protecting U.S. officials.

"Hell, I trained most of them and you want to put them on *me*? I can take care of myself."

*Fuckin' A, bubba.* Maybe Vic's ego was getting in the way, but at thirty-six years old he'd had a whole career of spec ops training. Offering him protection came as an insult.

Mike shook his head. "Hey, asshole, did I say you

couldn't? All I'm saying is we put some muscle around you. Eyes in back of your head."

Eyes in the back of his head. Mike had been his eyes for years now. Wasn't he the one who'd given Vic a job when he needed it? Now they were partners. Mike handled high-end security, and Vic handled the civilian contractor assignments. The neutralizing-terrorists stuff.

"There's no credible threat yet. I'm supposed to tie up manpower for a maybe?"

Mike shrugged. "But you think it's solid, or you wouldn't have come in here."

He had him there, and Vic scratched his head. The hammering in his ears went bye-bye, leaving behind the wilting end of the adrenaline rush.

"I brought a shit storm on us."

Mike rolled his eyes. "Are we having a moment here or what? Don't get ahead of yourself. Let's see what happens. Meantime, put a team together and I'll sign off."

"We may not need them, but I'll put something on paper."

"Right. Let's get someone to sweep your car and your apartment building. Just to be safe."

Vic nodded. "Already on it."

"Watch yourself," Mike said.

This sucked. He should fight this alone, but knew if this guy came after him, he'd need a team. The gut shredding began. People, maybe his friends, were going to die.

And it would be his fault.

GINA HAD THREE CHECKS FOR HER BROTHER TO SIGN, ONE OF which was for a company credit card maxed out by an overseas operative. Michael wouldn't be happy.

A quick stop in the ladies' room on the third floor allowed her to freshen up. She never knew when she'd run into Vic, but it always helped to be prepared. She fluffed her hair, checked her lipstick and gave herself a once-over in the full-length mirror. She wore the champagne pencil skirt and matching silk blouse her sister-in-law picked out. Not bad. Pretty darn good actually.

Roxann liked helping her choose age-appropriate clothes for the thirty-five-year-old she was, rather than the coed look she'd gotten used to. Gina liked her jeans and T-shirts, but maybe she was in a rut. A deep one. For four years now.

The romp on the beach with Vic made her realize she needed to make changes. To stop clinging to the person she'd been before Danny died. That person evaporated when a burning building collapsed on her husband and destroyed her world. Accepting the new normal hadn't come easily, and she'd been fighting it by not altering the tangible things like wearing clothes Danny liked or hanging his uniform in their bedroom closet so she'd see it every day. Keeping things the same meant preserving some part of her cherished husband.

This included focusing on their children. On making them whole when half the parent base had disappeared. Putting their needs first and hers last. Wasn't that what good mothers did? But somehow Gina the woman got lost, buried under the rubble of a burning building.

The time had come to dig out. Enter Roxann and her all-around good taste. Despite her penchant for classic clothes, Roxann could find things with a little funk to them. She made for a great sister-in-law, and Gina reminded Michael every day he'd better not blow it.

With a final flip of her hair, she left the ladies' room and headed for Michael's office. Vic stepped into the hallway, turned and smiled the wicked smile that always sent her heart into overdrive. Add the green eyes, the messy blond hair and the oh-so-sexy goatee, and a girl was done for.

"Hey, you," he said. "What's going on?"

Gina stopped a foot or two in front of him. Otherwise, she'd get whiplash trying to look up at all six foot five of him.

"I have checks for Michael to sign."

He glanced toward Michael's office, then back at her. Something was off. She searched his face, took in the rigid jaw, the crease between his brows and—*bam*—his eyes. Missing today was the twinkling mischief that promised a girl he'd put a smile on her face but wouldn't relinquish his emotional armor while doing so.

"Are you okay?" she asked. "You seem distracted."

He smiled the player smile this time. Like that would work on a woman raising three children. Puh-lease. Surely, she'd lost her mind thinking he'd admit something to her. "Forget I said anything. If you need to talk, let me know."

She stepped around him, but he reached for her and a *zing* shot through her arm. *Damn.* After that glorious night on the beach he couldn't touch her without her body betraying her. Not that he'd touched her since then. On the contrary, he usually acted like she had a skin rash.

"I'm sorry," he said. "You're right. I am distracted. No big deal."

"Fine. Just know my offer stands." She held up the checks. "I need to get these to Michael."

He pushed a curl from her cheek. What was with him today?

"Look at you."

"What?"

Vic shrugged. "You look...different."

Different? What the heck did that mean? "New outfit. Rox helped me with it."

"Ah."

Enough of this already. Because, really, she didn't have time. She was getting nowhere with him when all she wanted was to get *somewhere*. And then he went and did it. He tilted his head and parted his lips just so slightly and a burst of heat exploded inside her. Suddenly, the hallway seemed tight. Closing in as his stare filled the space. At any second, it would occur to him that he should attempt to mask his feelings. The idiot hadn't yet realized his ability to hide from her dissolved two years ago in her basement. That had been the first time she'd noticed *the look* and it still tortured her. Damn him for bringing it all back.

Her fingers twitched at the memory. Kneeling on top of the dryer battling the water that had shot from the pipe and doused her. And Vic staring at her in a way that made her miss having a man to curl up with.

"Holy shit," he had said.

The words cut through the sound of gushing water and penetrated her focused struggle with the valve. "The handle is stuck."

His gaze traveled along the ceiling, darting along the pipelines. Slow. Considering.

"Idiot," she screamed, "the valve is here."

He stepped around the large puddle forming on the cement floor and stormed to the back corner of the basement. "No kidding, but I'm not getting wet when I can cut the main supply."

"The main supply?" *What?*

And suddenly, the river slowed to a trickle. She stared at the pipe, gave it a whack with the wrench. *Bastard pipe.*

For two years she'd been living as a single mom, dealing with appliances that failed, shoveling snow, getting the car serviced. Never mind raising three kids whose moods shifted like swings in the wind. She been doing it all, hadn't she?

Without a man.

Until the flipping water valve got stuck. With Michael not around, she'd been forced to call Vic when all she wanted was to take a bat and smash that stupid valve to a million little bits. Just destroy that piece of crap. She pounded her fists on the washer because she didn't need this evil, blasted, hateful valve making her feel like she needed a man.

Vic stood a few feet from her, hands on his hips. *Did his lips quirk?* She swore they did. No, sir.

She flicked the wrench at him. "Don't you laugh. I'll come down there and beat you to death. You will be bloody if you laugh at me."

He remained silent. One of his better choices, because she was just mad enough to let him have it. She tossed the wrench down, pushed her saturated hair from her face. "I'm sorry I called you an idiot. That was mean." She held her hands wide. "Look at me! I'm soaked."

"Oh, I'm looking."

The rumble in his tone drew her attention and she found him, head tilted, lips slightly parted, eyes focused on her...chest.

The one encased in a soaking-wet tank top.

A *white* one.

With a sheer lace bra underneath. Lovely. Her very own wet T-shirt contest. She gasped and spun away because... well...*Vic*. Never before had he done this, and heat poured into her cheeks.

Two years she'd been without a man's hands on her. Two *long* years without passion. Without sex that left her loose limbed and quivering. And he had the nerve to look at her like he wanted nothing more than to put *his* hands on her.

Wait a second. Why not? She deserved attention. Didn't she?

Besides, he had great hands. Big hands that let a girl know he'd take care of her.

And then she lost her mind.

She jumped off the dryer and charged him. He stepped back. "No you don't, pal. You started this."

Grabbing his shirt, she pulled him down and kissed him with the furious lust of a woman who hadn't had a good screwing in twenty-four months.

He clenched her forearms. "Whoa, Gina." Yet his mouth was still on hers.

She shoved him backward. "Problem?"

"Uh, no. Yes."

Again with the tilted-head thing. "You're doing it again. The look."

"Hell yeah, because, holy shit, you're gorgeous. Between the shirt and the wet curls, you're like some kind of sea nymph. It's making me crazy."

"Okay, so we're on the same page here. The house is empty. Just you and me. Two consenting adults sharing some good old-fashioned fun."

"But."

She ran her fingers under his shirt. "But nothing. Wow, you have amazing abs."

He stepped back again. "Do you seriously want to do this? Because I've been hanging back. You green light me and we're on."

Hanging back? "You've been thinking about it? With me?"

"You just never noticed. You sure about this?"

"You bet I am."

He shoved her against the washer, dropped his jeans and hoisted her up for what she hoped would be a good, hot romp.

He didn't disappoint. On the contrary, he left her feeling just fine about the whole basement-flooding thing. Who knew that she and her brother's closest friend could spark that kind of inferno?

Vic set her on the floor, pulled up his jeans, and Gina dug a dry shirt out of the dryer. Where her wet one had gone was a mystery.

The sound of footsteps above slammed into her. Michael and Matt yelled and she tracked their footsteps from the living room to the kitchen.

Vic stared at the ceiling. "Crap."

At any second they'd be down the steps. She shoved her arms into the shirt. Matthew's. Gah! No time to find her own.

She spun around to button her shorts just as Michael and Matt halted at the bottom of the stairs. She whipped back and faced the openmouthed shock on Michael's face. His gaze moved from Gina, then to Vic, then ever so slowly to the floor.

Tank top found.

Uh-oh.

"Mattie," Michael said, taking in Gina's attire. "Go grab towels."

"The hose blew," Vic said.

*It sure did.* Gina twisted her lips to cage a laugh. How

ridiculous could she be? Her brother and son almost caught her having sex and she was laughing? Horrible.

Michael eyeballed Vic. "Are you fucking kidding me? My *sister*? The widow? With kids?"

*Uh-oh again.*

He shifted to Gina. "And you? You have to be nuts."

*Don't freak.* "Michael, I got soaked. I had clothes in the dryer." *Stop.* She shouldn't have to explain herself. Not to her brother.

He held his hands palm out. "I walked in here, with your thirteen-year-old son, and it appears we interrupted something. At the very least, it was reckless."

"Mike—"

"You shut up. I'm not talking to you now." He put his head down, cracked his neck. "Whatever this is. It's not good. For either of you. A man with a dangerous job and a vulnerable widow with three young kids... Gina, it's emotional suicide." He inched a step closer to Vic. "My goddamned *sister*? You'll wreck her life."

Gina huffed out a breath. "Knock it off. You don't know a thing about what went on here. You're completely out of line."

He snorted. "Am I? Have I said anything that's not true?"

No, he hadn't said anything that wasn't true. And now, Vic stood before her giving her the look that once again made her feel like the damned hallway had shrunk. After the basement incident Vic had kept those big hands of his, among other things, to himself. He'd been cordial. Disgustingly so. Like too much syrup on a stack of pancakes, and the sweetness made her ill. At times, she caught him staring and it infuriated her because they had never once discussed it. That was how it had been until Mike's wedding and their *second* act of spontaneous passion.

Again, Vic went dark, keeping to himself, being sickly sweet. And now she was done.

She grabbed his arm, hauled him into his office and slammed the door. "*Different.* Could you have come up with a more generic word?"

He gawked. "What?"

"What does different mean?"

"Your clothes. They're new, right? That's what I meant."

Of course. She'd given him the opening to talk about his feelings, to really *go* there and own up to his part in the off-the-charts sex, but nothing. Typical.

She propped a hip on the desk and sucked air through her nose. A burning sensation clawed from the pit of her stomach. "I'm in a rut. Trying to figure out who I am. All I am right now is Danny's widow or the kids' mom."

Tears slid down her cheeks and she swiped at them. How could she be crying over something so minor? How did she get to this place and where had she lost herself?

"Please don't cry. I hate that."

He hated it? Please. "Here's the thing, Vic. You're back to being the guy who wants to run screaming from me and *I* hate *that.* We need to talk about what happened with us."

He pinched his eyes shut, opened them again. "Why?"

This man was a major challenge. "Because I want to start dating again, have a man in my life, and there are times when you stare at me a certain way and it makes me think you could be that man. I need you to be honest with me."

He pressed his fingers into his forehead. "About what? I'm not sure what you want me to say."

"I want to know how you feel. I've been a widow for four years and in that time, I've had sex three times. Two of those times were with you, and if it was a blip, a way to pass time, whatever, then fine. But I need to know so I can move on."

"Who else did you have sex with?"

Was he insane? She'd just begged him to talk to her and he wanted to know who the other guy was. Crazy. "I'm not answering that. I don't ask you about your affairs."

He shrugged like she had a point.

"Wait, I will answer that. Why not? He's an accountant that Martha fixed me up with last year. Nice guy." She boosted herself off the desk and faced him. "No spark, though, not like on a beach in St. Barth or a flooded basement."

Vic inched toward her, his eyes on her in that way that made her cheeks fire. This was it. Finally, he'd talk to her.

"You fucked an accountant?"

**3**

---

*Man Law: Always duck and cover and hold on to your ass with both hands.*

SHIT ON A SHINGLE. DID HE *REALLY* SAY THAT? HE NEVER could deal with women. Blame it on his mother, the heroin addict.

Gina's eyes widened into big brown saucers. At any second, she'd go off on him. And then, oh baby, her eyes narrowed and she should have had smoke blowing out her nose. He was torn between wanting to jump out the window or tear her clothes off.

"That's what you're focusing on?" she yelled. "Who do you think you are asking me a question like that? Are you insane?"

That was it. He *was* insane. Had to be. He wanted this woman like he wanted his next breath. With that amazing rack and great ass, she had curves that sent his blood bulleting to the wrong places, and all he ever wanted was to touch her.

But it would never work. Not with his lifestyle. He could die at any time and she'd be alone. Again.

He stepped out of her reach. Just in case.

One fucker of a day so far.

"News flash, jackass," she said. "I wouldn't have *fucked* him, as you so eloquently put it, if you'd made yourself available."

Hey, now. What's that about? He'd have to play this cool. Contain the energy. Compartmentalize. He became a machine when it came to emotions, or lack thereof.

"It's *my* fault you thrashed some nine to fiver?" So much for playing it cool, but, hell, how did he catch the blame for that one?

She poked her finger at him. "You don't get to talk now."

All righty, then. She was on a roll, and as pissed as he was, he'd let her get it out. She had one of those tempers that burned out quick.

"What do you expect from me, Vic? I can't do casual sex, not the way I feel about you, and having a relationship? It's a joke. Even if you were capable of commitment, which God knows you're not."

"I'm capable."

She laughed, but it was sarcastic. "A relationship requires more than four weeks of dating, and from what I've seen, four weeks seems to be your limit."

"Now you get to do commentary on my life?"

That made her step back. Gina, above all else, was a reasonable woman. Mostly. If he couldn't comment on her life, why was it okay for her to comment on his?

She sighed and her shoulders slumped. "You're right. It's none of my business. Besides, what an awful thing to say."

He scratched the back of his head. "You're mad. It's okay."

"No one is entitled to be cruel to someone they care about." She leaned back into the desk. "You terrify me. With your job, I shouldn't let you into our lives. We'd get used to having you around and then one day, you don't come back, and my kids have lost another man. Bottom line, when you're ready to make changes and have a relationship with me, then you can ask about my social life. Until then, butt out."

Mike tore through the door, eyes burning. Shit.

"What's going on?"

"Nothing." Gina said. "We're talking."

"Yeah, hello, half the floor can hear you talking about banging some accountant." He glared at Vic. "What the hell? This is an office. I warned you about this."

He opened his mouth, but Mike had turned to Gina. "Whatever this is, take it outside my building."

Gina's shoulders flew back. "Michael!"

"No. I told you too. He's not going to give up playing cowboy. You know it. You'll give in, though, and when he comes home in a body bag, you'll grieve all over again." Michael shook his head. "I guess losing your first husband wasn't enough for you."

Now he'd gone too far. Mike had an explosive temper and sometimes said dumbass things, which Vic could tolerate, but not this time. He put his hand on Mike's chest. "You made your point. Shut up."

Michael pushed him off. "You're screwing up my sister's life."

"He is not," Gina said in a loud voice.

Michael grunted, locked his lips together and stormed off.

Vic eased his head back and stared at the ceiling. Could it possibly still be the same day? "Not good."

Gina put her hands over her eyes. *Please don't cry. Please.* If she started to cry, he'd put a bullet in his head.

"Are you okay?"

Heading toward the door, she said, "No, I'm not. I'm seriously pissed at you."

THAT EVENING VIC PUSHED THROUGH MIKE AND ROXANN'S kitchen door just as she slid a tray of lasagna into the oven. The smell of cheese and garlic assaulted him and his stomach howled. Roxann ordered the food from a restaurant, because, even though she enjoyed hosting family get-togethers, everyone knew she couldn't cook.

"Sit," she said to him.

"Actually," he said, holding up the empty bottle of wine, "your mom wants more of this red and there's none out there."

Roxann pointed to one of the chairs at the kitchen table.

He stayed standing. He knew Roxi well enough to know she had something on her mind, and it most likely involved the smackdown in his office, but he wouldn't let himself get sucked into some lame-ass conversation about how he screwed up. "What do you need?"

"I need you to have a lobotomy."

Oh, what the fuck? "I'm outta here."

She beat him to the door. "No, you don't. Have a seat."

"Rox, it's been a hellacious day. I'm not up for this."

"You're not going to let Gina go, are you?"

Vic analyzed her. What the hell kind of angle could she be playing?

"You obviously have feelings for her, or you wouldn't have behaved so poorly today."

He sat. "Did Mike tell you? Or Gina?"

"Gina."

"Good. I'm not sure how much Mike knows—I'm assuming you know about what happened on the beach?"

Roxi nodded and he tried to ignore the burning in his cheeks. "Like I said, I don't know how much Mike knows. Hopefully not a lot, and I need it to stay that way. He gets nuts about this subject."

"Tell me about it. I live with him."

With his elbows propped on the table, Vic lowered his head into his hands. "I'm tired." His Southern drawl slipped and he smacked his lips together. He'd learned to hide the accent, but at times it made itself evident.

Roxi squeezed his wrist. "I know, but you have to fix this. I'll deal with Michael. He was wrong to interfere. It's not fair to Gina, though. Did you at least apologize?"

Vic eyed the door.

"You didn't?" Roxann shook her head.

"Sort of."

She put up her hands. "Did you say the words *I'm sorry?* Nothing else counts."

He scrubbed his hands over his face. What. The. *Fuck.* "She's got me all twisted up. I'm trying to do the right thing. Mike asked me to stay away, given the dangerous job and all, and I do care about Gina. I don't want her to get hurt again."

Roxann sighed.

He had to make her understand. "Rox, I love my job and I'm good at it. I can't throw away years of training."

"So, it's the job or Gina? No happy medium?"

"No. I'm alone for a reason. I don't have to worry about anyone but me."

Good thing too, because right now, with this Sirhan crap, he only had himself to worry about.

"Why couldn't you help run the business rather than going into the field?"

Vic scoffed. "You're not listening. I *want* to be in the middle of it. I like it."

Gina came through the door. And glared at Vic.

"Rox, I'm sorry," she said. "Lily isn't feeling well and we're going to head home. Michael said he'd take us."

Roxann puckered her lips. That couldn't be good for him.

"Vic can take you."

*What?* "Huh?"

"I need Michael to help me here. The boys can stay and have dinner. We'll bring them later. You take care of Lily."

The two of them stared at her, but Rox had that blonde girl smile going for her and Vic didn't want to argue. Not in her own home. At least some of his aunt's lessons had stuck.

"Sure," he said.

"Great," Gina said.

"Wonderful," Roxann said.

LILY FELL ASLEEP IN THE CAR. POOR KID WAS DEAD ON HER feet. Vic pulled his Tahoe into the driveway behind Gina's house and parked next to her mini SUV. The narrow alley had houses packed tight on both sides, and when a car went barreling through, Vic had the urge to holler at the driver to slow down. What if Lily had been playing in the driveway? Asshole.

The evening sun faded fast, but the temperature was hanging in there. He looked up at the sky—no clouds. Stars would abound. A good night for a sail.

"I'll carry her in," he said.

"It's okay. I'll wake her up. Roxann is waiting dinner for you."

He snorted. "Roxann is not waiting and you know it."

Nothing doin' on that idea. She sent enough food with Gina to feed them for three days. No, Roxann pretty much beat him over the head with the idea he should *not* come back. She wanted him to square things with Gina. *He* wanted to square things with Gina. He couldn't take her being pissed at him.

Vic opened the rear passenger door and scooped Lily up. The kid was a peanut. "We need to talk," he said.

"Let me get her settled first."

He cradled Lily in his arms and got a whiff of strawberries. Probably her shampoo. Lily was obsessed with strawberries. She ate them nonstop, wore them on her clothes, her barrettes, her socks. Whatever she could think of. Sweet kid. He kissed her on the forehead.

"She feels hot. Does she have a fever?"

"I think so. I'll give her something."

"Is she going to be okay?" Damn, he adored Lily.

"It's probably the stomach flu."

Vic went through the kitchen and dining room to the living room. Gina's house had to be a hundred years old. One of those old brick deals that could withstand the worst hurricane-force winds. The carpet had a broken-in feel he liked. He hated houses resembling museums. He didn't want to get screamed at when he accidentally dumped a beer.

He marched up the creaking steps into Lily's room and deposited her on the bed. He glanced around the pretty room. A typical little girl space with dolls on the shelves and pink bed linens. One tall dresser, white with pink trim, and a framed picture of her dad on top sat along the far wall. Oh, and how could he have guessed? Strawberries on the wallpaper.

He snorted. "I'll wait downstairs. We'll talk when you're done here."

Talking. His favorite thing in the world. *Kill me now.*

VIC HAD SET FOOD AND DISHES ON THE TABLE. GINA STOOD IN the doorway of her little kitchen trying to remember the last time she'd found a meal ready for her. Danny had done it, but she couldn't place when and the agony that came with being a widow shattered her rib cage. Losing the memory of those little moments destroyed her. How could she not remember the last time her husband, her high school sweetheart and a man she'd treasured, had prepared a meal? She'd taken too much for granted back then.

After Danny died, she repainted the kitchen a bright, sunny yellow. Mealtime had been family time and they'd spent countless hours huddled around the table, laughing, telling stories, hearing about everyone's day. In the beginning, the memories were too painful and altering the kitchen seemed like a fresh start. She and the kids still did family time, but there was now a new cherry table for four to go with the updated wall color.

Vic stuck his head up from the refrigerator. "Salad dressing?"

"On the shelf. Toward the back. The kids can't remember to put it on the door." She looked at the table again. He'd even put her place setting in the spot she usually sat. "This is nice. Thank you."

He cracked open the bottle of salad dressing. "I hope you don't mind, but I'm eating too. I'm starved and it'll probably take me the next hour to figure out how to convince you I'm sorry. I figure we can eat while I talk."

She smiled at his logic. Nothing came between a man and a good meal. "You're allowed to eat. Just because I'm mad at you doesn't mean I never want to see you again."

Scraping the chair back for her, Vic held out a hand and she sat down. At least they were being civil.

Gina began doling out food. "I'm confused about today. We seem to be stuck between friends and something more."

This would be torture for Vic, but why should they beat around the bush? Sweat peppered his upper lip. Sweat? Over a conversation? This man was completely terrified of emotional upheaval.

"Here it is," he said. "When you told me you'd been with someone else, it surprised me. I try not to think about you being on dates. I also don't bring dates around when I know you'll be there."

The fork stopped midway to her mouth. "You do that?"

He huffed. "Can you give me some credit for being a decent guy? I don't think it would be right to put some girl in front of you after what happened downstairs. And on the beach."

"I wasn't flaunting that I'd been with someone. At least, I didn't set out to."

He propped his elbows on the table. "I'm sorry for being shitty to you. Like every other time my emotions take over, I acted like an ass. I'm sorry."

Gina took her half-eaten meal to the sink. She needed something to do. Were they really having this conversation? Would it get them anywhere? She stared out the kitchen window at the house on the other side of the alley. The Jeffersons lived there, and every time Danny would see them, he'd sing the theme song from the old sitcom. She could still hear him. *"Movin' on up..."* She laughed at the thought.

"You know, after Danny died, one of his firefighter friends brought me a letter he'd written." She stopped. Swallowed hard. Let the chill running through her subside. "He must have sensed something might happen, because he wrote it a few months before he died."

She turned toward the table.

Vic shifted in his chair. "You shouldn't tell me this. It's between you and Danny."

"It's okay. I need for you to understand." She took the seat next to Vic. She'd never told anyone about the letter and felt a pang of something inside. Regret? Guilt for sharing Danny's thoughts?

She shook it off. "He apologized for leaving me to raise three kids. He shared his hopes for the kids, things he wanted me to tell them, but the important thing was he asked me to give them a stable home. To make them as comfortable as I could without a dad."

Gina stopped, cleared her clogging throat. She grabbed a napkin from the table, blew her nose.

"Please. Let's not do this."

Vic's lips went white. Probably from the pressure of squeezing them shut. He had to learn to relax about this stuff. He was easygoing about everything else, but anything involving emotions seemed taboo with him.

"I need you to understand," she said.

"It doesn't matter."

"Yes, it does. Suppose you and I decide we want to be a couple, and I start bringing you around. We have dinners together, go places with the kids. They'd get used to it. They love you anyway, so it would be easy for them."

With a nod, he said, "It would be easy for me too."

"I don't know what your *real* job is. I think I make pretty accurate assumptions because I run the company checks. I see your expense reports. I know you've been in Afghanistan and Israel over the last two months. Those are dangerous places. If you become part of our lives and I have to sit home while you're on a trip, I'll go crazy. I would always wonder if you're okay. Heck, I wonder a little bit now. If we were a couple, it would distract me from giving my kids what my husband asked. Part of having a stable environment is having a mother who is consistent with her emotions."

Vic shrugged. "I get that. Believe me. It's why I'm not married. It's why I never let myself get close to thinking about it. I don't want to check in. I need to stay focused and I can't do that when I get emotional. You saw it today."

The phone rang. Gina thought about ignoring it, but what if it was one of the boys? She grabbed the cordless from the base on the wall, checked the ID.

"It's Michael's number." She clicked the talk button. "Hello? Hi, Rox. Lily's fine. She's sleeping. Vic and I are talking... Hmmm. Are you sure? No, I don't mind."

She hung up. Oh boy.

"What's up?" he asked, putting his dirty dish in the sink.

"The boys are staying there tonight. They want to watch *Friday the 13th* on Michael's new television."

Vic laughed. "I don't blame them. It's a kick-ass TV."

"Boys and their toys. Anyway, are we going anywhere with this conversation?"

Leaning against the counter, dressed in his faded jeans and his beat-up sandals, he finally relaxed.

"We probably understand each other better."

Gina went to him but stayed back a foot. No sense getting too close and self-combusting. Whenever she entered his orbit, something in her brain went whacky and all she wanted was to cuddle up with him.

"We can't continue to avoid each other," she said. "If we're not going to move forward, we should feel free to date other people. You're at all of our family functions. Why should you feel like you can't bring women around?"

"I don't like that idea."

Holding her hands palm up, Gina asked, "What are we going to do, spend the next ten years not bringing dates around? That's not okay with me. I want to be able to have someone in my life again. I don't *need* it, but I'd like companionship. I'd like my kids to have a man around."

And if Vic couldn't be that man, she had to let him go. Disappointment crept into her heart. Maybe she wouldn't get over lusting after him, but she'd live with it. She'd had practice.

Gina held his attention as he took a deep breath and shook his head. "It shouldn't be this hard."

For a thirty-six-year-old man who'd seen so much death, he was clueless. "When you care about someone, it should be hard. We can't continue to do this. It's not fair to either one of us. It doesn't mean we can't care about each other."

God, this sucked. Her body went numb. They weren't even a couple and it felt like a breakup. Or maybe a loss of hope. She had hope for her children, but when it came to her own life, she wasn't sure anymore. She had to raise three kids. *Her* life had to wait.

Gina swiped at her eyes. And now she was crying. Fabulous.

Vic wrapped his arms around her and squeezed. "I can't give you what you need. I want to. I really do, but I can't find the compromise."

Settling her head against his chest, she inhaled. Vic

always had a clean, salty-air scent and it tore something inside of her loose. She ran her hands over his back, just for a second, to savor it. He stroked her hair and she glanced up at him, the silence in the room causing her lungs to strain. She should break the contact. Step back.

And then he kissed her.

*Oh, no. No, no, no. Not doing this.*

But his kiss was an unexpected gentle touch of his lips, so different from the night on the beach. Last time had been fast and searing. This kiss had her falling, falling, falling. *Just enjoy it. Only for a few seconds.* Then she'd push him away.

His goatee pricked her chin, but she didn't want to stop. Ever. Not when her body craved his warmth. They connected on too many levels for it to end.

"We should stop, right?" Vic asked, kissing her again.

For a man who didn't like to talk, why the hell was he talking?

"Probably," she replied without removing her hands from his butt. How her hands got there, she had no idea.

Then he backed her into the counter and it was all over.

**4**

---

*Man Law: Never get suckered into a chick flick.*

"HOW THE HELL DOES THIS HAPPEN?"

Vic maneuvered Gina against the counter and sucked wind because, selfish prick that he was, he'd nailed her. Right there in the kitchen.

She laughed, and the sound bounced off the walls and made him smile. But her flushed cheeks and messy hair? That was the kicker. Yep, thoroughly thrashed. He wanted this constantly. He couldn't help himself.

"We have no willpower," Gina said. "We are truly pathetic."

She laughed again and Vic leaned in to run his fingers through her massive curls. He kissed her and stepped back to get rid of the condom before sliding his jeans up. She wriggled her skirt down and adjusted it. The skirt was convenient. Blame it on the goddamned skirt. If she'd had jeans on, maybe they would have slowed down enough to think it through. Maybe that was the problem the last time too. She'd had a dress on the night of Mike's wedding. Gina needed to invest in some friggin' pants.

Yeah, like *that* would work. He spent way too much time thinking about getting her naked to convince himself they would have stopped.

"Okay." She pulled her long hair into a knot behind her head. "Another simultaneous brain fart. Let's just move on."

"Yep. We can do this."

She squeezed his forearms. "We're consenting adults. We're entitled to these little mess-ups. It doesn't mean we shouldn't stick with our plan of moving on with our lives."

Our plan? Try *her* plan.

He tucked his shirt in. "I never agreed to that."

Gina narrowed her eyes. "Yes, you did. Just a few minutes ago."

He shook his head. "Nope. You wanted me to agree, but I didn't. I didn't say anything. But hey, who knows? Maybe some great guy, fucker that he is, will come along. Knock yourself out. It'll bug me, but I'll understand. Me? *I* can handle spending the next ten years not bringing women around you."

He hadn't had a serious relationship in years anyway, so it wouldn't be a problem. He'd date. Just not in front of Gina.

Being the most emotionally bankrupt person on earth came in handy sometimes. He'd never bothered to tell anyone he loved them. Not even his aunt, who'd taken in her screwed-up eleven-year-old nephew because his mother wanted drugs more than him. She put up with every ounce of bullshit he could hand her and he never told the woman he loved her. He wasn't proud of that dismal fact, but it said a lot about his ability to keep his emotions in check.

*Asshole.*

"We're no further along than we were before," Gina said, her voice clipped.

"Pretty much. Yeah."

She threw her hands over her face. "It'll never end."

"Mommy?"

She spun to the doorway. Lily stood there in her pink nightgown and her shoulder-length curls flying in all directions. Gina's face went red. She was probably thinking the same thing he was. Busted by one of her kids. Again. Jeez-O-Pete, if Lily had come in ten minutes earlier, she would have gotten an interesting lesson on the birds and the bees. Vic swallowed hard. What a mess.

"Hi, baby. Are you okay?"

"Stomach hurts. Can I have some ginger ale?" Lily gazed up at him. "Hi, Vic."

He knelt in front of her and tugged on her hair. "What's up, squirt? You got some nastiness in your belly?"

Bobbing her head, Lily took the cup from Gina. "Can I watch our movie, Mama?"

"It's almost eight-thirty. Aren't you tired?"

"I just took a nap."

Gina and Vic laughed. Couldn't argue that one.

"Sure, honey. For a little while. I'll watch with you."

"Okay," Lily said, grabbing Vic's hand. "You can watch too. Right?"

Oh, hell. She was looking at him with her dad's big blue eyes and the crazy hair, and his chest imploded. Gina's shit-eating grin didn't help.

"*Dirty Dancing,*" she said. "Can't beat it for a Friday night. We even skip the adult parts."

Her lips tipped up into a wicked half smile, clearly daring him to bow out on the favorite chick movie of all time.

What a witch.

"You bet, Lil. I'd love to watch a movie with you and your mom."

And that was no lie.

AT ELEVEN O'CLOCK THE NEXT MORNING, GINA, KNEE DEEP IN her twice-monthly ironing extravaganza, heard Jake and Matt come through the back door with Michael in tow. She glanced up as the boys made their way into the living room.

The room resembled a ransacked clothing factory, but the kids were used to it and Michael just laughed. The ironing had an organized chaos to it. Clothes were sorted by kid, stacked on her grandmother's oak dining table and, after they'd been pressed, hung on a rolling clothes rack in the adjoining living room. Once she waded through a pile, she'd take the clothes upstairs and start the next batch.

Really, the ironing was more about therapy than wrinkles, because the quiet, mundane process gave her battered brain refuge.

"Hi, Mom," twelve-year-old Jake said, kissing her on the cheek before heading to his room.

"Going upstairs," a soon-to-be-sixteen-and-perpetually-crabby Matthew said.

Grinding her teeth, Gina forced herself not to say anything sarcastic. Would it hurt the kid to say good morning to his mother?

"Hey," Michael said.

Her brother wore his standard Saturday outfit of crisp jeans and a white T-shirt. "Good morning."

Michael raised his eyebrows at the chilly tone and flopped onto the well-worn plaid couch Danny had loved. Suddenly, the living room felt outdated and Gina made a mental note to talk to the kids about getting new furniture. She never changed anything without having a conversation with them. Particularly when it involved things their father had enjoyed.

"How's Lily?" Michael asked.

"Better. She didn't vomit at all and there's no fever. The Woodlands called and invited her to the park. I figured the fresh air would do her good."

From upstairs, Matthew's stereo thumped and Gina contemplated yelling for him to lower it. But why bother? He wouldn't hear her anyway. She let it go.

"Listen, G," Michael said. "I'm sorry about yesterday. I was out of line."

She smiled. "Roxann got to you, huh?"

"Oh, yeah." He rested his head back and closed his eyes.

Roxann must have blasted him. Excellent work.

"I feel like a shitheel."

Gina snorted. "Good to know."

She should probably cut him some slack, but, no, not this time. He'd gone too far yesterday. She understood his overprotective nature. She'd encouraged it by not reining him in over the past few years, which was tough to admit, but she had to take responsibility for the monster she'd helped create. *Dr. Frankenstein, what have you done?* After the miserable scene in the office yesterday, Michael had to stop meddling.

Gina set the iron in the safety holder and sat in the recliner across from him. A dull throb began at her temples. She so did not want to have this conversation.

"I know you think you're doing the right thing," she said. "But Vic and I need to work this out. I feel bad you think you're in the middle, but really, you're not. *You* put yourself in the middle."

Michael narrowed his eyes. "Maybe I have, but his life-style doesn't lend itself to a white-picket-fence-and-three-kids scenario."

Ouch. Did she really need that kick in the gut?

"And you don't think I know that?"

"He takes chances with his life and I don't want to see you hurt again."

"But it's my choice to make."

Michael sighed. "Maybe, but I remember those days when the kids wouldn't show up for school."

"Oh, here we go." Time for more ironing. He *had* to go there. Had to remind her of the one time she'd let herself forget that, as a parent, she'd given up the right to self-destruct. He didn't do it often, but when he did, every muscle in her body became so rigid, she should have snapped in half.

Michael stood. "I'd get the call from the principal and come over to find you in bed. You were so depressed you couldn't get the kids to school. I was scared. I kept thinking you would do something crazy."

Gina gripped the iron tighter. Maybe she'd whack him with it. "I was grieving. The only thing left of my husband was a piece of his jaw, so until you've lived my life, don't lecture me."

"I'm not—"

"And besides," she interrupted, thankful Matthew's stereo was so loud. "I would never have done anything stupid like killing myself. I'm a responsible parent and you know it."

He stepped closer, took the iron out of her hand and set it down. "You're a great parent. And I'm not patronizing you either. At the time, all I knew was I had to come over here every morning and haul your ass out of bed. Little by little you got better and now you're smiling again." He blew out a breath. "I know you and Vic would be good together, but until he finishes playing cowboy, you shouldn't get involved."

Too late. She had spent the last two years trying not to get emotional, but after St. Barth, she was already there. Maybe she and Vic weren't a couple, but they were definitely, in some twisted way, *involved*. How to explain this to Michael?

"If anything happens to him, I'll still be devastated. Just because we aren't—" she made imaginary quote marks, "—involved doesn't mean I don't care."

He looked away. "I think you're lonely and vulnerable. And Vic is... He's Vic, a great guy, and I can see you two together, but I worry."

"You see me as vulnerable, but I'm not. You'll always think of me as your baby sister, but I don't need you to fight my battles."

Rubbing her sweaty hands over her denim shorts, Gina grabbed a shirt off Matt's pile. Her dry eyes blurred and she rubbed at them. She needed a nap.

"I think you're emotionally vulnerable," Michael said, dropping onto the couch again. She wasn't the only one exhausted by this conversation.

"Vic's a terrific friend to put up with you dictating how he should live his life."

"I'm not doing that."

Gina laughed. "You're telling him he can't date me."

"Whatever."

She set the iron down and sat next to him. "I know you're afraid for me, and I think it's great you love me."

"But?"

She smiled. "It's unfair. Vic and I are adults. We're

reasonable people—most of the time, anyway. Take yourself out of the middle, Michael. We'll both be much happier. I don't want to be alone for the rest of my life. I'm not saying Vic's the guy for me, but I want to be able to decide on my own. I'm smart enough not to sacrifice my children's well-being, and that's all you should be concerned with."

After taking a deep breath, Michael stared at her with those dark eyes that could send a person to their knees. Her stomach jumped, but she persevered. "You need to apologize to Vic."

She didn't mean to throw a lot at Michael this morning, but it seemed better to hit him with it all at once. Get it over with.

"I'll think about it."

Stubborn man. She let out an exaggerated sigh. She'd have to clock him with the iron before this was over. "While you're doing it, think about how great Roxann makes you feel, and remember me. What do I have?"

And there it was. He finally understood. Their eyes met and for a split second he didn't move, but she knew by the way his jaw unclenched that he finally understood. The joy Roxann brought Michael hadn't happened with his first wife. Not even close.

He stood, stuck his hands in his pockets and shrugged. "I guess we're done here, then?"

"Pretty much." She kissed him on the cheek. Her brother was a pain in the ass, but he was a good man. "Go home, Michael. Do something with your wife."

He smiled. "Yeah. We're heading up to the lake house for the night."

"Good for you guys." She hugged him. "Be careful, and I love you."

Michael stepped back, held her at arm's length. "I love you too, even if I'm a jerk sometimes."

She laughed. "I know, but stay out of my life. I've got enough problems, and it's not going to get any easier."

COFFEE. MORE COFFEE. VIC DRAINED THE LAST OF HIS CUP AND slid it to the edge of his desk. Only oh-nine-thirty and he'd hit his self-imposed two-cup limit. He was *not* a Monday morning person. He'd gotten up early, though.

He'd driven out to the farm, the four hundred acres of land owned by Taylor Security located thirty-five miles south of the city. They'd purchased it two years earlier for training. The restored farmhouse now contained a gym, seven bedrooms and a monster conference room with state-of-the-art electronics.

Vic liked to practice shooting there for a couple of hours a few times a week. They actually hired a farmer every year to make sure they got corn. The guys would create mazes and have their training buddies set up targets in unknown spots for them to fire at.

This morning, Vic hit the gym and practiced alone for two hours with his trusty Sig .45. He loved that freakin' gun. Get hit with a round from that baby and you'd most likely not get up. Almost eight pounds of rompin', stompin' dynamite. They'd seen a lot of action together.

Practice sessions at the farm, with the quiet wind and perfect sunrises, always gave Vic a sense of calm. The land sat in the middle of nowhere, the nearest house miles away, and cops didn't bother coming around. This morning's workout had given him the distraction he needed, but now he was at his desk digging through one of the piles in search of a report Mike wanted him to read. He found it toward the bottom. To the uninformed, his desk looked like a war zone, chaos everywhere.

He had piles. Sort of. He couldn't see the top of the mahogany desk, but knew where everything was, and who needed to see wood?

Mike had been after him to do some decorating, but he didn't have time for that crap. Vic let the painters slap a coat of beige on the walls and called it good. He had what he needed. A couple of leather guest chairs and a small table for impromptu meetings. The only pictures on the walls were photos of American flags from all over the country. Vic had a thing for American flags. Why not? Considering he was a citizen of the finest country in the world. Hoo-ah!

Mike's assistant brought in a large envelope and dropped it in front of him. He grabbed the manila envelope, spotted his name typed on a label, no address. A courier delivery. He ran his fingers up and down the envelope feeling for anything unusual. Nothing.

After tearing it open, he dumped the contents. Three five by seven photographs landed face down on the desk. This would not be good. He flipped the photographs over.

Lily.

At the park.

These photographs were recent. Lily wearing a pink shirt with a giant strawberry on it and pink shorts. He'd seen her wearing that shirt last week. He scrutinized the next photograph. Him carrying Lily into the house Friday night.

"Son of a bitch."

The final photograph was another of Lily leaving the park.

*It's that easy* was handwritten on it.

The picture stung his skin and he dropped it. An insane

roar began in the pit of his stomach. The warrior wanting action. And the fear. The fear brought out the warrior. He knew how to contain it. Make it work.

Sitting back in his chair, he worked on his breathing. He had no doubt who sent these photos. This was it. Game on.

The sheikh probably knew enough about Vic to realize he wouldn't be afraid of a fight. No. The sheikh was a smart guy. He'd get to Vic through the people he cared about.

Wasn't this some fucking irony? He'd spent most of his adult life alone, partly because he never wanted to endanger a wife and kids. Lily wasn't even his and he still put her in harm's way.

Tension coiled around him and worked its way to his shoulders. Balling his fist, he sent the pencil cup flying against the wall. He'd need more than that to tame his temper.

He buzzed the assistant. "Who delivered the envelope?"

"It came by messenger. Is there a problem?"

*There's a problem all right.* "Where's Mike?"

"In his office."

Vic snatched the photos, shot down the hall to Mike's office to find he had a couple of middle-management guys in with him.

"Sorry to interrupt. I need a minute," Vic said.

Mike focused on him and something registered. "No problem. We can finish later."

With a brief nod toward Vic, the two men left.

"You look spooked," Mike said.

Spooked wasn't the word. Crapping his pants would be more like it. Vic dropped the pictures on the pristine desk.

Mike inspected the photos. "What the hell is this?"

When he looked up, his eyes had the same fire Vic often saw in the mirror.

"A messenger just delivered them. One was from Friday night. I carried Lily into the house. Was she at the park over the weekend?"

Mike nodded. "Saturday. Is this what I think it is?"

"I'm guessing my friend the sheikh sent them."

Mike's face hardened to cement. He stood, put his hands over his face, then fisted them. *Go ahead, pal, hit me, I deserve it.* His friend resembled Dr. Bruce Banner just before he mutated into the Incredible Hulk.

"Fuck," Mike said.

"I worked up a few scenarios. I didn't anticipate *this*, but I can improvise. I'll put a couple of guys on them. I've got Tiny and Duck ready to go."

Mike's phone buzzed. "Call for Vic," the assistant said. "Some Sheikh Khalid Sirhan."

They gawked at each other. The combat buzz streamed in Vic's system, his nerves on alert. Every sound in the room became louder, every smell a little stronger. This was what he lived for.

"Take it," Mike said.

"Give us one minute." Vic said into the phone. "Count a full sixty seconds and put him through."

He needed the minute to get his head square.

Already in action, Mike pulled out a digital recorder, a pad and pen. "Is your head on straight?"

Straight enough to know he wanted to tear this fucker to pieces. Threatening seven-year-old civilians was beyond evil.

"You bet," he said.

Years of combat training taught him to suck air through his nose and tense his arms until the muscles were about to burst. He let the breath out, released his muscles, and a warm relaxing sensation spread through him, allowing him to clear his mind for the task ahead.

Mike's line buzzed and, as usual, the machine within Vic took over. He punched the speaker button. "Vic Andrews."

He was not going to show this guy one ounce of respect. The title didn't mean dick. And the name? Khalid Sirhan. Vic did a quick translation and came up with *immortal wolf*. They'd see how immortal.

"You know who this is?" Sirhan said. The lilting Middle Eastern accent usually had a calming effect on Vic, but not from this asshole.

"Yeah, and I got your package."

"She's a lovely girl," Sirhan said.

*Oh, crap.* Vic's stomach went frickin' haywire and Mike had the Bruce Banner thing going on again.

"And she's going to stay lovely." He held out his hand, giving Mike the silent version of *Calm your ass down, pussnuts.*

"We shall see," the sheikh said. "You have done me a disservice. I expect reparations."

"And what?" he said. "You think I'm going to let you roll in here and do harm to this little girl? You must be bat-shit. I'll kill you first."

Mike puckered his lips as he jotted notes. The strategizing face.

"It seems you have little faith in my power. I found you, didn't I?"

Sitting down and propping his feet on the desk, Vic settled in for the chat. "I'd be impressed if I were hard to find."

"You Americans. Anyone can be betrayed for money."

Mike rolled his eyes and flipped the sheikh the bird.

"What are we talking about here?" Vic asked. "You want my head on a stick or what?"

"I could kill you if I wanted."

He laughed. "You think?"

"The point is moot. Men like you do not fear death. It is part of your world. I have other plans for you."

Yeah, this asshole was going to torture him by terrorizing the people he cared about. Just freakin' beautiful. Those pictures of Lily had the sickness rolling in his belly again. This conversation was going nowhere.

"Listen, Sirhan, it's been great talking to you, but if this conversation isn't leading up to a big bang, I've got work to do."

The line went dead. Sheikh Elvis had left the building.

With a punch to the speaker button, Mike said, "*That* was a waste of time."

"Not really. He's smart enough to know I got wind my cover was blown. This is part of the game for him, twisted fucker that he is."

Vic picked up the phone again. "I'm gonna send Tiny over to Lily's summer camp. Have him keep an eye on things."

Next to Mike, Tiny was his go-to guy. Not many people knew Vic and the former Marine were cousins. They had, in fact, lived together like brothers after Vic's loony mother dumped him on his aunt.

He liked to keep his private life under wraps. Parading his loved ones around, as the current situation proved, could be catastrophic.

"One of us has to tell Gina." Mike ran his hands through his hair. He'd aged ten years in the last fifteen minutes. "This is a fucked-up world."

Wasn't it the truth?

"Where are you?" Vic asked when Tiny answered his phone. "I need you to get over to St. Theresa's school. Lily is in day camp over there. Call me when you arrive."

Gina didn't know it yet, but Tiny was about to become part of her round-the-clock security detail.

Vic hung up. "He's on his way."

That's what he loved about these guys. Nobody wasted time asking questions. They went where ordered and asked questions later.

"Mike, I'm sorry—"

He put up his hands. "I know what you're thinking and it's bullshit. You did a job. Nobody expected you to get sold out. We'll fix this."

Oh, they'd fix it. Vic wasn't sure how, but he knew it would involve a lot of blood. Probably his own.

"The only thing we know," Mike said, "is Lily may be the target."

That shriveled his balls. Innocent little Lily mixed up in his mess.

"He could also be playing us," Vic said.

"We need to be ready for anything."

Anything could be a whole lot of things. Visions of car bombs, home invasions and rapes snapped in his mind. He was most definitely going to blow his cookies when he left Mike's office.

"I'll tell Gina," he said. "It's my situation."

Mike leaned back in his chair, ran his fingers over his lips a few times and nodded. She wouldn't sleep until this was all over and it made Vic's insides burn. He hated to give her more grief.

"I'll call St. Theresa's," Mike said, "and let them know I'm sending people over to help with security. I'll tell them they're getting use of Taylor Security's brand-new community support initiative. I'm going to lie to a nun."

"Yeah, well, it beats the truth. And God'll forgive you. I'll head over to the school after I talk to Gina."

This was why Vic didn't do relationships. He never wanted to sit in front of a mother and tell her that her child faced danger because of him.

And now he had to do just that.

## 5

*Man Law: Always avoid emotional women.*

VIC WALKED BY ROWS OF DULL GRAY CUBICLES IN THE TAYLOR Security accounting department and shivered at the sound of clacking keyboards and low murmurs. The place gave him the creeps. Mike went for the industrial look in the open areas. Even the carpeting screamed b-o-r-i-n-g.

"Good morning, Mr. Andrews," Gina's cubemate said.

"Hey, Martha."

Gina, phone to her ear, turned and smiled. He liked her chaotic curls better than the pulled back do she wore this morning, but whatever. He supposed the ice-queen hair went with the navy pants suit that was more Roxann than Gina, but what did he know? Women were always changing things up.

"Well, hi there," she said when her call ended.

Her happy demeanor at seeing him would change fast. He smiled because, hey, smiling at Gina was easy.

"Got a minute?" He tried to sound casual, but how many times had he walked into accounting, rather than calling her, when he needed something?

Her smile went bye-bye and he knew she thought this had something to do with Friday night and their kitchen aerobics. In a way, she'd be right.

"Everything okay?"

Vic jerked his head toward the conference room. No way would he do this in front of an audience.

GINA CLOSED THE CONFERENCE ROOM DOOR. "WHAT'S wrong?"

Vic leaned against the wall and gestured for her to sit. He was acting squirrelly again.

She took the nearest seat in an effort to hasten whatever news he would deliver. He dropped three photographs in front of her and, after wiping her sweaty hands on her slacks, she picked them up.

"Why are you taking pictures of Lily?"

"I'm not."

A protective maternal instinct sparked. "Then who is?"

He rubbed his forehead and the sliver of panic Gina had been squashing threatened to break free.

"I'm going to give it to you straight," he said. "I don't know how else to do it."

This would be bad. "Honesty is best. I'm a big girl."

He nodded. "I did a job in Israel last month—I can't give you the details—but a man died and now his brother, a sheikh, wants my ass in a sling."

Israel. A sheikh. Vic's ass in a sling. Why was he telling her this? "What does that have to do with Lily?"

Vic dragged his fingers against his forehead again, this

time hard enough to turn his knuckles white. A stranger would think maybe he had a headache, but she'd studied him for hours. He went to Herculean efforts to keep his emotions in check. Not much rattled him.

She clasped her hands together and squeezed. "Is my daughter in danger?"

He pulled a chair and sat, putting his big hands over hers. Their warmth somehow diminished the jitters. Whatever the problem, Vic would help her.

"All I know," he said, "is this guy wants to mess with me. He had someone following me, taking those pictures. They saw me with you and Lily and must have assumed we were a couple. He wants me to think Lily is in danger and, well, this is a bad dude."

"How bad?"

He stared right into her eyes. "Bad enough he's on a government watch list."

"A *terrorist*?"

He nodded. "I'm sorry."

"So, he's capable of harming her?" Thoughts of her beautiful little girl in her pink strawberry T-shirt prompted tears. *Dammit.* She swiped at them. She would not get hysterical. Hysteria, she had learned from Danny's death, got her nowhere but into a bottle of meds.

Vic squeezed her hand. "I promise you nothing will happen to Lily."

Was he kidding? She, of all people, couldn't believe that. She bit back the sudden irritation and focused on him. "You can't promise me that."

She'd dealt with tragedy before, and empty promises couldn't erase it.

He nodded. "You're right, but we'll do everything we can to keep her safe. I called my buddy at the State Department and told him the sheikh might be in Chicago. They're all over it. They want this guy, Gina."

"We can count on them to help?"

Vic shrugged. "As much as they can. Lynx is a good guy. If he can help, he will."

The oil painting over Vic's head suddenly won Gina's attention. She focused on it and tried to organize her twirling thoughts.

Lily.

She shot out of her chair. "I have to get Lily."

He grabbed her arm. "She's fine. Tiny is at St. Theresa's now. I'm going there when we're done here. We've got a couple of other guys heading over also. Mike called the school, told them Taylor was giving them a year's worth of free security. Some bullshit about a community support initiative." He smiled. "Your brother has become a spin doctor."

Gina nodded, her mind zooming ahead. "I'm going with you. I want to get my baby and bring her home. The boys too."

The boys. Jake was on a field trip with the science club and Matthew—he'd better be at Keith's, or he would be in big trouble. He'd reached the age where babysitters or camp gave him a rash. Gina had put him on a short leash for the summer to see how he did. So far, he hadn't disappointed her, but they weren't even out of June yet.

"I need to get my purse and cell phone." With Vic on her heels, quick strides carried her to her desk. She'd call Matt and Jake from the car.

Her knees wobbled, but she willed herself to stand tall. She'd get through this. Her family would stay intact. It had to.

She refused to lose one of her children.

. . .

VIC PULLED INTO GINA'S DRIVEWAY AND SPOTTED COWBOY Roy in his signature snakeskin boots and Wrangler jeans standing on the back stoop. Mike and Roy had come ahead and gone through the house to clear it. All had been quiet.

"Who's that man, Mama?" Lily asked from the backseat.

Gina slid Vic a sideways glance. "He's a friend of Vic and Uncle Michael's, honey. He wanted to come by and visit. Is that okay?"

"Sure," she said, shrugging.

He glimpsed Lily in the rearview. "He's a nice guy, Lily. I've known him a long time." He swung toward her. "Stay in the car a second, okay? I'm going to come around and open the door for you."

Her eyes went wide. "Just like the movies!"

That made Gina laugh. "Yep. We can pretend Vic is prince charming."

*Ha. Good luck with that one, babe.* He was as close to prince charming as a serial killer. Technically, he *was* a serial killer, but somehow the government made it honorable. And on some level, he knew what he did helped fight terrorism, and knowing it kept him sane when the demons crawled into his mind while he slept.

Roy came off the porch and stood next to the car while Gina and Lily got out. Vic ambled behind them with Roy on the side, just in case a stray bullet happened by.

What a thought.

He tensed his body, let the brutal squeeze of muscle sink in and counted to ten before releasing his breath. The moment of panic went away.

Gina darted up the stairs, through the back door into the kitchen. Who could blame her for being spooked?

Vic turned to Roy. "Monk's out front."

"Roger that." He stepped back out the door to keep watch.

"Is he leaving?" Lily asked.

"Um, no," Gina said. "He's going to stay outside for a while. Why don't you go upstairs and put your things away? Maybe we'll go to Uncle Michael's and use the pool."

Use the pool? Was she smokin' crack? Yeah, Mike lived in a secure building, but the pool was on the roof. Thoughts of choppers and snipers ran through his brain. Okay, maybe a little paranoia wormed its way in too.

"You should stay inside," he said after Lily went upstairs.

"And how do I explain *that* to my children?"

How the hell should he know? He didn't know squat about kids. Still, he felt a pang of guilt over having put her in this situation. "I don't know and I'm sorry."

"I know you're sorry. You've told me three times." She leaned against the counter in the very spot where they'd done the deed on Friday night. "Sorry doesn't help, so stop saying it. I need you to tell me what our new *security* entails."

Vic sighed. "It entails you and the kids keeping your asses inside. If you go out, you go with one of the guys."

She glowered at him with *the* face. The one where she narrowed her eyes and puckered her lips. The mentally-dismembering-your-body face.

"Jake and Lily won't ask a lot of questions," she said. "But Matthew? He's a problem."

Matt would be the ball breaker. Maybe Gina should tell him the truth. He would be sixteen soon and considered himself the man in the house. It still seemed a lot of pressure for a teenager.

"Do you think I should tell him the truth?" Gina, the mind reader—how the hell did she do that?—asked.

He sat and rubbed his gritty eyes. "Hell, I don't know. Part of me thinks it's a good idea, but I'm not a parent."

"Could you have handled it when you were his age?"

"That's different. My mother walked out on me. I had enough anger to fight ten sheiks. Matt's anger is different. It doesn't rage like mine did. He knows his father loved him."

Whoa? What the fuck? When did this become Dr. Phil?

Gina, still leaning against the counter, unfolded her arms. Body language for *I'm open to this. You can talk to me.*

*No freakin' way. Kill me now.*

After a minute, she had the *aha* moment that he wouldn't admit to his emotional shortcomings.

"You're probably right," she said, "but I won't lie to him. When he asks, I'll tell him a watered-down version of the truth. I'll have to since we won't be going anywhere unaccompanied until this is over."

"Nobody leaves this house without an escort. No negotiation."

Just as she was about to mouth off, Matt came through the front door and shouted that he was home.

"In the kitchen," Gina yelled back.

"What's with the goon out front?" Matt carried his skateboard and wore a pair of ratty jeans and an equally ratty blue T-shirt. "Oh, hey," he said when he saw Vic.

Since the night on the beach, Matt had been giving him the hairy eyeball. A subtle hairy eyeball, but definitely there. That may have gone back a couple of years to the day he barged into the basement and found his mother in his clothes. The kid wasn't stupid.

"What's up, pal?" Vic gave Matt a fist bump.

"Is he one your friends? Sorry about the goon comment."

Vic shrugged. "He's been called worse."

"Thanks for coming home so quick," Gina said. "Have a seat. I need to talk to you about something."

Holy shit, the kid's face went four funky shades of green, and Vic thought Matt would vomit right there. Gina rushed to him, put her hands on his cheeks.

"No. Honey, everything's fine. I'm so sorry."

She hugged him and Vic's chest tightened. A similar scene probably unfolded the day Matt found out his father was dead.

"Mom, don't do that to me." Matt pulled away and jammed his fingers into his eyes. "I'll be right back."

He took off, and when Gina turned back to Vic, she threw her hands over her face and starting bawling.

Great. Women crying. Not *exactly* his specialty.

Not knowing what else to do, he dropped into a chair, pulled her onto his lap and kissed the back of her shoulder. "I'll fix this. I will."

Then she did something she'd never done before. She spun around, buried her pretty face in his neck and locked her arms around him to finish her cry. Selfish son of a bitch that he was, he was stoked to hold her. He'd brought chaos into her life and he had the audacity to enjoy this? She should cut off his balls. Well, maybe cutting off his balls went to the extreme, but there had to be some sort of punishment.

He ran his hands down her back, but they couldn't spend too much time here, because he needed her to focus. "Matt'll be back any second. Can you pull it together or should I intersect him?"

Shooting to attention, she rushed to the sink and

splashed water on her face. "I can't believe I just did that. What if he'd walked in on me crying?"

"He didn't. Stop worrying about it. Do you want me to talk to him?"

Would he really know what to say to this kid?

With her back still to him, Gina wiped her face with a kitchen towel. "I don't know."

"Neither do I, but maybe I can lay it out for him. He won't freak if I'm here."

She did a yes-no thing with her head and Vic prayed she'd tell him no. He wasn't afraid of many things, but this scared the crap out of him. He wasn't equipped for family drama. His aunt's house hadn't packed much drama. None he had seen, anyway, and he forced himself to block out the first eleven years of his life with Mommy Dearest. It was easier than thinking about the johns who came and went so his mother could feed her addiction.

"Maybe we can do it together?" She turned toward him. "He might ask questions I don't know how to answer."

And what made her think he could? No clue. He'd roll with it. "If it's what you want. I'll do whatever you need."

## 6

*Man Law: Never get mixed up with family squabbles.*

GINA POINTED TO A CHAIR AT THE KITCHEN TABLE. "HAVE A seat, buddy."

This would be a tough conversation. And having Mr. Anti-Emotion help her would make it even more interesting.

Slanting a glance toward Vic, Matthew dropped into the chair. The recent tension between them ran fast and strong, and she didn't understand it. Then again, Matt enjoyed being crabby to everyone lately.

"Does he have to be here?"

"Hey," she said. "*He* has a name and *you* will use it. Besides, I want him here."

What the heck? She hadn't even started and she had lost control of the situation.

"Gina," Vic said, leaning back and crossing his arms, "let's not sweat the small stuff."

Now *he* was going to tell her how to discipline her son? He was supposed to be helping her. "You're a guest in our home. I want him to be respectful."

He shrugged.

"Whatever," Matt said.

She hated that all-purpose response but clamped her jaw shut.

"Why am I here?"

Trying to explain this without freaking Matthew out would be a challenge. She took a silent breath and shifted toward Vic for support. Mr. Impatient held his hand out.

"The man out front works for Uncle Michael and Vic. There's another man out back. They're going to be hanging around for a while."

"So?"

Vic grunted and Gina shot him a look. He needed to let her handle this. He was in a support role, whether he liked it or not.

"Can you stop being a smart-ass for five minutes?" Gina asked.

Matt jerked a shoulder.

Progress. Wonderful.

"Uncle Michael and Vic sometimes get involved with dangerous situations. I don't know the details, but someone made threatening remarks against us. Uncle Michael wants us to have security as a precaution."

With Matthew, the best approach would be to make it Michael's idea. He respected his uncle and wouldn't question his decision. Michael had been the father figure since Danny died and took no guff from Matt. Maybe she could learn something from the approach, but Michael didn't have to live with a teenager. He could yell all he wanted and leave. She had to clean up the mess and, sometimes, her sanity depended on choosing her battles.

"They're just going to sit around outside?"

"Yes," Gina said. "They'll go with us when we leave the house. I need you to help me with this, Matthew. You are not to go anywhere without Vic or one of the guys with you."

Matt offered another sideways glance at Vic. "I don't get it. Why do I need a babysitter? I didn't do anything wrong."

"Can I say something?" Vic asked.

"Sure," Gina said.

"You didn't do anything wrong. I got into a bad deal at work. Some guys have been following me and saw me bringing your mom and Lily home the other night. They assumed your mom and I are a couple. They think they can screw with me by using your mom and Lily. We want to be cautious here."

Suddenly her son wasn't fifteen and three quarters anymore and his sun-kissed brown hair wasn't two inches longer than it should be. He was her cute little boy wanting to understand something beyond his years.

"*Are* you a couple?" Matt asked Gina, his eyes wide and a little wary.

An explosion of surprise rocked her. She hadn't antici-pated *that* question.

She touched Matt's hand. "We are not a couple. Vic's our friend."

When he squinted, his eyes held a beady meanness and a weight settled in her chest. He didn't believe her. How disappointing.

"I know you're lying," Matt said.

"Hey," Gina snapped.

Forget disappointment. The reeling anger whirled inside her, pounding, whooshing in her ears. She stood and leaned on the counter for a mom time-out. She had never lied to Matthew. Not when Danny had been trapped in a burning building. Not when he didn't understand why he couldn't see his dad's body, and not the hundreds of times it would have been easier to lie and avoid a meltdown. On the contrary, she thought things through until she wanted to drop from exhaustion. She always found ways to be honest without giving him more than he could emotionally handle. And now he called her a liar?

"I saw you on the beach after Uncle Mike's wedding."

Oh, no. Had he seen them having sex? She swiveled to Vic, who hadn't moved an inch. *Help me.*

Taking his cue, he said, "What do you think you saw?"

The only response was an icy glare.

"What?" Vic said. "Just say it."

"I saw you kiss her. Don't tell me you didn't, because you'd be a liar too. You're both liars!"

Vic, to his credit, remained stone still with his arms folded across his chest, his face relaxed, not a care in the world.

"First of all," he said, his voice firm. "Don't scream at me. If you were a little older, I'd kick your ass all over the back alley."

Whoa. Nobody was kicking anybody's ass around here, but before she could say it, Matthew jumped out of his chair.

"No," he yelled.

Vic grabbed his arm in a motion so quick Gina almost missed it. For a big guy he could move.

Vic handled Matthew's temper the way Michael did. Straight on, with no pleasantries. When Michael yelled, Matthew reacted with a typical teenage sulk, but with Vic, his face became cherry-red.

"She was supposed to be taking care of us," Matthew yelled. "She dumped us on Grandma so she could make out with *you.*" He spun to Gina. "I hate you."

The room closed in. Gina grabbed the edge of the table and concentrated on breathing. Nothing made sense.

The hate part she could deal with. Kids said that all the time, but the vicious tone gutted her.

"Oh, please," Vic said, his voice an octave lower and a whole lot scarier.

Gina had never heard this voice. "Vic, it's okay."

"No, it's not." He turned to Matthew and in that same low voice said, "You don't know shit about being dumped. When I was eleven years old my heroin-addict mother sent me to live with my aunt because I was too much of a burden. I was interfering with her getting her next fix. She didn't know who my father was, so she left me."

Matthew's mouth dropped open. He'd never heard about Vic's childhood and, to Gina's knowledge, never bothered to ask.

"I didn't see her for three years," Vic continued. "*You* don't get to bitch about being dumped until you've *been* dumped."

He stopped, bit down on his bottom lip, shot out of his chair and leaned against the refrigerator.

She'd never noticed before, but Vic had a definite routine to corral his emotions. The breathing, the tensing muscles, the time-out. She'd learned more about him in ten seconds than she'd learned in ten years.

His unusual outburst left Gina unable to move. The men in her life were giving her a whole new set of circumstances to deal with. Vic needed to talk, hopefully to her, about what his mother had done to him. The anger and disappointment, she knew, could suffocate a person.

"Don't you ever let me hear you accuse your mother of not taking care of you. She busts her ass to keep you kids happy and she doesn't deserve this crap."

"Screw you," Matt said, his voice cracking and losing the desired effect.

Her smart-ass teenager was hurting. He just didn't want to admit it. Oddly, Matthew and Vic were more alike than they'd ever know.

"That's enough," she finally said, but Matt was already heading to the door.

He stood with his back to them for a second, maybe to say something, but then wiped his eyes. Crying. Gina fought the urge to go to him. It would only anger him more to be treated like a child. At least they were getting somewhere. She preferred crying to hostility.

"Can I go now?"

"Are you all right?" she asked.

"Yeah."

"Then go. Come back when you settle down and are ready to apologize."

And won't *that* be fun?

## 7

*Man Law: Never admit you screwed up.*

"I SCREWED UP," VIC SAID, SCRATCHING HIS HEAD WITH BOTH hands.

*Crap.* He was supposed to be helping her and he went off on her kid. He never imagined himself parent material. This episode sealed the lid on his fatherhood potential.

"I don't think you did," Gina said. "I hate to see him upset, but it felt good to have someone take my side for a change. You have no idea the effort I put into being honest with him, and for him to accuse me of lying? I just don't get it."

She sighed and stared at the empty kitchen doorway.

"He saw us on the beach."

Vic nodded. "I saw him in the window that night. I figured you did too. He couldn't have seen us—" he waved his hand, "—you know. We were too far down the beach."

She walked to him. "He's never seen me kissing any man but Danny. That's what this was about. It's not you."

"Yeah, but it's not me I give a shit about. He needs to start treating you better."

Gina's face went slack and she stepped back as if he'd sucker punched her. At this point, he'd lost count of his fuckups. Someone get a scorecard.

"Now *you're* going to start? Why not? Let's make this jump-on-Gina day."

"I may be out of line here—"

"You think?"

"You wanted my help."

That closed her mouth. She pounded her palms on her forehead. "You're right. I brought it on myself."

She was already mad—why not take it all the way? She needed to straighten this kid out before he became a miserable bastard. Vic, as CEO of Miserable Bastards Incorporated, knew about miserable bastards.

"All I'm saying is you're good to him. He was dealt a shitty hand, but at least he knew his father loved him. And you? Jesus, what you do for him is amazing."

A curl flopped in front of her eye and he moved to push it away, but opted to put his hands in his pockets where they'd be safe. Touching her always translated to a major screwup. Or, depending on how he looked at it, a major screw. Gina analyzed his face.

Never a good sign when a woman did that.

"I'm sorry your mother left you. I can't imagine what that feels like."

*And there it is, folks.* The pity. He could defuse this quick. He'd had years of practice.

"It feels like what it is. She didn't love me enough to stick around. At least she put me somewhere I'd have a good life. I'm grateful for it."

And that was why, all these years later, he let her live in a condo he owned in Louisiana. He paid the mortgage and the utilities and had groceries delivered once a week. He wouldn't give her money, because she'd only buy drugs, but she had a roof over her head and food in her belly. He would give her exactly what she'd given him.

"Do you talk to your mother?"

He shrugged. "We don't have a lot to say."

How could she understand? Gina and Mikey had a good mother. One who always made Vic feel like one of the family by inviting him for meals and visiting him when he was sick. Or kicking his ass when it needed kicking. A mother like Gina was to her son.

"Do you want me to talk to Matt? Apologize?" Vic asked.

"Maybe later. He needs to apologize to you too. He'll cool off and—in about thirty minutes—he'll come back. He always does. When he cries, he knows he's wrong. He just can't admit it right away."

Vic looked at his watch. Three o'clock already. He'd been out of the office most of the afternoon. "I gotta get back. I'm waiting on Lynx's call, and he won't call my cell. He's a pain in my ass."

Gina laughed. "Somehow, I think we're all a pain in the ass."

Smiling at that was easy. His whole life seemed to be a pain in the ass recently. "Not everyone."

When she began rocking on her toes, he knew he had to leave. The same crazy tension was back, upsetting the molecules around him, and he was starting to sweat. If he didn't get the hell out of there, they'd be all over each other. At least he'd learned something after the last three episodes of frantic humping.

"Gotta go." He kissed her on both cheeks. "You're doing great with this mess. I'm in awe. Thank you for not splintering me for going off on him."

She laughed. "We're only on day one. It could still happen."

WHEN VIC LEFT, ALL THE ENERGY IN THE SUNNY YELLOW kitchen went with him. He had this magical way of creating excitement, good or bad, anywhere he went.

Talking to Matt was first up. She'd put her life on hold for her children, and she'd do it again, but she wanted a little respect.

"Mama?" Lily called from the living room.

"In here, baby."

Lily stepped into the doorway, all brown curls and cute little nose, and something warm bloomed in Gina's stomach.

"I think Matt is crying again," she said. "Why does he *do* that?"

Gina snorted. "I'm going up to talk to him. How about you pick a board game for us to play? Maybe Monopoly Junior?"

"Okay. I'm banker."

All was right in Lily's sheltered world. Unless you grew up with Vic's mother, life could be simple at seven.

Then there was Matthew.

Rolling the stiffness from her shoulders, Gina drew a deep breath and closed her eyes. It would get worse before it got better, but she could handle it. Respect would once again reside in her home. Even if it killed her.

"Hey," Matt said from the doorway, and the sudden sound of his voice made her yelp.

"You scared me." She laughed at herself, but the sight of her dejected son with his red, swollen eyes bit into her. She hated this for him. "I was just coming up."

Matthew dropped his chin to his chest, shuffled his feet. "I'm sorry, Mom."

The backbone she'd grown just a few minutes earlier started to give way. No. Respect would reign supreme. She folded her arms.

"I know you're sorry and I know you didn't mean what you said."

"I didn't. I swear."

"It doesn't make it right."

"I know."

"You've been crabby to me for months now, Matthew, and I'm done. You can change your behavior or your butt will be parked in the house every day."

"Mom, I said I was sorry."

"To make sure you understand me, I want to see some changes. That means coming home on time, putting a smile on your face in the morning and not smart-mouthing me. You'll also apologize to Vic."

Matt's eyes got big and wild. "What? Why? He was crappy to me too."

"Watch your mouth. You gave as good as you got."

With Matt shaking his head in stunned silence, Gina felt an awkward sliver of hope. Control could be a beautiful thing. She and Matt weren't going to be friends after this, but she would live with it. She had to be his mother, not his friend.

He turned to go.

"I'm not done yet."

He halted, inched back to her with a long face.

"Matthew, I love you more than you can ever know, and I'm trying to be respectful of your feelings by telling you what's going on. I understand your frustration with Vic, but he wants to help. He's concerned for us and that's all you should be focusing on."

"But I don't want you going out with him."

*So* not focusing. It had to be a testosterone issue because the men in her life tended to concentrate on exactly what she didn't want them to. If she had the energy, she would have laughed.

"I will always be here for you, but there are parts of my life that are private. My relationship with Vic is not your concern. All you need to know is if I date someone, it'll be someone who wants to spend time with all of us." She stopped, took a breath. "Honey, just because your dad isn't here anymore doesn't mean I don't still love him. He was an amazing man and I ache for him every day. No one will *ever* replace him. Ever."

Tears slid down Matt's cheeks. He swiped at them and put his hands in his pockets again.

God, this stunk.

"Whatever," he said.

Ugh. "Fine, but you're still going to apologize to Vic."

"I don't want to."

Gina stifled a grunt. She'd like to list all the things she didn't want to do. It would take days. Life stunk that way. "Well, too bad. You're mad at him for something that isn't his fault. You liked Vic before you saw us on the beach and you know it. Now he's the enemy because we kissed? I don't think so."

Matt's glare should have incinerated her. "I don't have to like him just because you say so."

Gina sighed. Arguing with a teenager was fruitless. She leaned against the counter and prayed for patience.

"I'm thirty-five years old, Matthew."

"So?"

"I know you don't want me to date. But what happens when you kids are all grown and out of the house?"

More shuffling of the feet and a shrug.

"Look at me."

He brought his gaze to hers and his dark blue eyes softened, becoming recognizable again.

"I will be alone," she said. "Probably living in this house, and I can promise you it's not what your father wanted. Your dad knew how dangerous his job was. He wanted us, expected us, to keep living our lives. I don't know if I'll ever meet someone I want to marry, but I want some companionship. If there is someone I'd like to spend time with—"

"I know it's Vic. I know it."

"Now you're acting like a brat. Is that what you want?"

"Can I go now?"

She shrugged. "Sure. Go to your room and think about it. You'll realize I'm right, but whether you do or not, you *will* apologize to Vic."

He left the kitchen. "Don't try to sneak out your window either. Monk and Roy will catch you and I'll lock you in this house for a month. Bet on it."

His only response was to bang his way upstairs and slam his door.

What else was new? Her head weighed forty pounds, but at least she wasn't a pushover. She couldn't be happy, but she could be satisfied.

"I'm ready," Lily yelled from the dining room table.

"I'll be right there," Gina said to the only happy child in

the house. Ooh, she'd better tell Monk and Roy to watch Matt's window for an ornery teenager trying to escape.

Jake came in the front door. "Mom, I'm home!"

Now there were two happy children in the house, a crabby teenager and one satisfied mom.

Maybe life could begin again.

## 8

*Man Law: Always know where your enemy is.*

"WHAT HAVE WE GOT ON THIS GUY?"

Vic marched into the executive conference room at Taylor Security. Three operatives and one support staffer convened at the table. Tiny sat near the window, Duck and Billy across from him. Duck had just come back from a stint in Iraq and hadn't shaved the thick beard he'd sported over there. Billy had been sitting on ice waiting for his next job. All three of these men were top-notch operators. He trusted these guys and wanted their help.

"Sirhan hasn't come into the states. Not under his real name anyway," Janet Fink, the only woman in the room said. Janet, a blonde in her early thirties with round cheeks and a big smile, had done a tour with the CIA and was, in Vic's opinion, one of the best damned support people he had ever seen. She could do amazing things with a computer.

"My State Department contact just called," he said. "Sirhan went underground."

He glanced at his notes. "There's been no chatter regarding Sirhan. Some of his underlings were on the move, but nowhere near Chicago."

"Well, that sucks," Tiny said.

"Whoever took the pictures of Lily," Vic continued, "had to have been a new cell or they would have been flagged coming into the States."

"That's what we figured," Mike said, coming into the conference room and taking his seat at the other end of the table. Mike, though not the suit-and-tie type, was usually all buttoned up. Right now, his shirtsleeves were rolled to his elbows and his five o'clock shadow appeared heavier than normal. Everyone in the room must have noticed the difference, because all eyes focused on him.

"We don't know who we're looking for," Vic said.

Mike stuck his bottom lip out. "Not yet, anyway."

"I'm still working on a couple of things," Janet said. "Maybe your guy can follow up on them for us if I can't come up with anything?"

"Like what?"

"A list of Sirhan's aliases for one. I was able to find some of them, but I know there are more."

Vic made a note. "I'll check on it."

"Tiny, you're on Lily. Pick her up at the house in the morning and get her to daycare."

"Roger," Tiny said, scratching his buzzed head. With longer hair, Tiny could easily be mistaken for Vic's brother. Though Tiny's eyes were blue, they shared the same facial structure and build.

"Duck and Billy, you're on the boys. Work it out," he said. "Mike and I will handle Gina. Roy and Monk will stay on the house. We're going to rotate on the house. I've got a couple of other guys flying in to help, but until they get here, we're doing double duty. Questions?"

"If Sirhan's here," Duck said, "and we spot him, do we neutralize him?"

Neutralize. As in permanently.

"If you have to, yes. Obviously, the government would like to get their hands on this guy. If we can deliver him, score one for our team, but that's not our responsibility right now. Keeping Gina and the kids in one piece is."

Throwing his pen on the table, Mike sat forward. "Let's not be afraid to break the bank on this. My sister and her family could be targets. No idea is too expensive or too stupid. Got it?"

They all agreed.

"If we need more manpower, we'll add it," Vic chimed in. "Janet, holler for whatever you need to keep the intel coming. I'll do what I can with my government contacts."

"Sure thing," she said.

"We're done here. Guys, head over to the house. The kids and Gina are all home now. Work out a schedule with Monk and Roy. Include me on it."

The staff filed out. He and Mike stayed in their seats and Vic propped his feet on the table. "This is fucked."

Mike rubbed his hands over his eyes. "Big-time."

"I went a round with Matt earlier."

"I heard."

He snorted. "Kid's a piece of work."

"Yeah. Thanks for taking care of it. He thinks because he's bigger than her, he can push her around."

That made Vic laugh. Gina may have given Matt a wide berth, but she had it in her to fuck up his world. "He's young yet. He'll learn."

"Amen, brother. Anyway, she's making him apologize to you, so you're going to be summoned."

"Oh, that'll be pleasant. The kid wants me in his crosshairs."

"You'll get used to it. He's testing you. Figuring out which buttons will light you up. He did it with me after his dad died and my role got bigger."

Testing him? "He played me?"

Mike grinned. "Like a fiddle, pal."

"Well, holy shit." Vic laughed. "The kid's pretty good."

"Yep. Now you'll know next time. And there *will* be a next time."

FIRST THING TUESDAY MORNING, GINA STOOD IN THE stairwell outside of the Taylor Security executive offices. She stared at the back of the door and steeled herself for the negotiation she was about to engage in.

Knowing Vic could be unreasonable when he wanted to be—no, really?—Gina prepared a speech. She fluffed her hair and gave her black blazer a good yank. She could do this.

She marched toward Vic's office and knocked on the open door. "Hi."

Frank Sinatra crooned softly from the stereo behind the desk. Sinatra? Who'd have thought?

He glanced up from the computer screen and she spotted dark circles framing the bottoms of his eyes. Fatigue. He would work through it, though. She knew he could go days on ten minutes of sleep.

"Did I keep you too late last night?"

"Don't I wish," he joked.

Her insides became jelly.

After coming over the night before so Matt could apologize, Vic had stayed and gone over every inch of the house to determine where they needed to upgrade the security system. The house wasn't that big, but he'd walked through it at least a dozen times. Exhausted from the day and wanting only to sleep, she'd finally thrown him out. The last thing she needed was him in the house when she was in bed. *Can we say distraction?*

"I need to talk to you." She squeezed her butt cheeks together to remind herself to be strong.

He leaned into the armrest of his chair. "What's up?"

The black pullover he wore gave him a *GQ* sexy look and her cheeks boiled. *Don't think about it.* She needed this. "I forgot to mention I have somewhere to go Saturday night."

He froze, his whole-body rigid. She hadn't even said anything yet and he was getting mad.

"You have to be joking. You expect *me* to escort you on a date? No way. Talk to your brother."

He went back to his computer. He thought she had a date? Oh. My. God. Of course he did. Saturday was date night and she'd just walked in acting nervous. After what had happened the week before, she should have been prepared for this. Every explanation lodged in her throat, but she managed a squeak. Wonderful.

"It's not a date. I should have said that. Sorry."

In a matter of seconds his demeanor changed. The hard angles of his face softened and he dropped his head in his hands. "No. *I'm* sorry. I'm tired and I jumped to a wrong conclusion."

Now they both felt bad. Why did this always seem to be the way with them? Gina sat in one of the guest chairs.

"I promised I'd fill in with the band on Saturday night at Mizzy's. Rochelle needs the night off."

Before Danny died, Gina had performed with a popular bar band and, after the accident, in an effort to be home with the kids in the evenings, she'd given up singing. Occasionally the group called her to fill in and she jumped at the chance. Performing professionally had always been her dream, but marrying Danny was also a dream, and when the kids arrived, she'd reshuffled everything, leaving her hope of a career unfulfilled. And still nagging at her.

These opportunities to fill in were the beginning stages of her quest to find herself again, and she'd fight for it.

Vic's mouth hung open as if she'd sauntered into his office wearing a leather catsuit and carrying a whip. Actually, he'd probably like that. She held up a hand, her prepared speech ready to go.

"I know you're going to tell me it's too dangerous, but I'd like to figure out a way to make this work. I don't mind making exceptions, but I gave my word I'd do this. Besides, I'm excited about it."

"Yeah, but, Gina, it's a huge, stinking bar. It probably holds three, four hundred people."

"I know."

He sat back. Stared at her.

She straightened enough to let him know she wouldn't give in. Nope. She hadn't asked to be put into a situation where she couldn't go places alone. Why should she have to give up something so important to her?

Vic leaned forward, hit the speaker button on his phone and dialed four numbers. An internal call.

"What?" Michael's voice boomed.

"Smackdown with your sister about to happen."

"On my way."

They disconnected.

Why did they need Michael? They were adults. They could figure this out. "Was that necessary?"

Vic put up two hands. "I don't want you going off on me."

"I won't. I'm telling you what's on my schedule."

"Yeah, but I'm getting irritated and, as you've seen—right in this office in fact—I'm not the most rational guy when I get emotional. Maybe I'm not thinking straight on this. When Mike gets here, we'll ask him what he thinks."

"I don't care what Michael thinks. You need to help me find a way to do it."

Now *she* was getting mad. And sounding like a brat, which she didn't want either. She had a lot of restrictions on her life, and she accepted them as part of single parenthood, but being told what she could and couldn't do? Not a chance.

"What's up?" Michael said from the doorway.

Gina shifted sideways, squeezing the armrest of the chair to help her focus. "I'm supposed to sing Saturday night."

"Oh."

"Yeah," Vic snorted. "*Oh.*"

"That's a problem, G."

"Yes!" Vic, all big smiles, pointed at Michael with both hands. "My man. Thank you."

She stood. Oh no. No. No. No. They were not going to pull a boys' club scenario on her. "Guys, I don't want to be unreasonable about this. Think of me as one of your high-end clients. Tiffany Limone. Think of me as Tiffany, who needs to go to an event. You wouldn't tell her no."

"Totally different," Vic said. "Tiffany is a whack-job. You're not."

Michael laughed and Gina ground her teeth together.

"This is not funny. All I'm asking is you give it some thought, some honest-to-God thought. After that, if you tell me it's too dangerous, I'll back off, but don't brush me aside. This is important to me."

Michael sighed. Vic folded his arms. She didn't care if she'd pissed him off. If they had taken her request seriously, she wouldn't have had a hissy fit. She didn't mind getting mad and hollering, but whining was not her style. Neither one of them spoke. Fine.

"You can let me know what you come up with." She strode out, leaving them both staring at her.

Mizzy's.

What a fucking nightmare.

Vic stood dead center on the dance floor and did a slow three-sixty. He blew out a breath. The place had a huge two-story open area in the middle, and various side corridors with rooms extending to the outer walls. The cavernous building, with its cement walls and exposed beams, had an eerie quality to it, and Vic didn't like it.

He checked his watch. Eighteen-hundred hours. Three and a half hours before Gina went on. They had some time before the place opened, but he, Mike, Tiny and twenty other Taylor Security operators had met the owner outside the locked building. Vic wanted his guys to be the first ones in to check the place out.

Not surprisingly, the owner had no problems with the additional security. How many nightclubs received free security from a top firm because a band member had a stalker? At least that's what they told him.

"I'm all set," Gizmo, their electronics whiz said as he came into the room. "I swept the whole place."

"No whackadoo terrorists hiding anywhere?" Vic asked, only half joking.

"Nope."

"The metal detector at the front entrance is ready?"

"Yep."

"And the guys at the door have handheld scanners in case someone's keys go off and they need to be double-checked?"

Giz rolled his eyes. "Yes. All the other emergency doors will be guarded by security. No one is getting into the building without going through the main entrance."

"Okay. We can let the employees in through the front door."

Mike walked in, wearing his weekend ensemble of jeans and a T-shirt. He'd go home before Gina's show and change into slacks and a dress shirt. Mikey was a sharp, if not predictable, dresser. Vic would stay in his battered cargo pants and not so crisp T-shirt. He liked to blend into the crowd.

"I just walked the perimeter," Mike said. "It's clear."

"You checked the second-floor fire escapes?"

Mike scoffed at him.

"Right. She's your sister. I'll check again before I leave, just in case."

"Suit yourself. I never thought I'd see the day *you* were high-strung."

"She's in this goatfuck because of me and could get killed." The idea of Gina on a slab curled around his spine, gnawed its way up. What happened to the emotionally bankrupt machine he'd been a week ago? The machine chose *now* to take a vacation?

"And she'll be fine because of you. Get over yourself."

"Yeah, yeah, yeah. Thanks, Mommy," he said. "Don't you need to be somewhere?"

"Other than this therapy session?"

Vic laughed. He wasn't the only one who knew what buttons to push. "Fuck you."

"I'm going home to shower. Roxi is coming tonight," Mike said.

Oh, just great. Now Vic had to worry about Roxann too? What the hell?

"I'll head over in a while and get Gina. Tiny'll bring the kids over to your place when Gina and I leave. She wants them in your building. She's freaking out about that. The woman doesn't care that she's going to be on stage in front of hundreds of people but she wants the kids on total lockdown."

Inclining his head, Mike said, "She's a mother. That's what they do. My building is safer anyway."

Mike lived in a swanky high-rise with mucho security. Tiny and Roy would watch the apartment from inside the building, and Gina would feel better about the whole effing thing.

It had been one bizarre week and the strain had dug in. Vic and Mike had been running Gina wherever she needed to go. No easy feat with a single mother who needed groceries and dry cleaning. Not to mention sports, dance classes and the litany of other kid-related activities.

The lack of time Gina spent on herself stood out. So far, she'd been to an exercise class once after work. That was it. He got the impression this was normal. Maybe, with the guys on the kids day and night, Vic would encourage Gina to take up a hobby or something. Maybe he'd take her for a sail.

All in all, he was one tired son of a bitch. He could

handle battlefield stress, but the histrionics over lost tutus were a whole different matter.

Not a peep from Sirhan though. Vic had no idea what the fucker was up to. Blood pumped through his veins like an out-of-control freight train. His head should have exploded from the pressure. He tensed his arm muscles, held his breath and let it all go.

"I'm outta here," Tiny said from the second story railing. He'd just finished a second walk-through. "Doors are good."

"Okay. When you leave, tell the guys to stay near those doors. I don't care how early it is—I want the outside of this building crawling with security."

Nobody would sneak in. Not tonight.

"The kids just left with Tiny and Roy," Vic called up to Gina, still in her room getting ready. "I've got my men watching the front and back of the house, and we'll set the alarm before we go."

The hall closet at the base of the stairs called to him. He'd checked it once already, but what the hell? He opened the door and checked it again.

"You're a bundle of nerves," Gina said, smiling at him as she came down from the second floor.

Forget his nerves because, holy shit, she had on one hell of a pair of tight black jeans and an equally tight V-neck shirt. Gina was sportin' some cleavage tonight. Va-va-va-voom. Did he suddenly hear burlesque music somewhere?

Throw in the wild curls and spike heels and he had himself one hell of a bombshell. Lush curves from top to bottom. All he wanted was to get her out of those clothes. Despite having done the deed with her three times, he'd never had the pleasure of seeing Gina butt-naked, and it suddenly became a priority.

And yes, he had a hard-on.

A massive one.

*And* she spotted it.

Jesus H. Christ. Talk about the eight-hundred-pound gorilla in the room.

Gina stood on the bottom step, her nose inches from his, but she moved even closer, her warm breath on his face. "Is that a pickle in your pocket?"

She tried to keep a straight face but, with that corny-ass line, burst out laughing.

Funny thing. Her throaty belly laugh eased the constricted muscles in his shoulders.

"Now that we've established you are smoking hot tonight—" Vic held his hand out, "—shall we go?"

"Despite my X-rated thoughts right now, we shall."

He grunted. "Don't even go there, sister."

A silent and kid-free house did not bode well for his raging body. Considering they had already proved their expertise when it came to lightning-fast sex. He grabbed Gina's hand and hauled ass to the back door. All he had to do was get her into the car and to Mizzy's. He just couldn't look at her in the process. Piece of cake.

He was so screwed.

VIC TAPPED HIS FEET WAITING FOR GINA TO GO ON. HE SAT ten feet from the stage at, quite possibly, the smallest table in the universe. Roxann snagged the seat to his left and Mike the one across from him. The funky dance music, decibels too loud, made his head pound.

The lighting, if it could be called that, sucked. Tiny

fixtures hung from the rafters, throwing shadows over the crowd. He saw enough to know Roxann looked great in jeans and a white button-down shirt with a chunky belt at her hips. She wore her blond hair pulled back, accentuating her cheekbones and the fact that she didn't belong in this place. She had class written all over her. She and Mike didn't necessarily blend in, but they didn't have to.

His cell phone buzzed and he unclipped it from his belt. Text from Bobby V. at the door. All was quiet. Mike glanced over and Vic gave him a thumbs-up.

Mike leaned in and yelled, "They should be starting soon."

"Yeah."

Vic knew Gina performed occasionally, but he never went to see her. Out of respect for Mike, he had stayed away, but this was different. Technically, this would be considered work.

Someone bumped his shoulder and he scooted his chair back to give himself extra room. Unfortunately, people crammed in shoulder to shoulder and stacked themselves three deep at the bar. They'd all be loaded by the end of the night, and what a mess it would be.

The pulsing under his skin began and he scratched at his arm in a hopeless attempt to minimize it. His nervous energy had returned. He'd always hated nightclubs. They were a hotbed for bad behavior. He didn't mind a shot-and-a-beer bar so much, but these monster nightclubs could be a nuisance.

Roxann leaned over, bumped his shoulder. "How are you doing?"

Tonight was the first he'd seen her since she'd skewered him in her kitchen.

"I'm good. You okay?"

She smiled a goofy, no-teeth smile.

"What?" he asked.

When she put her hand on his shoulder, Mike's eyes shifted in their direction. He didn't like Roxi touching other men. Probably a holdover from his cheating ex-wife. Roxann was solid and Mike knew it, but old habits lived on.

"You're nervous," she said.

He backed out of her reach before Mike blew an artery. "I'm wound up. There's a difference."

What a load of dog shit. He was nervous as hell. Something had him edgy. Years spent in the military, and the training that went with it, had his instincts working overtime. The thumping music zoned him into his immediate surroundings. He'd blocked out the sound yet everything around him heightened. A woman at the next table wore heavy perfume and the flowery scent instigated a sneeze. Someone laughed from the table on the other side when he could barely hear Roxann talking. His instincts had saved his life on more than one occasion and something in this place was definitely off.

The band took the stage and Gina, her outfit showing off every inch of her slammin' body, made all thoughts of bad guys disappear. *Oh, crap. Don't think about the V-neck T-shirt.* All he needed was another boner. With his luck, Roxann would notice and she'd be mortified.

"She looks fantastic," Roxann said, smiling.

Mike shrugged. He'd always been vocal about not liking his sister's sexy clothes.

"She always looks fantastic," Vic said, earning a glower. He pointed to his head. "I've got eyes."

Mike ignored him.

After the blowout last week, Mike hadn't said anything to him about his potential involvement with Gina. Probably because Roxann had threatened to castrate him if he interfered again. She had the touch with reining him in.

Roxann angled toward Mike and said something while stroking the back of his head. Vic had seen her do it a hundred times, but this time he clenched his teeth. No one ever touched him in the intimate way people do when they've been together awhile. Why it suddenly bugged him may have had something to do with the petite brunette on stage.

The waitress put his water, a beer and a vodka on the rocks on the table. Vic told the girl to run a tab and, after giving him the I'm-available-if-you're-interested stare, she strutted away. She was hotter than an August day, and a few weeks earlier he'd have been all over that action. Not now, though. He didn't have it in him. Not with his feelings about Gina twisting him up.

The band kicked into the Springsteen classic "Man's Job." Nice. They obviously knew the crowd pleasers.

This song had a butt load of harmony, and Gina snapped her fingers, swinging those beautiful hips. She hit a high note, threw her head back and—oh boy, ladies and gentlemen—left the atmosphere. He'd never seen her like this, and had to smile. This must be freedom for her. Gina the dead firefighter's wife gone. Gina the mother taking a break. This was just Gina.

Their eyes locked and Vic, knowing the next few lines, hummed along.

Yes, loving Gina would be a man's job. His insides disintegrated. What the hell was going on with him? Could he handle being the man in her life? Could he make the changes necessary even to be in the running?

His phone vibrated again. Vic shook himself out of his

mental stupor and checked the ID. A text message that everything was quiet out back. So far so good.

Gina stepped up to sing lead. Now, this would be fun. Vic surveyed the area, making sure no one approached the stage. He couldn't imagine anyone penetrating the security they'd put in place, but something still dogged him. As crowded as this joint was, anything could happen.

She adjusted the microphone to her height. "Hey, everybody."

A couple of boneheads a few tables over hooted and hollered, and Vic and Mike both turned. Drunks. This early. *Fuck.*

"How about a little Aretha?" Gina asked, leaving Vic enthralled with the easygoing girl on stage.

The crowd whooped as the band broke into "Chain of Fools" and Gina's bluesy voice belted out the first line of the song. Her singing voice had a richness to it he'd never heard, and he smiled at the newness of it.

Hell, even Roxann sang along.

Gina had gone to the far-off place again, bumping those hips, letting the music take her away from her problems. Any man in the place, besides Mike of course, would be crazy not to want her.

When she got to the second verse, she set her sights on Vic and pointed at him. Say what?

Mike shifted in his seat and Vic couldn't blame him, because his own legs had liquefied. People focused on him and the walls crowded in bit by bit until all the oxygen had been squeezed out. *Hey, floor, how about swallowing me whole?* Vic didn't know whether to be mortified, pissed off or happy that Gina thought about him that way.

This up-and-down thing with her made him nuts. Totally

fucking certifiable. He wanted her 24-7, but how the hell could they make something out of their broken lives? With her responsibilities and his baggage, it would be one hell of a heavy load for them to carry. He inhaled again, let his active mind simmer. Maybe they could carry the load together.

He sat straight, noticed Mike looking everywhere but at him and almost laughed. Any other time, Vic would have capitalized on his discomfort, but not tonight.

Mike would have to live with the situation, because Vic knew one thing for sure. He wanted Gina in his life.

"We're going to take a short break and be back." Gina waved and glanced at the table as she left the stage. *Oh yeah, you'll hear from me on this stunt.*

The crowd continued applauding until the DJ cranked up Beyoncé.

Vic drummed his fingers on the table for a second. "I'll be right back."

Roxann had a whopper of a shit-eating grin on her face, but Mike not so much. Vic couldn't worry about it.

He had to talk to Gina.

Gina came out of the backstage ladies' room, pulled her phone from her purse to check on the kids and ran smack into a guy wandering the long narrow hallway. "I'm sorry," she gasped, grabbing his arm to keep herself from going over.

Three other doors—two dressing rooms and a storage room—dotted the long hallway, and she wondered why he'd be backstage. Maybe he worked at the club.

The guy grabbed her other arm. "No, problem, gorgeous. You okay?"

His shaved head and body-appraising leer gave her chill

bumps. *Creepy*. When he zeroed in on her breasts, unease snapped at her and she burrowed into the wall. She smelled alcohol. Great. The music from the bar blared and the dressing room doors were closed. Where the hell was the band?

"I'm fine, thanks. Just heading back to my friends." She tried to sidestep him.

Maybe if he knew people were close, he'd go away.

As she moved, he put an arm on each side of her, caging her in.

All those self-defense tactics Michael had drilled into her were about to be put to use. She knew not to go for the crotch first. Men expected it. Plus, he was a big guy, maybe six feet, and she'd have to hit him hard enough to ensure he wouldn't recover fast and grab her. She'd poke him in the eyes. Or maybe a chop to the throat and then blast him with a knee to the groin. But that would really piss him off. She'd try reasoning first.

With her hand on his chest, she pushed. "You need to back off."

The drunk, already only inches away, took a step closer. "Or what?"

So much for reasoning.

"She asked you to back off."

The drunk swiveled his head and found Vic standing behind him. Thank God. The breath she'd been holding burst free. With his talent for soundlessly sneaking up on people, no wonder Vic excelled at the covert stuff.

The drunk's hands remained on the wall and Gina contemplated giving him that shot to the balls.

"What?" he asked.

Vic's jaw tensed, but otherwise he didn't indicate what he might be thinking.

The guy finally faced Vic. Well, Vic's chest anyway and she covered her mouth to stifle a laugh. Tough guy wasn't so tough anymore.

Vic got into the drunk's space. "You like intimidating women?"

"Who the fuck are you?"

"Security." He jerked his thumb. "Beat it, asshole."

Rearing back and nearly knocking her with his elbow —*jerk*—the drunk took a swing at Vic.

So not a good idea.

Vic swept his right leg out, knocked the idiot off his feet, rolled him to his belly and jammed his knee between his shoulder blades. *That'll hold him.*

"Now, look, numb-nuts. I'm really not in the mood to rip your arms off and shove 'em up your ass. I'm going to let you up and have someone escort you out. You are not staying here tonight."

Gina stepped out of the way and stood behind Vic in case the drunk did anything stupid.

"Let. Me. Up," the jerk wheezed.

Vic, ever the gentlemen, held his hand out for the guy, shoved him against the wall face-first and held him there. He unclipped his phone and dialed.

"Meet me by the back hallway. We got someone needing help out."

He turned to her. "Wait here. I need to talk to you."

"Okay, but I've only got five minutes before we go back on."

"I'll be quick," he said. "Unless this dipshit gives me a hard time and I have to throw him off the roof."

He gave the guy a shove and headed to the end of the hallway, where he dumped him off. Good riddance. Vic strode toward her and she steeled herself for a lecture on personal safety.

"Are you okay?" He took her hand and entwined his fingers with hers.

"I'm fine."

"Why didn't you drop him?"

"I was about to let him have it when you walked up. I figured I'd try reasoning with him first."

"Next time, forget reasoning. He could have hurt you."

Gina checked her watch. Only three minutes before they went back on stage. Vic, still holding her hand, took a step closer. She'd backed herself into the spot where the drunk had pinned her. This time she liked the closeness.

No doubt he wanted to ream her about getting carried away during "Chain of Fools." He was lucky that was all she did, because she'd been thinking about jumping him since the pickle-in-your-pocket incident. She had no willpower when it came to this man.

"I'm sorry if I embarrassed you," she said.

He smiled wide. "You didn't embarrass me. Mike needed CPR, but I'm fine."

A laugh bubbled out. Poor Michael.

"So," he said, "you want to have dinner with me next weekend?"

Just like that. *Boom!* He'd asked her on a date. At least she thought it was a date. They'd been spending a lot of time together over the past week. It could be a friendly thing.

"Uh...a date dinner or a friend's dinner?"

"I think we're friends, right?"

She nodded.

"Have I ever asked you out to dinner?"

His eyes were getting greener by the second and sweat dripped down her back. "No."

"Then I guess it's a date."

"Uh."

He stepped back, held up two hands. "I know we haven't settled the whole thing about my job, but like you said last week, we're stuck. We've gotta go one way or the other, and I want to go forward. We may decide we hate each other."

"Unlikely."

"Still. We don't know if we'd even work out, and we're worried about the kids and what could happen. I'm not going anywhere until this Sirhan crap is settled. Let's take advantage of the time."

Why, oh why, did this make sense to her? Really, what were they so worried about? They might go out on a couple of dates and decide they drove each other crazy. They could just stay friends if it didn't work out.

"Gina, let's go," someone called from the stage, but neither of them moved. Her heart thumped louder than the music in the club and she battled her better judgment.

"I have to go. Can we finish this later?"

He dropped his head, but stepped back, his jaw tight.

"You're taking me home later, right?"

"I'll meet you here," he said.

"Okay. Think about where you're taking me to dinner next week. I like anything. Particularly if you'll be dessert."


The answer was yes.

Vic tried smacking her on the butt, but she scooted away. He grabbed the back of her pants, spun her around and kissed the hell out of her. Plastered against the wall, her lush skin pressed into him. He knew he'd done the right thing. They'd be great together.

"Hey," one of the band guys said, storming around the corner and seeing Gina being mauled. "Oh. Sorry. We're ready."

Vic grunted. His pants were bulging. Again. He wondered if men ever died from too many hard-ons. "I'm ready too," he whispered in her ear.

She laughed. "I guess you'll have to stay that way."

"What else is new?"

## 9

*Man Law: Never wonder if you should have thrown the asshole off the roof.*

VIC DRAGGED HIS TIRED ASS INTO HIS OFFICE, SET HIS COFFEE down and dropped into the desk chair. Why did Mondays always have to happen on Monday? Why couldn't Friday happen on Monday? Jeez, he was worn thin, his brain whacking out on him. Friday on Monday? What the hell?

He unbuttoned his sleeves and rolled them up. He'd worn a nice shirt and dress pants today. Mike always wanted everyone all spit and polish when clients visited. As long as he didn't need to do a song and dance, he didn't give a shit. Right now he wanted a bed. And for a change, he wanted to sleep in it. Alone.

After taking Gina home Saturday night he'd stayed to help the guys keep an eye on the house. With the kids sleeping at Mike's and Gina alone in the house, it seemed the right thing to do. Only problem was, Gina the aerobics queen had a 9:00 a.m. step class on Sunday mornings. Then came the normal grocery shopping, kids' birthday parties, sports, blah, blah, blah. He'd finally dropped into bed at midnight but was so overtired sleep wouldn't come.

If he didn't get some downtime soon, he'd go ballistic and that wouldn't be pretty.

With a quick tap his laptop whirred to life. A couple of clicks later he was into his email. Sixty-four messages. He'd be here all morning.

Leaning forward, he scrolled through the list, deleted all the junk and reduced the number to fifty. Not bad. The first four were operatives checking in. Old Marty got himself shot in the foot, literally, by some pissed-off Iraqi and needed medical attention. Wasn't Marty the guy who'd complained that protection details were boring? That'd teach him.

The next email came from one of those websites where people upload their home movies and send them to friends. The subject line said Howdy Doody Sent You a Video.

Assuming the virus protection would do its job, he clicked the link.

The video popped onto the computer screen and Vic jerked his head back. "What the..."

Gina, wearing the wicked V-neck T-shirt and tight pants, belted out "Chain of Fools." This was from Saturday night. Fuck a duck. He clicked back to the email. Howdy Doody? Who the hell used Howdy Doody as a screen name? Gina's voice boomed in Vic's ears and he took a deep breath, tensed his muscles, let the breath out. The roaring in his head quieted.

*Stop and think about this.* He clicked back to the video and studied it. Grainy. Probably a cheap cell phone. He pictured the bar in his head. The stage, the crowded tables, the bad lighting. He locked it into his brain and focused on the computer. The video was shot from roughly the same area where he'd been sitting. Maybe a little to the left, but the same vicinity. The cameraman swiveled the camera on himself and smiled.

*Son of a bitch.*

The drunk who'd harassed Gina in the hallway.

"Yo." A voice came from the doorway and Vic nearly bolted from his chair.

Tiny, dressed in Dockers and a blue pullover, threw up his hands "Whoa. Sorry, dude. Didn't mean to startle you."

He went back to his computer but waved Tiny over. "Take a look at this."

"Hey," he said from behind Vic's chair. "It's Gina. Cool. She's pretty good. You shoot this?"

Vic sat back. "No. That's what's pissing me off. It's from Saturday night. And check this." He hit the rewind button on the screen until they got to the man's face.

Tiny shrugged. "Who is it?"

"That's the dickhead that cornered Gina."

"Huh?"

Vic didn't have time for a lengthy explanation. "You wanna focus here or what? This asshole must have gotten my name and the company I work for from someone at the club. How else would he have my email address?"

The phone buzzed. "Vic?" the assistant said.

Why couldn't that goddamned phone burst into flames? "What?"

"Khalid Sirhan. Line one."

A thought bashed its way into Vic's skull and he gripped the edge of the desk. Oh, no. Couldn't be.

"Whoa," Tiny said for the second time since he'd walked in.

"Tell Mike I need him in here," he told the assistant, then grabbed a pen and paper and shoved it at Tiny. "Take notes."

"Got it."

Vic hit line one. "Sirhan? How you doin' today?" he asked in his practiced, happiest-guy-in-the-world voice.

"You got my email?"

He fisted both hands.

"Which one would that be?"

"The one of your lovely lady."

Yep. No more hoping Sirhan wasn't behind the video. *Okay. Work this problem. Concentrate.* He had to control his temper and not let this fucker get to him.

"Tell me the guy that shot it was one of yours." He laughed. "I knew I should have thrown that bastard off the roof."

Tiny curled his lip and gaped at Vic like he'd lost it.

"Well," Sirhan sighed, "it was unfortunate for my friend you arrived when you did. Much can happen to a woman in five minutes. Particularly one with her assets, and he was disappointed not to have sampled."

Vic pictured tearing Sirhan's head off and shoving it up his ass. That was about the only thing keeping him from blowing his oats right on the desk. Did someone just put his stomach through a grinder?

He didn't want to be talking to this asshole about Gina, but showing his discomfort? Not an option. "Sirhan, please. That numb-nuts, pain-in-the-ass fuckwad couldn't get it up enough to sample. Besides, she'd have taken him down long before that. My girl can pack a punch."

His girl? What the hell was he saying? If anything he should deny he and Gina were a couple. Realistically, though, Sirhan wouldn't have believed him. Plus, he didn't want to underestimate the sheikh's not-so-merry men. They had managed to rattle Vic already and that was saying something.

"It does not matter now," Sirhan said. "There will be next time. Maybe the little girl. You never know."

Tiny, who'd obviously heard enough, vaulted out of his chair and stormed from the office. Vic couldn't blame him and did a quick ten count to calm his raging blood pressure.

"What I know," he said, "is that your amateur bunch of pissants won't get anywhere near that little girl. You'd better stick with me. I'm a lot more fun."

The line went dead.

The bile swelled in his throat and he tried to swallow it back. *Don't get sick. Don't let him win.* But, Lily. Precious, pretty Lily. Ah, shit. With no time to spare, Vic grabbed his garbage can and heaved until his empty body shuddered from the intensity. The thought of Lily being raped would never leave his mind.

"Are you all right?" The assistant asked from the doorway. She, along with the rest of the floor, probably heard him coughing up his breakfast.

"Yeah, but I'll need a new garbage can. I'll take care of this one."

Tiny came back in. Handed Vic a wet paper towel.

"Thanks," he said, leaning his head back and spreading the towel on his face. The cool wetness took the burn from his cheeks, and the throbbing in his head settled to a dull beat.

"What can I do?" Tiny asked.

Vic pulled the towel from his face. "Cuz, you're going to help me find this fucker. I'm done waiting on his ass."

. . .

FORTY MINUTES LATER, AFTER A QUICK MEETING WITH THE support people and a shower in the building's gym—a desperate and futile attempt to wash away the filth Sirhan had dumped on him—Vic tracked Mike down. No way would a terrorist beat him.

He stepped into Mike's office. "Hey."

Mike did a double take on the dress shirt Vic wore. "Sorry I couldn't join you before. I had a client here. Nice shirt."

"I borrowed a clean one from your stash. Another call from our friend Sirhan."

"And you needed a clean shirt?"

Vic nodded. "Yep."

"This guy getting to you?"

"What's getting to me," he said, dropping onto the couch, "is this waiting around with my thumb up my ass. I just met with the team and we're gonna see if we can flush him out."

"How?"

"The old-fashioned way. I told Jimmy, Dutch and Billy to hit the streets, ask questions. Maybe some lowlife some-where knows something. Janet's working on where he's calling from. My guess is he's around. Maybe not in the city, but close. He's not dumb enough to call from a traceable line, but you never know."

"What'd he say to you?" Mike wanted to know.

And now Vic needed to decide if he'd tell Mike the truth about the video and the threats Sirhan made. Mikey would go ape-shit and Vic didn't want him going over the edge before anything really got going. Why let his best friend worry over something that might only be an empty threat? Nope. Better to keep it quiet.

Besides, Vic had the situation under control. He hoped.

"You think Roxi will let me tap into Phil?"

Mike leaned forward, rested his elbows on the desk. "You're not going to tell me what he said *and* you want my wife's help?"

Vic shrugged. "She is the publisher of the second largest daily newspaper in this city and Phil, as you know, is the best investigative reporter around."

"Here's the deal." Mike sat back again. "I do not want Roxann involved in this. You call her and ask her about Phil, but *you* tell her to stay out of it."

For the first time all day, Vic laughed. "You're using me for an end run?"

"You want this, you do it my way. If I tell her to stay out of it, she'll do it anyway. If you tell her, she'll listen."

Vic stood, shook his head. Marriage. Go figure. "I'll talk to her."

"And get my shirt cleaned before you bring it back."

Right. Any more calls from Sirhan and he would be buying two new shirts. One for Mike and one for himself. Not only that, but he had just lied. Technically he'd lied by omission, but it still counted. How the hell could a guy tell his closest friend some scumbag threatened to rape his seven-year-old niece? Mike would eventually find out because, well, he was Mike. Nothing stayed out of his range for long. He would deal with the fallout later. And knowing Mike, it wouldn't be easy.

It might even cost him their friendship.


"Hey, Rox," Vic said when she came on the line.

"You read my mind. I was going to call you this afternoon."

Roxann calling him. Hmmm.

"Oh?"

"Gina and I are going shopping tonight."

Gina going shopping? He didn't know this. Did she think she'd be going alone?

"Michael is going with us," Roxann said.

"Poor schmuck."

"That's what he said. I need to know where you're taking Gina on this big date Friday night."

What was Roxann up to? "Why?"

She sighed. "Nothing is easy lately."

"You brought it up, sister."

"For crying out loud, she wants to buy a new dress and asked me to help. I have no idea where you're taking her. How am I supposed to find something appropriate?"

Gina wanted to buy a new outfit. To go on a date with him. A sudden warmth worked its way through his system.

"I'm not telling you where I'm taking her. I want it to be a surprise, and I don't trust you."

"Excuse me?" Roxann shot, ready to do battle.

"*But* I'll tell you it's nothing too fancy. I'll be wearing a sport coat. Probably dress pants. Does that help?"

"So we're talking casual elegance here?"

Vic smiled. "Now you're fishing. That's all you're getting. I'm changing the subject back to why I called you."

Laughing, Roxi asked, "Okay. What can I do for you?"

"Can I borrow Phil?"

"For what?"

He had her attention. He had never asked for Phil's help before, and Roxann's big story radar probably went haywire.

"Hey now, you can't get involved. I'll be deep-sixed by Mike, and I've got other problems right now. I don't need him riding my ass. Promise me you'll stay out of this. You already know what you need to."

"Which isn't a whole lot since all you and Michael will tell me is some bad guy is mad at you."

"And that's all you need to know. Rox, if I didn't think the *Banner* could get a helluva story out of this, I wouldn't ask. Can I call Phil?"

Vic sat back and waited. Typically, she couldn't resist the pull of a big story.

She sighed again. "Fine. I'll tell Phil to expect your call. I'll clear it with his editor. And won't that make me popular?"

"Thanks, Roxi. You're the best."

"Yeah, but you still won't tell me where you're taking Gina."

"Nope. Gotta fly."

He hung up and spun his chair to the window. Things were looking up. If he had anything to do with it, old Sirhan was about to get a butt load of firepower coming his way.

The hunter about to become the hunted.

## 10

*Man Law: Never try to figure out a woman's logic.*

VIC STEPPED UP TO GINA'S BACK DOOR AND GOT A WOLF whistle from Billy, on guard duty for the night.

"Fuck off," Vic said.

He had to admit he looked sharp in his gray slacks and black sport coat. He'd even worn a new white dress shirt.

"I may bang you myself," Billy said, risking an ass kicking.

Vic gave him a good dose of the death glare and knocked on the door. A minute later Gina appeared in front of him and the spit in his mouth dried up.

"Whoa." He took in what was possibly the sexiest dress he'd ever seen. He wanted to nibble that bit of bare shoulder. And forget about the newly styled curls. He loved her old hairstyle, but she'd gotten a good two inches hacked off, and her hair now framed her face and accentuated her dark eyes. Wow. Friggin' stunning.

Billy, being the nosy bum he was, stepped over, beheld Gina and dropped to his knees. Asshole.

Gina laughed. "You guys are great for my ego."

"Where's your pride?" Vic asked. "Keep this up and I'll revoke your man card."

He put a hand on Billy's shoulder, shoved him sideways, and he went over like a dead tree. "Go find your own girl. I got dibs on this one."

He stepped into the house and closed the door. "You look amazing. That dress should be on *America's Most Wanted*."

Gina did a little twirl. "Roxann helped me pick it out. Check out these shoes."

They were black with a single strap across the front and five-inch heels. He had no idea how she walked in them.

"Don't they hurt?"

She laughed. "Of course they hurt. I'm hoping we won't be doing a lot of standing."

Hell, if he had his way, they'd be horizontal already. Something weird happened, because his cheeks got hot. Could he actually be blushing? Wussy boy.

"Nope. Not a lot of standing happening tonight," he said.

He listened for kid noises and asked, "Kids already gone?"

"Michael and Rox picked them up a while ago. They're going up to the lake house for the night. Tiny went too."

It just got better and better. Kids gone for the whole damn night. He'd gone to heaven. No doubt.

"You ready to go?"

"I am. I told Michael I'd call a few times to check on the kids. I hope you don't mind."

"Don't mind at all. Let's roll. I got a big night planned for you."

"I want to talk about something first."

Not even out the door yet and it sounded like he was in trouble. Not good.

"Sure," he said, not sure at all.

"I don't think we should have sex tonight."

Okay, then. Not what he expected her to say and, prick that he was, his heart nosedived right to his feet. But he could be an understanding guy, at least try to see what her fucked-up logic might be.

"You're disappointed," Gina said, turning away from him.

He grabbed her arm. "If I'm being honest—and that's what you always want—hell yeah, I'm disappointed. Our past history should tell you I pretty much want you all the time. I don't think there's anything wrong with that."

"I think it's important that we start over," she said. "Treat this like the first date of two people that don't know each other. I want us to be sure the chemistry is there without the sex. Does that make sense?"

Women. They drove him crazy.

"It doesn't make sense to me, but I'm useless where women are concerned."

"You're not useless. I don't know why you think that."

He held up both hands. No sense rehashing his baggage. "We've been friends a long time. How do we pretend we don't know each other? I know you'll eat fish but prefer a good steak. I know you love sunny days and getting a tan even if it's bad for you. I know you like country music, but you're too chicken to tell your rock-n-roll friends. Hell, I know what every inch of your body feels like when it's under mine." He stopped, thought for a minute. "If you don't want to have sex, we won't, but I don't think we can pretend this is a normal first date."

Her eyes narrowed to slits, and she pursed her lips. He'd gotten her thinking.

"I see what you're saying, but I think we need to make sure we like each other outside of the bedroom."

Was she out of her mind? How could she not know he liked her? If he didn't, he wouldn't be trying to thrash her every chance he got. For Christ's sake, why was this so complicated?

"Aha!" Vic waved his finger. "There's where your theory falls apart."

"Huh?"

"We've never had sex in a bedroom. We've done it on the beach, against the damned washer and we've done it in your kitchen, but never in a bedroom. Case closed. Let's go."

Gina laughed and folded her arms. "You don't expect me to go for that, do you?"

Striding to the back door, he put his hand on the knob. "I just want to get the hell out of this house and take you on a date. Can we forget about everything for a few hours and have a nice time?"

He opened the door when she started toward him.

"Okay, but I'm not having sex with you tonight."

"I'm available," Billy yelled from outside.

Vic winced. Freaking great. He'd hear about this for the next twenty years. They cruised by Billy and Vic pointed at him. "Don't forget I own you."

Billy stopped laughing. Vic had pages and pages of blackmail material on these guys, and he got extra lucky with Billy, because he had pictures from the night Billy tried to pick up a woman who was a man in drag. Good times, that.

Vic snorted and opened the car door for Gina. "The house is locked. Call me if anything comes up."

Nothing better come up. That was all he had to say. He didn't want to be disturbed while he had Gina all to himself.

GINA SCANNED THE MARINA AS VIC OPENED THE CAR DOOR. Moist lake air surrounded her and in three seconds, her curls would go rampant, but not a problem. The hairstylist assured her the new styling products would keep frizz at bay. The sky held a few fluffy clouds with a backdrop of orange and pink from the setting sun. The usual smattering of airplanes circled, waiting to land at O'Hare.

All in all, a great night for a sail, but were they really dressed for it? She didn't think so. Large sailboats and speedboats rocked quietly in their slots. She looked around for Vic's but didn't see it. A motor hummed as a cigarette boat made its way out of the marina to open water.

"Curious?" Vic asked, leading her down the dock.

"I'm wondering how I'm climbing onto a sailboat in these shoes."

"You're not climbing onto a sailboat. You're climbing onto that."

He pointed to the end of the dock where a luxury yacht sat, its motor idling. A gangplank rested against the dock, and Gina glimpsed a uniformed man at the deck's rail.

"I don't understand. I thought we were going to dinner."

"We are. On that." He pointed to the yacht again.

Warmth filled her. The yacht had to be a hundred and fifty feet long, gleaming white with three decks and, with the dusk sky behind it, could have been something out of a travel book.

"I don't understand," she said again, feeling like an idiot. "Are you teasing me? I'll have to hurt you if you're teasing me."

Vic smiled. Not the player smile, though. The real one that came out when he seemed truly entertained. A slightly crooked incisor peeked out and she couldn't help grinning.

"I'm not teasing you," he said. "Let's go. They're waiting for us."

With his hand resting on her back, he guided her to the gangplank. She stepped up to it and stopped. This was for her. Truly? "Who owns this boat?"

She couldn't help it. She had to know.

"A client who owes me a favor. A big one. I've been saving it for something good."

"And dinner with me qualifies?"

"Absolutely."

She glanced at the yacht, then back to him. Her body ached. It had to be coming apart. There was no other explanation for the implosion inside her. He'd done this for *her*. He'd taken the time to make it happen. He could have made a dinner reservation somewhere and she'd have been satisfied. Her eyes began to pulse and she slapped her hands over them to hide the tears. Typically, she cried at the end of a date, not the beginning.

Without saying anything he pulled her into his arms and kissed the top of her head. He knew her well enough to know she'd be embarrassed. He waited and, after a minute, she pulled her hands away, wrapped her arms around his waist.

"Thank you."

"It's not over yet. You might hate me by the time we dock again." He glanced around. "I'd really like to get you inside until we get on the lake."

Gina started up the gangplank. "Is someone watching us?"

"I don't want to risk it. Just so you know, a couple of the

guys are going to be tagging along in another boat. I don't think anyone will bother us, but it's a big lake with lots of access points. It's a precaution."

The captain waited at the rail and introduced himself. They had a crew of eight on hand to serve their needs. Eight people. For the two of them. It should have been funny, but somehow, in the midst of all this luxury, it fit.

Vic led her inside the cabin and Gina's gaze traveled along the enormous interior. What a wonder. Large windows lined the sides and the lake sparkled beyond them. Three leather sofas sat in the middle of the space with a couple of wingback chairs and ottomans. The walls, painted a soft taupe, had dark oak trim and the soft overhead lights gave a feeling of warmth. Gina let out a low whistle.

"Yeah," Vic said. "Not too shabby. We'll hang here until we get on the water. We're going to eat on deck. If that's okay?"

Was it okay? Surely, he had to be joking. "That sounds great."

It had been a long time since she felt that way about sharing a meal with a man.

The lights of the Navy Pier Ferris wheel glittered in the distant darkness while the skyline loomed in a brilliant array of blues and reds and white. Perfect weather for a perfect night. Gina tilted her head toward the winking stars and breathed in. Chicago was a magnificent city, and seeing the tall buildings against the lakefront made her appreciate having city life and a beach all in one.

Vic stepped behind her, slid his sport coat over her shoulders and ran his hands down her arms. She'd give him a week to cut that out. Then again, a week might not be long enough. Odd how she had missed the simple things like a touch from the man she cared for.

"The wind is kicking up," he said.

"A little, but the fresh air feels good."

He leaned into her and said, "Good enough to score me some points and get you to rethink that no-sex thing?"

She laughed. One-track mind.

"You're not answering," he said.

Damn straight she wasn't. "So—" she faced him, "—what did you have to do to get use of this floating palace?"

The dim overhead lighting fell across his face and his eyes zeroed in on her.

"Can you talk about it?" she asked.

He hesitated a moment then said, "Monk, Billy, Tiny and I pulled the owner's daughter out of a makeshift jungle prison in Colombia."

Gee, just a normal day at the office. Gina gaped at him.

"What?" he asked.

"It's a good thing, what you do. I'll never understand your love of the danger, but it's honorable and I can see why you do it."

He shrugged. "I wouldn't say I love the danger."

"But you get a rush from it. Part of you enjoys the dark side and that's okay. It makes you who you are."

Vic leaned in, pushed a curl from her cheek. "Honey, it's a job. The military trained me and I wanted to use those skills in the private sector. And thank God for dumb-ass hotel heiresses or I'd be unemployed."

They both laughed. "Doubtful," Gina said. "I have to say, as a parent, I can't imagine how that man felt when you brought his child home."

Just a foot from her, the warmth of his body reached her and she moved closer. He smelled male, clean, and all she wanted was to crawl inside him. She grabbed his shirt and hauled him down for a lip-lock and, oh yes, the heat was there, firing her system.

He wrapped his arms around her, and his hands wandered up and down her body, slowly exploring and making her legs tingle.

More. That was what she wanted, and he must have anticipated the primal urge, because his hands were suddenly on her breasts. Oh yes. She hadn't been touched like this in a long time and the heat drilled deeper into her core. *I'm going to ignite this whole damn boat.*

She left behind the lonely young widow and was now a desirable and wanted woman. He slowed the kiss's furious pace, and disappointment dropped on her. He pulled away an inch, giving her the classic Vic grin.

"That no-sex thing isn't sounding so good right now, is it?"

It really would have been fun to clock him, but he was right. She'd turned into an inferno in his arms.

Something about him made her always want to go fast. As if it wouldn't last and she needed to experience him before it ended.

She ran her hands up his shirt. "Teasing me won't get you laid tonight. Just remember that. *Wonder* Butt."

"Excuse me?"

She laughed. "Martha nicknamed you Wonder Butt."

Martha, her fifty-something cubemate, got all hot and bothered whenever Vic came into the accounting department.

His shoulders sagged. He opened his mouth, shut it again, and then said, "Are you kidding?"

"Nope."

"How widespread is that?"

She burst out laughing and, still in his arms, eased around to stare out over the rail. "I think it's contained to accounting, but if you're not nice to me, I can change that."

He leaned in; his body solid against hers. "You're a witch," he whispered and kissed her neck.

If she could stay like this, just for a little while, she'd be happy. And that was saying something, because being happy with Vic had never entered her realm of thinking.

None of this could come to any good.

She'd take the time she could get, and then they'd go on with their lives.

The emotional rubble he'd leave behind would be murder. And Vic would give her emotional rubble. He couldn't help it, and she had to accept it. She couldn't live with a man who faced constant danger.

Not again.

## 11

*Man Law: Always stay sharp.*

"IS IT REALLY OVER?" GINA SIGHED AS THEY WALKED DOWN the dock after leaving the yacht.

Vic laughed. How could anyone not love Gina? She always said what was on her mind. Maybe he could learn. "Afraid so, babe. Gotta give the floating palace back."

She turned toward the yacht. He'd have to see if he could snag the big tub another time. Seeing her have fun made him want to do this for her again. Dare he say it made him happy?

Him? Happy?

His view of happy had become wildly skewed recently. He thought the job made him happy, but he wasn't so sure anymore. The constant training, working his body to the brink, got old. Not to mention the nightmares. He'd stopped counting the lives he had taken over the years, but they haunted him at night.

*Forget it. Push it aside. Do the work and shut the hell up.*

Not wanting to spend too much time in the open, he grabbed Gina's hand to keep her moving. Something had his nerves firing. He had the guys check the lot and everything seemed quiet, but his senses still buzzed.

He got to the Tahoe and opened the door for Gina while scanning the area from the corner of his eye. Typical line up of cars. A couple of Mercedes, a few Beemers. The Ferrari was a sweet ride, and he would have loved to slide behind the wheel of that baby. Then he spotted the Chevy and everything went slow motion. The other cars disappeared from his mind, and his arms stung. What the hell was a beat-up eighty-five Chevy doing here?

Best he could tell, the car was empty. The employees couldn't park here. The owners' lot required a parking pass and employees didn't get one. Someone owning one of these boats wouldn't be driving that piece-of-shit car.

Not about to leave Gina to check it out, Vic slid his phone out of his pocket and dialed Monk. He stepped sideways to block the lake breeze but kept an eye on the Chevy. Gina knocked on the window and put her hands out palms up. He held up a finger.

"Did you check out this Chevy?" Vic asked when Monk answered.

"It's locked, nobody in it. We checked your car too. It's clean."

"Did you get the plates?"

"Yeah, but it's late and I can't find Janet. I'll have her run it in the morning."

"Roger," Vic said and hung up.

*Shit.* Who owned that fucking car? He checked his watch. Twelve-forty. Did he have Phil's cell number? A top-notch crime reporter would have a P.D. source who could run a plate at any hour, and Phil said he'd try to help when needed. He scrolled through his phone's contact list. Nothing for Phil's cell. Crap. He'd have to remedy that.

Gina opened the door, her lips tight with that frustrated-mother look. "What's wrong?"

"Nothing. I'm coming." He shut the door again, shoved his windblown and very annoying hair out of his face and moved to the driver's side of the truck. Still eyeing the Chevy, he reached around to his back and grabbed his trusty Sig. Gina sat staring out the window when he got in, so he slid the gun into the side pocket of the door. No sense upsetting her any further. He'd managed to keep the gun hidden all night. Why blow a great evening?

She finally turned to him. "Is everything okay?"

After a minute of debating with himself he nodded toward the battered car. "The cars parked here. That piece of crap doesn't belong."

She glanced out her window. "Oh."

"Don't worry about it. Monk will check it out. It could be a lead. Who knows?" He started the truck. "Let's get outta here."

He pulled onto jam-packed Lake Shore Drive to make his way to the North Side. No easy task with cars zooming by. He punched the gas to keep up with traffic. A busy night in Chi town.

Gina reached over, tapped on the radio and switched the station. He gave her a what-the-fuck face.

"What?" she asked.

"Man law violation." He flipped the station back. "Standard operating procedure. Whoever is driving chooses the music."

She waved him off. "That's just dumb."

"Oh, honey," he laughed. "You've got a lot to learn. There's a whole code we men live by. Ask Mike."

He checked the rearview. Switched lanes. He'd have to spend time educating Gina on man laws. He glanced at the mirror again. A car three back switched lanes with him. Was it a beat-up Chevy? Despite the lights lining Lakeshore Drive, he couldn't see well enough in the dark to know for sure. He shot back across two lanes and took the Addison exit ramp.

Gina grabbed the door handle and squeezed. "Wow. What is with the driving? Where are you going?"

He checked again. Shit. He'd picked up a tail. Two cars back. It had to be that Chevy. He stopped at a traffic light. Nobody moving from the car. He slid a sideways glance at Gina's wild-eyed expression.

"I think we have company." He dialed his phone.

She sucked in air. "Oh my God."

"Where are you?" Vic asked when Monk answered.

"Just got to Oak Street. What's up?"

"Turn around. I think someone is tailing me. I'm about to hit Addison. I'll drive around until you catch up."

The light turned green and Vic checked his mirror. Yep. Still there.

"So, what are we doing about this?" Gina asked, her voice a little squeaky. A nervous habit he'd noticed early on. She'd make a terrible spec ops person, but her honesty was the thing he loved most about her.

He picked a random one-way street and turned right. Parked cars lined both sides of the street, but most of the houses were dark, their inhabitants probably sleeping. "When Monk catches up to us, I'll lose this guy. Once I do that, Monk'll follow him and see where he goes."

"Sounds pretty simple."

He took a quick glance at her and shrugged. "If it works."

She fumbled in her purse. "I need to call Michael and check on the kids."

"Fine. But I'd know if there was a problem. Call anyway so you're not worried about them."

Vic's phone rang. "You back there?" he asked, sitting a little straighter in his seat.

He stuck his earpiece in so he could have both hands on the wheel while he talked with Monk.

"Yeah. I just turned onto Montrose. I think I see you. Four, five cars up. You're stopped in front of a dry cleaners?"

"Bingo. You're right behind my tail. Is it that Chevy from the lot? I can't tell from here."

"Roger that. Two people in the car."

"Is it?" Gina asked.

She hadn't yet learned the art of keeping quiet when he wanted to think. Vic held up a finger. She'd have to wait a sec.

"Okay," he said. "I'm gonna ditch this asshole. You stay with him and see where he goes."

"You want us to talk to him?"

"No. Just find out where he goes. We'll run the plate and the address and see what we've got. Let's get somebody on him. Do *not* lose this guy, Monk."

"Got it, boss."

He clicked off. Gina lowered her hands to her lap and furiously tapped them against her legs. Holy hell, the tension in the car could give a man a heart attack.

"Sorry. I had to think. Kids okay?"

"They're fine. Michael wants you to call. Keep him updated."

He squeezed her hand. "This is not a problem. The guys

will take care of it. I just wanna know who's back there. Nobody will get hurt. Okay?"

She nodded. "I hate this, but thank you. I'm okay. I trust you."

Not too bad, considering he'd thrown her life into a snake pit filled with terrorists. He pulled his hand away, put it back on the wheel. He had to find an alley, and Gina knew this neighborhood. Might as well keep her mind busy.

"Isn't there a long alley used for garbage pickup around here? I think it's behind a bunch of stores or something."

"Yes," she said, pointing out the windshield. "Turn right on the next block."

He checked the rearview. The Chevy was still three cars back. If he timed it right, he could swing the turn, haul ass into the alley and kill his lights. With any luck, the black Tahoe would be invisible, his tail would cruise by and Monk could take over.

"When I get to the corner, hang on, because I'm gonna floor it and go screaming into that alley. With the lights off, they shouldn't see us."

Gina, looking doe-eyed again, nodded.

He got to the corner, waited for the green light, made the turn and floored it. He reached the alley and—oh shit— someone had parked too close to the corner. The turn would be way too tight. Son of a bitch. They could easily swerve into the side of the building.

Adrenaline shot through him, making his arms and legs tingle again. He could do this, no problem.

*Concentrate.*

*Time it.*

*Wait.*

*Now.*

Gina plastered herself against the seat and said something, but it fizzled. Or maybe he blocked it out. He cut the wheel. The back end of the SUV fishtailed, but they hadn't hit anything yet. He killed the lights and shot down the alley, hoping he didn't hit a bystander and make them roadkill.

Halfway through the alley he checked his rearview. Took a breath. Let his body come down from the surge. Gina swung around and stared out the back window.

"Was that them?" she asked, panic lighting her voice.

Vic dialed Monk. "I think so."

"Yo," Monk said. "Nice piece of work there. I see you haven't forgotten everything you've learned."

"Yeah. You got 'em?"

"You bet your ass I do. I'll call you when we get somewhere."

"I have to tell you," Gina said, walking through her back door, "that scared the hell out of me."

Vic shut the door behind him. "Not your typical first-date stuff, huh?"

He wasn't kidding about that. The edge of the thrill had worn off and her body reacted by changing to lead and forcing her to drag it around. How did these guys do this for a living and not suffer from constant fatigue?

After kicking the killer high heels off, she leaned against the kitchen counter and almost heard her feet groan. "Not typical, but I wouldn't trade it. Dinner was amazing. Thank you."

He walked to her, hoisted her onto the counter and leaned in. His breath tickled her cheek and her insides coiled with anticipation. Why did she always respond to him this way?

"You are way too short," he said. "You're going to need a stepstool every time I want to kiss you."

Gina opened her legs so he could move closer. He wiggled his eyebrows.

A laugh was the only response she had. "I was giving you more room. I didn't mean it *that* way."

Not at the time anyway.

He had that smug grin on his face again and she smacked his arm. "Just shut up and kiss me."

*Please.*

Taunting her, he stepped back. She grabbed him by the shirt, hauled him to her and flattened herself against him for a mind-frying kiss.

He groaned. "That dragging-me-by-the-shirt thing. I love it. Remember that."

If she could crawl into his skin, it wouldn't be enough. She slid her hands up his chest and around his neck, drew him closer and wrapped her legs around him. The bulge in his pants pressed against her—*oh baby!*—sending a swirl of heat through her midsection. And all of a sudden, the no-sex theory seemed rather stupid.

The kids were gone. They'd have all night together. His hands explored and their lips collided in a glorious frenzy. She imagined them naked in bed together, and she'd have that big beautiful body all to herself. Finally, they could go slow and not rush it.

The swirl of heat funneled into a furnace blast.

A noise from the back porch snapped her to attention.

No.

Billy.

Out back.

The blinds were down, but with him standing on the porch just feet away, he might hear them through the walls.

She backed away, sucked in a breath.

"I know," Vic said. "No sex tonight."

"Not that. It's Billy. He'll hear us."

Vic moved away, put his head down. "Crap."

"What?"

He held his hands out. "You said no sex. That's what you said."

She snorted. "*You're* having a crisis of conscience. Mr. Anti-Emotion. Are you kidding me? Forget what I said. I changed my mind."

She jumped down from the counter and stalked him. He was *so* having sex with her tonight. Wicked bad sex. *Gymnastic* sex. Did he have any idea the effect he had on her? She hadn't experienced this kind of need in years. Goodbye numbness, because Vic made her feel anything but numb.

He angled around her, walked through the small dining room to the living room. That wouldn't help. Roy was on the *front* porch. Even when they were alone, they weren't alone. She grabbed the back of Vic's shirt, pulled it free from his waistband, but he slapped her hand away.

"No," he said. "This is a reaction to what happened in the car. It's an adrenaline rush. It happens to men in combat all the time. We get hard-ons from the action. You're probably having some female version of it."

Gina clenched her fists, let the sizzling frustration settle in. He was such an idiot. "What are you talking about? I didn't feel this way until you put me up on that counter. Maybe I thought about the last time we were together there. I don't know, but I can promise you it has nothing to do with that car following us. This, hot man in my life, is lust. Plenty of it."

"Hey," he hollered, pointing his finger at her and paying

no mind to Roy possibly hearing. "You were pretty friggin' adamant about not wanting sex. I'm trying to be a good guy here and not take advantage." He raked his hands through his hair and stalked the room. "I mean, seriously, if you want to get thrashed, I'll thrash you like you've never been thrashed, but you told me no."

He stopped pacing and stood in front of the sofa, his shirt half-untucked, his blond hair a shaggy mess, looking at her like she'd gone insane. Oh, she wanted to get thrashed, all right.

And he'd be the guy to do it.

Someone knocked on the front door.

"Oh, come on." Vic went to the door, checked the peep hole and flung the door open. Roy was standing there.

"What's the yelling?"

"We're fine," Vic said. "Just me trying to figure out the female persuasion, and you know how good I am at *that*."

"Dude," Roy said, fighting a laugh. "You tripping or something?"

Whatever happened to the days when people had sex without these distractions? "For the love of Pete," Gina said, marching to the door. "We're okay, Roy. Thanks."

She shut the door, clapped her hands together. "Well, then. This is not going how I thought it would. Maybe we should take a few minutes to calm down. How about some coffee? I only have decaf."

She might as well do something with her hands, because they obviously were not going to be on Vic any time soon. She could only blame herself for saying she didn't want to mess around. She'd never make *that* mistake again.

Vic dropped himself onto the well-worn couch and stretched his long legs. "No coffee. Thanks."

His cell phone rang and he pulled it from his pocket, checked the ID and hit the button.

"What's up? Got it. Wait till he gets there and then take off. Get some sleep. Yeah. Thanks."

He hung up, tossed the phone on the coffee table.

"That was Monk. They tailed the car to a house on the South Side. We'll run the plates and the location in the morning." He rubbed his eyes. "I'm so freaking tired."

Gina sat next to him. "Why don't you get some sleep? I've got two empty bedrooms upstairs." She smiled big. "I could put you in Lily's room with all the strawberries. I know how much you love them."

He managed to laugh. "Thanks, but I'm okay. I'm better than okay. I had a great time tonight, and that doesn't happen a lot."

"Me too."

Vic flipped her hair over her shoulder. "We'll borrow the boat again."

The stillness in the air didn't feel right. Something in the room had changed. He cleared his throat, which only made the feeling worse. They'd gone from blazing hot to ice-cold. They had to talk about it.

"Can we talk about what just happened?" she asked, knowing his unabashed love of talking about his emotions.

To her surprise, he nodded. "You need to be sure. I don't want you to regret it."

She slouched back in the sofa and shook her head. Would she ever understand him? "Why would you think that? I didn't regret it the other times."

He tilted his head back and huffed. "I'm a literal guy. You told me no sex and then you changed your mind. I wanted to make sure you changed it for the right reasons and not because you were, well, wound up."

This was a good man. Emotionally stunted, but with a heart as big as the Grand Canyon. She leaned over, rested her head on his shoulder. "I see your point. Sorry I confused you."

"I want you to be sure, and I know you weren't tonight." He kissed the top of her head, let his hand roam down her back and suddenly the energy stormed back into the room.

Her brain might not have been sure, but her body seemed pretty damned determined.

Why was this so difficult? Until Vic, she'd never thrown herself at a man and she certainly wouldn't have expected to be rejected. She ran her hand down the buttons of his shirt. "So, no sex tonight."

He groaned. "I've got a headache."

# 12

---

*Man Law: Always avoid complications.*

GINA OPENED HER EYES AND SQUINTED AT THE RED GLARE OF the digital clock. Three-thirty. Ugh. A muffled sound on the front porch, just below her bedroom window, rocked her to a sitting position. An intruder? Her heart hammered and she surveyed the room.

Moonlight slanted through the crack in the blinds. Nothing there. Now she was paranoid. Great. She took three deep breaths and laughed at herself.

A man's rumbled laughter sounded from below. Vic's laugh. He was still here?

Throwing the covers off, she went to the window and pressed her ear against the closed blinds. Vic and Roy must be on the front porch.

Maybe she'd head down there and visit with them. She wasn't getting any restful sleep anyway. She opened the closet door and yanked on the pull chain. Light flooded the closet. She stood for a second staring straight ahead at Danny's firefighter uniform. Four years and she hadn't moved it. The most she'd done was brush the dust off the shoulders.

"Oh my." She stroked the sleeve of the uniform.

A pang danced in her chest. Regret? Loss? She didn't know. She shifted and scrutinized the room. The same blue curtains, the same off-white bedspread with blue trim, the same light blue walls. Just as it had been when she had shared this room with Danny.

She wanted to use the kids as an excuse, that they didn't need her bringing men around, but four years later, she couldn't do it anymore. The loneliness closed in on her. She had allowed herself to become rooted in being a widow. Taking a risk on someone, getting hurt, frightened her. Rightly so, but it had to end.

She'd become anesthetized to the opposite sex. And then, two years ago, in her basement, a little piece of her came to life again. It took hold and hadn't let go. Twenty-four agonizing months.

She turned back to the uniform, pulled it down and hugged it to her. "I miss you and I still love you. Always will, but I'm ready to bring another man into this room. I've never done that before. I haven't wanted to, but now I do. As much as I want to hang on, I have to let you go."

She stood for a minute, crushing the uniform to her, trying to breathe in any remnant of Danny's scent, but nothing remained. Time had stolen it. Stripped it from her.

Danny was gone.

"Okay, Gina," she said aloud. "Time to get a life." She set the uniform back, kissing the sleeve before she scooted it out of sight. She'd keep it in the back of the closet for safe-keeping but wouldn't look at it every day.

She breathed in and the load lifted from her. The sadness faded. She let the weightless feeling surround her and enjoyed the obscure pleasure in it. Maybe Danny had somehow given her permission to take this step.

She yanked her bathrobe from the hanger, slipped it on over her nightshirt and took a minute to steady her quaking nerves for this next big step.

"Did you hear about Marty?" Vic asked Roy.

Vic should have gone home an hour ago, but he figured he'd give Roy a break, let him catch a combat nap and grab something to eat. When Roy returned, they started shooting the shit and here they were, on the porch in Gina's red rocking chairs. A relaxing breeze, no bad guys in sight. A perfect summer evening.

"That dumb-ass," Roy said shaking his head. "Who gets himself shot in the foot?"

Vic normally didn't find screwups amusing, but Marty hopping around on one foot gave him a good belly laugh. Lately, Gina had been making him laugh, too, but he wouldn't read anything into it. They were spending a lot of time together. That was all.

"He's coming home until his foot heals," he said. "He can't be hobbling after some diplomat on it. That'd be nice, huh? The body man on crutches? Dipshit."

The front door opened, and Vic and Roy both jumped from their chairs. Pressure bolted up Vic's spine and he reached for the gun at his waist. After getting tailed that evening, he wasn't taking any chances. Gina stepped onto the porch and he jammed the gun into the holster again. Holy crap. She'd startled him.

"Everything okay?" he asked.

"Uh-huh." She eyed him and his lame attempt to conceal the gun with his arm. "I couldn't sleep."

With his body on the down slope of the rush, he noticed Gina had scrubbed her skin clean of all makeup. Not that she wore a lot anyway, but he'd never seen her without makeup. With the bathrobe and her hair in a ponytail on top of her head, well, too damned cute.

"I'm sorry if we woke you," Roy said.

She waved him off. "I'm restless tonight."

She wasn't the only one. Vic hoped his pants wouldn't suddenly go snug around the crotch.

Gina glanced back in the house, then at Vic. "Can I talk to you a minute?"

Talk.

*Kill. Me. Now.* She wanted to talk. He hated talking. "Sure."

He wiped his sweaty hands on his pants and followed her into the house where she flipped on the lights and closed the door behind them. Maybe she was dumping him after one date. Wouldn't that be his luck? But they'd had a good time. Aside from the terrorist following them and the no-sex fight. All in all, a pretty good date.

"What's up?"

She scratched the back of her neck. "You were right about before. The no-sex thing. I wasn't ready."

Vic slid onto the arm of the recliner. He hated staring down at her and if he sat, they'd be eye level. "Okay. I'm glad we made the right decision, then. Is that what you wanted to tell me?"

She nodded. "Yep. Mostly."

Whew. Maybe she wasn't dumping him. She moved toward him, slid her arm around his shoulder and settled her leg on top of his. Nope, not getting the dumping feeling here.

"I figured it out, though," she said. "It's the bed."

He'd heard some good excuses, but that one took the prize. He puckered his lips to stifle a grin. "The bed?"

"You're confused again, aren't you?"

"Totally lost."

They both laughed.

"I can clarify. The times we had sex. That's all it was. Just sex. A frenzied rush to relieve the tension." She stopped, sighed. "Well, we screwed each other."

Thinking about sex with her sent his blood plunging south. He tried to get up, but she didn't move. "Yep. Got it. We're good."

"I'm not done."

Of course she wasn't. "Sorry."

"I've been upstairs, sleeping on and off, and when I heard you down here, I figured I'd visit. But when I opened the closet, I saw Danny's uniform and it hit me."

He had the urge to tell her not to say it. Selfish bastard that he was, he didn't want to talk about Danny. "What?"

"I don't want to screw you anymore."

*Oh, crap.* Now, that hurt. Dumped for a dead guy. He nodded. "Okay. That's all you had to say."

Everything inside him ached, but not a physical pain. Physical pain he could deal with. This was a widespread, chest-caving-in kind of dull ache, and he hated the weakness of it. He closed his eyes, got hold of his emotions. *Pain is just weakness leaving the body. That's all. Deal with it.*

"Hey," she said, getting his attention. He opened his eyes and she smiled at him. "I want to make love to you. In a bed. No frenzied rush."

What the hell? This was like being thrown around in

rough surf. Just a brutal pounding. He sagged back against the chair. No wonder he stayed away from the emotional stuff. Who could take all this shit? "Wow."

"Yeah, wow. I adored Danny and I've been hanging on to him out of loyalty. I convinced myself that sex with you wasn't a relationship. Bringing someone into my bedroom is different. That room has a lot of meaning to me, and I don't want to be reckless." She put her palms against her forehead. "Does that sound stupid?"

Was he supposed to answer that? Could be one of those fucked-up rhetorical questions.

She widened her eyes. "*Does* it?"

He *was* supposed to answer. Shit. "No. Not at all. I think it's—I don't know—remarkable that you know yourself that well. Danny was a lucky guy and I'm freaking out because I'm the guy you want to bring into that room."

And what right did he have? He'd make her life a war zone and, unless he could figure out a way to not cut loose after a few weeks, he'd hurt her.

"It's freaking me out too," she said. "But I'm not worried about it. I'm excited. This is a big step for me, and you helped me get there."

She stood, grabbed his hand and tugged him forward. Oh, no. He couldn't move. Nope. He should stay glued to the fucking chair because he knew what was next. She wanted them to go upstairs. He'd been thinking about this for months...and suddenly he didn't want to? What sane guy would say no?

But this was more than getting laid. Emotions would be involved and he'd screw it up. He always did. Danny had been a good man and Vic didn't deserve to take his place.

Gina bent over, got nose to nose with him. "There are no ghosts in my bedroom. I'm ready. Now stop thinking and take me to bed." She smiled. "If you don't, I may have to take Billy up on his offer."

Billy?

As if.

Vic gave her a gentle push backward and jumped up. "Screw that. What are we waiting for?"

He opened the front door and told Roy he'd be a while. Hopefully a long while. He locked the door, flipped the lights off and followed Gina upstairs. Roy's imagination would be running wild, but he wouldn't say anything. He knew Vic well enough not to give him crap about Gina. Other women, yes, but not her.

Waiting for him at the top of the stairs, Gina held out her hand. He took it and she led him down the short hallway to her bedroom, but his mind refused to absorb it as fact.

Things were about to get a whole lot more complicated.

"So, this is it." Gina held her arms wide. "My bedroom."

It occurred to her that Vic had never been in here. "It's a little small," she said, her nerves doing a jitterbug up her arms. "We gave the boys the bigger room."

Vic leaned on the doorjamb, inspected the room. "I don't think it's small."

"You can come in, you know. I won't bite."

He laughed and stepped in. "Well, that's a damn shame."

When he got close, she took note of the dark, puffy rings around his eyes and the five o'clock shadow. Tired. Maybe too tired. They should forget the whole thing. Shouldn't they? If they did, she could stop the gymnastics in her head, but that wouldn't make her happy either. Ugh. She'd give him the option. "You look tired. Do you just want to sleep? That would be fine too."

In three steps he reached her and slipped the belt off of her robe. "Not a chance, sweet cheeks. I've been a nice guy long enough."

He slid the robe off her shoulders, but she held it for a second. "I don't want to rush this. Okay?"

"Fine with me. You're my main focus these days, and I've got all the time in the world for whatever you want."

Zing! No denying the major innuendo behind that statement. She let the belt go. Bye-bye robe.

Nervous excitement bubbled just below her skin. Could he be feeling it too? This knowledge of everything changing between them. They'd been together before, but not like this. This was new and the anticipation heightened her curiosity.

"I'm nervous." Oh, very seductive.

She wished she'd thought to change out of her sleeveless nightshirt into something sexier. White cotton just didn't cut it. Of course, she'd have to wipe the dust off the sexy stuff, but at least she still owned some things. And they fit.

"I'm nervous too," he said. "It's a rush, isn't it?"

He reached down, grabbed the hem of her nightshirt and stopped. "I just want to see you. I've never seen you naked and I've been thinking about it." He paused. "Is that okay?"

She nodded and he tugged the nightshirt over her head.

The brush of his fingertips against her belly rippled through her and she forced herself not to grab him. She always rushed things with him. Always attacked him.

"You okay?"

"Yep. Trying not to rush."

He pushed her backward onto the bed. "I know, but it's better this way."

He gave her body a detailed inspection and she shivered. Men didn't look at her this way anymore, and she suddenly wanted her robe back.

"You have one hell of an amazing body."

"My ass is too big." How romantic.

He knelt next to her, flipped her onto her belly.

"Let me see this." He ran his hands over her back and ass while she prayed for a thirty-second rewind. How embarrassing.

"I love your ass. Who thinks it's too big? I'll kill them."

She snorted a laugh into her pillow until he straddled her legs and began kneading the tight muscles along her spine.

"Oh, that feels good," she said.

Vic laughed, leaned forward and kissed her cheek. "Gina Delgado, you little slut."

She shifted and he moved to the side, propped his head in one hand while moving the other over her shoulder, down her breasts. His fingertips were calloused but his touch soft, and Gina closed her eyes to enjoy the tingle moving through her lower body.

"Why am I the only one naked?"

He shrugged. "Because it's a major turn-on for me. Maybe I'll have you run around naked all the time."

"I'm for equality," she said, working the buttons of his shirt. "And I want these clothes off you."

When she got to the bottom, they both sat up and she pushed the shirt off his shoulders, but he wore a sleeveless T-shirt underneath. Too many damn shirts. She moved her hands underneath, over his solid abs, up to his shoulders, and pulled it off.

"Much better. Don't you think?"

"You're in charge right now."

She raised her eyebrows. "Oh, I like that idea. Now the pants."

"I got it." He rolled off the bed, pulled his gun from the holster and stuck it in her nightstand. She'd have to get used to the weapon's constant presence. Even when she couldn't see it, she knew he had it on him. The pants and briefs went next. A boxer briefs guy. She'd never noticed before.

The sight of him naked, the long, lean muscles, caused her nerves to bubble again. She'd known him over ten years and had barely seen him with his shirt off. Now he was naked in her bed.

And what a sight. He spent hours in the gym, and the proof of it stood in front of her. His body was part of his job and, as she'd heard him say, required maintenance. A faded round scar—probably a bullet hole—sat on his right shoulder, and she ran her fingers over it. Vic came off as an easygoing guy, but underneath lived a disciplined and dangerous machine.

Gina snuggled closer to him, reached up and pulled his head toward her. She kissed him hard, only wanting to feel the colliding tongues and clashing lips. She wanted him in a way she hadn't experienced in a long time and took strength in it. One of the insulating layers, the excess weight confining her, had come off, leaving her exhilarated and vulnerable at the same time.

Rolling on top of her, Vic trailed kisses down her neck, her shoulders, her breasts—oh God—she melted into the bed as his hands and mouth worked across her body. It had been too long since she'd felt this pleasure, and she fought the urge to hurry it along.

"You're making me nuts. I can't stand it."

"Do you like it?" he asked.

"Absolutely."

His erection pressed against her thigh, and her throat clogged. This time was different than the times before. The awareness of his touch was more important than rushing. She'd dreamed of him like this. How did she get this lucky?

"I'm flat-out crazy about you," she said, smothering his face with kisses. "You make me feel like a beautiful, desirable woman and, after three kids, that's a gift. I think about you day and night. I dream about having you inside me."

Did she really say all that to him? Maybe she needed to learn some restraint in the honesty department before he ran screaming from the house. This was a man with commitment issues, and she'd just poured her heart out.

"I love that," he said, kissing her nose.

"I'm sorry, I can't wait." She locked her legs around him as he slid into her. Oh yes.

He smiled at her and rolled his eyes up, and she laughed. She knew they'd both get as good as they gave. Everything in her somehow came free with him. All the issues went away.

They moved together as if they'd done this a thousand times and knew the nuances of each other's bodies. The squeezing in her lower belly began. She knew what was coming, that colossal shattering she'd learned to live without. For so long her body had held her captive until this pleasure seemed foreign to her, and now she had it again. Every nerve ending tingled and, when she opened her eyes, she found Vic watching her. Smiling a big toothy grin. Mr. Smug.

She laughed. "I should slap you."

"Kinky." He groaned when she tightened herself around him.

She could play smug too.

"Keep that up and this is going to be over quick," he said.

She slammed her eyes closed and a light show exploded inside her head. A cry tore free and she relaxed into it, let each wave of relief flow over her until her body refused to move.

Vic began moving again, bringing her back.

"Now it's your turn," she said, still working her hips and talking dirty to him. Talking dirty? Oh. My. God.

"Oh boy, that'll do it." After a few seconds of her whispering, his body stiffened. He groaned and his breath came hard and fast, until he fell apart on top of her.

"Very nice," he said into her hair.

With their bodies still joined, he rolled to his side and hugged her close.

A sudden panic gurgled in her throat, and she swallowed it back. Forced it away before it took hold of her. *Forget the fear and the risk. Forget about not getting emotionally involved. It's too late anyway. Just enjoy. Enjoy the time you have.*

"You're too much." She kissed his chest and ran her hands down his belly. "I'll never survive you."

"Yeah, you will. I'll make sure."

"Well, if I don't, we'd better make it worthwhile."

## 13

---

*Man Law: Always get out fast.*

VIC ROLLED OVER, REACHED OUT A HAND. NO GINA. HE opened his eyes, squinted against the morning sun squeezing through the edge of the window blinds. He checked the clock. Oh-eight-thirty. They'd only slept a few hours and he wanted more.

The smell of bacon frying smothered his senses and he grinned.

"Breakfast."

When the heck had a woman last cooked him breakfast? Usually he was up and out fast. He didn't have the need to rush out today. He wouldn't mind going back to sleep, but he wanted to get his ass to the kitchen and see what Gina had waiting for him. Maybe she'd be naked. Not likely with Dutch on the morning security shift. But a man could dream.

He rolled out of bed and slipped into his pants and T-shirt, bemoaning the lack of clean clothes. He didn't want Gina embarrassed when the guys saw him leaving in last night's clothes. Some women were funny about stuff like that. They didn't want anyone knowing they'd done the deed. His aunt called it the walk of shame.

When he strolled into the kitchen, he found Gina at the stove wearing the fluffy cotton bathrobe and about as far from naked as she could get. Her hair curled wildly around her shoulders and he remembered rifling his hands through it just a few hours ago.

"Morning," he said, kissing her on the cheek.

She set the spatula down beside the pan of scrambled eggs, grabbed him by the shirt and hit him with a lip-lock. Now, *this* was living.

"Hey, handsome," she said when she was done mauling him. "Coffee is just about done."

He moved to the side. "I could say you shouldn't have made me breakfast, but really, it smells great and I'm damn glad."

She laughed. "I love a big breakfast on Saturday mornings. The kids have gotten used to it."

She put her hands on his waist and scooted him sideways. "Have a seat. You're in the way."

"Can I help?"

"Nope."

A knock sounded on the back door and Gina opened it just as Vic hit the chair.

"Hey, Monk," she said. "Come on in."

Monk wore his usual outfit of cargo pants and a black T-shirt, his dark hair hidden under a bandanna. He spotted Vic in his undershirt and raised his eyebrows, but Vic didn't imagine his renegade friend ever suffered embarrassment.

"Sorry to interrupt. Smells good in here."

Gina shoved a plate of bacon and eggs in front of Vic and went back to the stove humming a song he couldn't place.

"You're in a good mood today," Monk said to her.

She shot him a wide grin. "A night of good lovin' will do that do a girl."

"Ho," he said, high-fiving her, and they both burst out laughing.

*Holy shit.*

"Gina, what the hell?" Vic said, his mouth full of eggs. So much for her being embarrassed about the walk of shame. "Why not call Rox and take out an ad in the *Banner*?"

With the spatula in hand, she rolled her eyes. "Do you think he can't figure it out? You're sitting at my table eating breakfast in your undershirt. I'm in my robe, and your car has been in my driveway all night. These men are not stupid."

She smacked Monk on the arm. "Have a seat. There's plenty of food."

Muttering over his food about women making him crazy, Vic gawked at Monk settling in at the table. "Why are you here?"

"I tried your cell, but it was off. We'll talk about that later. A couple of guys *were* tailing you last night. Maybe you could have kept your phone on so we'd know you weren't dead?"

Oh, please. Monk hurtling headfirst into mommy mode. *Kill me now.*

Vic dropped his fork and it clanged against the table. "Back off, Mommy. The guys knew exactly where I was. They could have rung the damn doorbell."

"Coffee?" Gina held the pot up.

"Thank you, darlin'." Vic pushed his mug forward and

earned himself a nasty glare. Some women didn't like being called darlin' and, apparently, Gina was one of them. *Note to self: never call Gina darlin' again.* He didn't mean anything by it. It came from his Southern upbringing. He was sure he'd called her that before.

"Sorry," he said.

She smiled. "You're forgiven."

She sat down next to him with her own plate of food.

"What's up?" Vic asked Monk. "You have something for me?"

Monk, in the process of inhaling his food, stopped, wiped his mouth and hands with a napkin and pulled a piece of paper from his pocket. "Here's the plate number on the Chevy and the address of the house. The car is registered to Gerard Conlin. He's an American citizen, grew up in Idaho. The house is owned by some real estate investment company. Janet's running it down. Seems fishy to me."

After reading the piece of paper, Vic handed it to Gina. "Uh-huh. I'll get the name of the company from Janet and have Lynx check it all out. Maybe Conlin is on the radar."

Nothing sickened him more than an American citizen working for a terrorist.

Vic slid a gander at Gina, who busied herself eating breakfast. "What else?"

"Not much. We got a guy on Conlin and if he goes anywhere, we'll see what's what. You want us to talk to him?"

Talk to him? No. Vic definitely didn't want to *talk* to him. He'd like to beat him within an inch of his life, but he didn't want to talk to him. "Nah. Let's do a sneak and peek on the place. See if we can find anything."

That got Gina's attention and she gave him a hard stare. Was she going to get all high and mighty on him? He shrugged. "We're not gonna steal anything. Checking him out is all. He may lead us to Sirhan and we can put all this bullshit behind us. Don't you want your life back?"

She lurched up, took her plate to the sink and scraped it clean. "Not at the risk of one of you going to jail."

Monk's eyes moved from Gina back to Vic.

"We only go to jail if we get caught. We generally don't get caught."

Sarcasm had probably not been his best choice, because she whirled on him. "This is funny to you?"

Monk threw his napkin on the table. "I gotta go."

"Chicken," Vic hollered as he flew out the door. He turned to Gina, let out a breath. "It is *not* funny. It *is* part of what I do, though. I've played outside the lines a long time. I'm not sure I know any other way."

Never had he made a truer statement. He played dirty most of the time. Justifying it became part of getting to the greater good. She would have to adjust. Certain things he couldn't change.

She picked up the empty plate in front of him, took it to the sink. "From now on, I don't want to hear about it. I don't want the danger in my face."

With deliberate and jerky movements, she smacked the faucet on. She was *pissed*. And he knew it had more to do with Danny than him.

He got up, went to where she stood and shut the faucet. "I'm sorry. I wasn't thinking. I won't talk about it in front of you anymore."

She leaned into him, rested her head on his chest. "I don't want to spend my days worrying. I just can't do it."

Oh boy. They were right back where they started. He had a dangerous job and she couldn't be with a guy with a dangerous job.

The phone rang. Saved by the bell. Gina stepped back and reached for the cordless.

"It's Roxann."

She spent a couple of minutes on the phone then came back to him. "She's taking Lily for a pedicure. How does that happen? Do you know the last time I had a pedicure?"

Vic held up his hands and she said, "It's been a long time. You don't even want to see my feet."

No lie there. The body parts he had interest in had nothing to do with feet. He reached over and tugged on the belt of her robe.

"I'm not really a foot guy, anyway."

She arched an eyebrow, while his hands roamed inside her robe. "I can see that."

"What do you want to do today?" He leaned down, kissed her neck.

When her arms came around him, he licked behind her ear, and she groaned. "I want to screw your brains out, and then I want to drive up to the lake and see my family."

"Since you shouldn't go alone, I'll have to go with you." He trailed kisses down her neck. "Is that a problem?"

"Not if you keep kissing my neck like that."

He stepped back, grabbed her hand and hauled her toward the stairs. "Then let's get ourselves laid. We've got a busy day ahead of us."

## 14

*Man Law: Never mess with a guy's grill.*

"MONK TOLD ME YOU WERE TAILED LAST NIGHT," MIKE SAID, throwing Vic a towel after an intense game of Marco Polo with Jake.

The patio scorched Vic's feet and he slid into his flip-flops.

Matt lounged on one of the cushioned chairs, playing with his PSP. Gina sat next to him, soaking up the sun in a red bikini, and Vic smiled to himself. He now knew exactly what was under that bikini.

"Monk's got a big mouth," Vic said, toweling off.

"At least he told me about it, which is more than you did."

Mike in a pissy mood. *Lucky me.* "Nag, nag, nag. Get over it, Mary, or I'm divorcing you."

"Nice." Mike laughed. "I need a beer. Be right back."

Vic took in the beauty of Lake Geneva. The second deepest

lake in Wisconsin, one hundred and thirty-five feet deep and twenty-one miles around. Lush green trees dotted the lakefront, but not enough to obscure the views from the houses. And these were some houses. Big money here. Vic didn't usually go for the upscale stuff, but he loved this view. Something about the place let him forget about life and kick back.

The late-afternoon sun bounced off the water as speed and sail boats cruised by. Big fluffy clouds offered intermittent relief from the heat. Just a damn good day.

Mikey had done well for himself with this lakefront property. He'd bought it a few years earlier, leveled the existing structure and rebuilt to his specifications. Vic had made himself at home here many times, and Mike never seemed to mind. Even after Mike and Roxann got hitched, they'd always encouraged Vic to use the house when he wanted.

Vic thought about buying a place of his own up here, but that went away quick. Too permanent.

Mike handed him a beer and sat down at the patio table. "Janet get back to you on that address?"

"Yeah. The real estate company that owns the house is part of a shell company. She's running it down. My guess is our friend Sirhan owns it."

"Probably a good guess."

Vic draped the towel over his chair, sat and clinked his beer bottle against Mike's. They both took a slug.

Mike propped his sandaled feet on the table. "I got a call from the owner of the property that backs up to the farm."

What was this now? Vic and the guys had been out there late Thursday firing off rounds, but hell, that neighboring property was almost a thousand acres. The guy couldn't have heard anything.

"And?" Vic asked.

"He wants to sell it."

Vic's heart may have gone pitter-patter. He wasn't sure. "Don't tease me, Mikey."

"I'm not."

Vic leaned forward. Last year he had the idea of opening a training center where guys could brush up their special ops skills, but the farm didn't have enough acreage for what he had in mind, so he'd given up on it.

Being Mr. Proactive, Mike had approached the owner of the neighboring property and told the guy to call him if he ever wanted to sell.

"What does he want for it?" he asked, his mind going to the hefty fees they could charge.

"A lot, but I wasn't going to negotiate until I talked to you. Do you still want it?"

"Shit, yeah."

Mike tilted his head. "Easy, my friend. Think about this. I'll front the cash, but I'm not running this monster. I got enough headaches. It's your baby."

"What's my end?" He and Mike were great buddies, but business was business and money was money.

Mike shrugged. "Half."

Vic's eyes nearly popped from his head. Holy shit. "You're giving me fifty percent?"

"I'm not giving you jack. You'll earn every percentage point. All I'm going to do is sign the check. *You* will oversee construction; *you* will hire the staff and *you* will put up with the complaints. I want no part of it except to watch the cash roll in. It'll be a lot of work." Mike looked at him hard. "You get what I'm saying?"

Yeah. He got it. He clenched his teeth, tightened his forearms and released them. Let the frustration settle into his bones.

"You'll have to come off the road, Vic. This training center will be one hundred percent of your time. No more playing cowboy. Can you live with that?"

Matt's voice drew Vic's attention and Gina sat up, her dark hair glistening from her swim. She laughed at something Matt said and the sound of it floated in the air. They were getting along again.

Gina and the kids.

Could he give up his lifestyle to make room for them?

Staring back at Mike, he shook his head. Mike wasn't stupid. The son of a bitch was going to put Vic's feet to the fire and make him choose between the training center or the off-the-books work. Mike watched Gina's back by manipulating Vic into a career change. The guy had moments of sheer brilliance.

"What does this have to do with your sister?"

Mike shrugged. "That's up to you. I'm doing my best to stay out of it, but if you think you want a life with my sister, you know what it'll take. My wife thinks the universe is sending you a message with this training center thing and that it's time to make a change. I gotta admit, the timing is weird."

"No shit," he said.

Mike stood, patted his shoulder. "You let me know. I'm hungry. Who's hungry?" He yelled to Gina and Matt.

"I'll help you," she said, standing and slipping a cover up on. Too bad. Vic liked the other view.

"Let me call Roxann and see what's keeping them," Mike said. "Tiny's probably out of his mind by now."

"Vic, why don't you light the grill?" Gina asked, walking

by him and brushing her hand over his shoulders. He could get used to that.

He shook his head. "No can do."

Gina stopped, frowned at him. "Why?"

"Man law eighteen."

"Again with the man laws?"

"Tell her, Mike."

"Man law eighteen?" Mike dialed the cordless. "Never mess with a guy's grill. It's right there with electronics. If it has buttons and it belongs to a buddy, a guy can't touch it."

Her mouth flopped open and Vic couldn't resist giving her an I-told-you-so look.

"Truth," Mike said. "I'd bury him if he touched my grill." He went into the house to talk to Roxann on the phone.

Gina grunted. "Morons." She followed her brother into the house.

Matt snickered from his lounge chair, shooting poisonous darts at Vic. Enough already. Time to talk to the kid. Matt had been working his last nerve all afternoon. If he hadn't been Gina's son, he'd have gotten a talking to long ago. Well, the time had come.

Standing to stretch—cripes, he was tired—Vic yelled, "Mike, where are the boat keys?"

Mikey had a twenty-nine-foot Bayliner sitting at the dock begging for Vic's attention. Vic had actually picked that baby out. Mike, knowing zilch about boats, gave him a budget and told him to have a party. The blue and white boat had enough seating for ten, maybe twelve people, so if Mike's visitors wanted to cruise, they could all go. Vic knew the boat got good use, but he'd give her some extra TLC.

The screen door slid open and Mike tossed the keys out.

"Be back in half an hour." He started toward the dock. "Come on, kid, take a ride with me."

"I'll stay here," Matt said.

*Yeah. Bite me.* "It wasn't a request. Let's go."

The pain in the ass moved slow, but he got moving. By the time he got to the dock Vic had the boat fired up. He yelled to Matt to untie the lines and watched as the kid took his sweet time getting it done. *Kill. Me. Now.*

He guided the boat out of the no-wake zone, hit the throttle and shot toward the middle of the lake. On a nice Saturday, boats invaded the lake and it made going full throttle almost impossible. Besides, he didn't need to wreck Mike's boat. He'd find a quiet spot somewhere on the other side of the lake and let it rip.

By the time they hit top speed, the boat began bouncing off the lake with vicious thuds and the wind smacked at Matt's hair. The kid was doing his best not to smile, but Vic knew he had him. Matt was a boy, and boys liked fast cars and boats. At that age Vic had liked fast girls too, but he wasn't about to talk about that. Gina would rip his nuts off.

He eased up on the throttle, shut the engine and let the boat drift in the middle of the lake. He let out a breath and his humming body settled down. *Fun's over.*

The kid bolted straight when Vic moved to the bow and settled onto one of the bench seats to stretch his legs. "So, what's up? You still pissed at me?"

Matt shrugged.

"If you want me to treat you like a man," Vic said, "talk to me like a man. Otherwise, it's all bullshit." He had to get through to this kid.

When Matt stayed silent, Vic figured they'd be here awhile. Not a problem. He had patience. He'd spent hours doing worse things than floating around on a boat. "I'll sit here all night if you want."

"You can't keep me out here."

Vic jerked a shoulder. "You gonna swim back?"

"My mom will kill you."

"Probably."

He hadn't thought about that. He may have just screwed the pooch by dragging Matt out here. He'd deal with it later.

Matt narrowed his eyes and started grinding his teeth.

*Come on, kid. Let me have it. I know you want to blow your stack.*

Nothing. Just the damned teeth grinding.

Matt rested his head back against the seat and closed his eyes. Stubborn little shit. Vic had to smile. He'd been just as ornery at fifteen, and he suddenly felt sorry for putting his aunt through this fucking misery.

Ten minutes later, with only the chirping birds to keep the conversation going, Matt finally spoke. "I know you went out with my mom last night. She dumped us on Uncle Mike because of it."

Hadn't they been through this recently? Mike's warning about Matt pushing buttons rang in Vic's ear.

He leaned forward. "She didn't dump you. You know it, but you're trying to light me up. You got nothing this time. I *did* go out with your mom last night. She told me she talked to you and you didn't have a problem with it. Why are you pissed at me?"

The heat evaporated from Matt's eyes, but something else took residence. Confusion maybe. "I don't know. I just am."

That answer sucked. They were getting nowhere.

Vic scratched his head with both hands. "You're driving me bat-shit. It doesn't matter though. I'll still care about your mom. And I'm going to spend time with her. With all you guys. We're all here together today, aren't we?"

"So?"

"Your mom could have stayed in Chicago all weekend, but she wanted to be with you. She's not going to dump you. Maybe there will be nights when she and I go to the movies alone, but she and your dad did that when you guys were little. She didn't dump you then, right?"

"But—"

"No. Don't try to deny it. You can spend as much time as you want being pissed at me. I won't like it, but I'm used to aggression. It'll eat at you more than me. If you want to be miserable, knock yourself out." Vic stood. "I'm still going to date your mom."

He walked back to the boat's cockpit and fired the engine. Frustration knotted at his shoulders. Fucking teenagers. The mess of 'em should be put in some sort of coma. They should go from twelve to twenty and forget everything in between.

This bullshit was over. He wanted things with Matt to be good for Gina's sake, but he wouldn't pacify the kid. Fuck it.

They returned to the house in minutes, and Vic docked the boat and headed across the grass. The smell of sizzling meat hung in the air. The others had arrived. Lily sat at the patio table showing Gina her nails and Jake, God bless him, was still in the pool and probably half-shriveled by now. Tiny must have been in the house resting after being forced to spend all afternoon in a salon. Poor bastard.

"Hey," Matt said, trailing a few feet behind.

Vic stopped and turned to him.

"You got sunburn on your back."

Sunburn? That was all he had to say?

"Yeah," he said. "I forgot sunscreen. It'll hurt like a bi— uh—it'll hurt later." He might as well at least try to not swear around the kid. Although, Matt had a pretty good potty mouth himself.

Shuffling his feet, Matt nodded toward the lake. "Um, there's fireworks tonight. Maybe we can go out on the boat later and watch them?"

Haza! Forward motion. Vic wanted to leap with joy, but Matt had his eyes locked on him, waiting for a response. *Don't make too much of it. It's killing the kid to do it. Play it cool.*

He nodded. "Sure. We'll all go. It'll be fun."

"Yeah," Matt said, obviously not giving another inch.

Vic gave him a companionable shove. "You are a major pain in my ass, but I suppose, right now, you feel the same about me."

Matt laughed, and it was a good snorting laugh that made Vic smile. "Pretty much, yeah. We're stuck with each other."

"I can only hope, kid. I can only hope."

## 15

*Man Law: Never reflect on a bad childhood.*

"THAT HIM?" VIC ASKED FROM THE FRONT SEAT OF TINY'S NOT so tiny Hummer.

They'd gone to a lot of trouble weaving in and out of lanes and making illegal turns to ensure they weren't tailed, but could they be any more conspicuous in this monster? Sure the moonless night sky blanketed the area in darkness, but a Hummer was hard to miss even from the alley across the street.

Tiny observed the front of the beat-up, two-story brick house. "Yeah. That's Conlin."

"He's shorter than I expected."

Tiny gave him the famous you're-a-dumb-ass curled-lip look.

Vic flipped him off. "The guy hassling Gina at the bar was bigger. I thought maybe it was the same guy." Conlin got into the Chevy. "Are you sure he's gonna be gone awhile? If we're going to break into the guy's house, I don't want him running out for coffee and coming back quick."

Here they sat, in a neighborhood known for its gang violence and drug dealing, and Vic wanted to get moving. The pounding in his head had nothing to do with fear. No, this lifeless darkened street, with its dead trees and boarded up houses, reminded him too much of his early childhood. After a nice weekend with Gina, he didn't want to think about that. Particularly after he and Matt made nice. Score one for the kid, who stepped up and kept their little chat to himself.

"According to Janet," Tiny said, "Conlin works at a twenty-four-hour market stocking shelves. I called the place and they said he comes in at eleven."

"No roommates?"

"Not that we've seen."

When Conlin drove out of sight, they walked around the house to the back door. Tiny pulled out his penlight and turned it on before using a handkerchief to loosen the bulb on the porch. No sense having the place lit up while breaking and entering. Not that cops spent too much time around here anyway, but still. Vic put on a pair of latex gloves and pulled the small black case containing his lock-picking tools from his pocket. He chose his favorite pick along with a flathead screwdriver.

"Look at this piece of shit lock," he said. "I love these wafer-tumbler deals. They got these nice wide keyholes that make it so easy for me."

"Whatever," Tiny said, humoring him.

Vic slid the screwdriver into the keyhole, rotated it and applied the right amount of pressure. Almost there. With his other hand he inserted the pick, quickly pulled it out and felt the lock give. Bingo. The familiar rush of excitement swirled through him and he opened the door, waited a second for any beeps indicating an alarm—nothing—and stepped in. Tiny entered the kitchen behind him.

The house was a typical row house with the living room, dining room, kitchen front to back. The small stove light lit the entire kitchen, where a card table sat in the middle of the room with four folding chairs. The dank smell of old grease assaulted Vic, probably from the dirty dishes piled in the sink, and he held his breath. They trudged over the nasty-ass kitchen's sticky floor and into the living room.

A lit lamp sat on a folding tray next to a worn gray sofa that could have been green at one time. Vic sensed the overload of dust in the place settling on his skin. He'd need a shower after this.

"I'll take the upstairs." He handed Tiny a pair of gloves. "Use them so you don't leave prints. They'll also keep your hands clean in this cesspool."

"Got it." Tiny snapped the gloves on and moved directly to a trunk sitting in the corner of the otherwise empty dining room.

"Any idea how long he's been here?"

"Six months, I think."

Vic took the creaking stairs two at a time, thanking his almighty stars he didn't live in this dump. The place reeked of discarded food and the smell made his stomach hitch. What a way to spend a Sunday night. Particularly after a good day at the lake.

The upstairs hallway was dark and Vic pulled out his penlight. He stopped at the top, listened for any movement in the house.

Nothing.

The first door on the right was the bathroom and he

poked his head in. Fucking pigsty. Not going in there unless he had to.

The second door led to an empty bedroom. He'd come back to that one. The third and last door was another bedroom. A full-size mattress and box spring sat on the floor—no frame or headboard—and a chest of drawers against one wall. A folding card table sat in the other corner with a computer on it. He'd get to that in a minute. He went to the closet. People always hid shit in the closet, and he could never figure out why, because guys like him always went there first.

He rifled through the few pairs of pants and shirts. With the penlight in his mouth, he stepped inside and knocked on the walls to see if anything sounded different from one wall to the other.

The closet was a bust. Maybe Conlin wasn't so dumb after all.

Vic moved to the bed, lifted the mattress and, holding it up with one arm, ran the penlight over the gauzelike material of the box spring. Nothing.

Okay. Moving on. He went to the computer, booted it up and waited while it made that whirring sound. He heard Tiny coming up the stairs.

"Anything?" he asked, sticking his head in.

"No, but I'm about to check out the computer. Anything downstairs?"

"Just rotted something or other in the fridge. You check the bathroom yet?"

"Be my guest, pal," Vic said, secretly glad he didn't have to do it.

The piece-of-shit computer was taking a long time to boot up. Sirhan obviously wasn't paying his employees well. Vic sat back in the folding chair and stretched his legs.

When he slid his foot back, a piece of the 1970 shag carpeting came with it. Hmm.

Vic stood. "Tiny." A second later he came back in.

"What?"

Vic jerked his head toward the table. "Grab an end. We're gonna slide it this way."

Being careful not to dislodge the monitor, they moved the table and he bent to pull up the carpet. Hardwood. Damn nice hardwood too. He reached down, started knocking on the floorboards. The fourth one rattled.

*Yes.*

"Loose?" Tiny asked.

"Yep." He stepped to the side, pulled the carpet back and lifted the board.

Checking the one next to it, he found it loose and pulled it out. Tiny shined his penlight into the floor.

"Subfloor," he said.

Vic dropped to his knees. God help him, he'd have to throw these jeans out because who knew what kind of filth grew in this dump. He reached his arm under the boards and, before he got elbow deep, his fingers brushed against an object. "I got something and it isn't a dead animal."

"What is it?"

He wrapped his fingers around what felt like a stack of paper and pulled it out. He sat back on his heels and, with Tiny's penlight shining down, stared at a stack of hundred dollar bills neatly wrapped in a money band.

"Are there more?"

Vic stood, moved left a couple of feet and, with both hands, pushed on the boards. Four more loose. He pulled the boards up and shined the penlight onto stacks and stacks of hundred dollar bills.

"Fuck me," Tiny said. "There's gotta be fifty grand there.

This is not the neighborhood to have that kind of cash around."

"Unless you're a terrorist trying to hide it."

"There is that."

Vic pushed on the next few boards. Loose. He pulled those up and—*holy shit*—this guy had all sorts of goodies. With itchy fingers, he ran his hand over a few semiautomatics, an AK-47 and a sawed-off shotgun. Some hand grenades rested quietly next to a couple of handguns. One of which he recognized as a Colt .45. A real man-stopper Vic had used many times. If he'd had time, he would have checked every floorboard in the room. He was sure he'd find other treasures, but didn't want to take the time and risk getting caught. He wasn't law enforcement and he certainly didn't have a warrant. That would be Lynx's department. And there seemed to be enough here to get Conlin locked up.

"I'm going to put this all back together. You check the computer. I'm sure it's password protected, but give it a try. You got a flash drive to copy files?"

"Yeah," Tiny said. "If I can get in."

"When we're done here, I'll call Lynx and see if he can get a warrant for this place. If they lock Conlin up, maybe he'll squeal on where Sirhan is."

That would take some time, though, which sucked, but probable cause needed to be established before a warrant would be issued.

As suspected, the computer was password protected. Tiny shut it down and he and Vic moved the table to its original location. All in all, the sneak and peek only validated that Conlin was up to no good.

"Let's get out of this hole," he said, taking a final glance around the room to ensure they put everything in its rightful place. "Don't forget to fix the light bulb on the porch. We don't need Conlin suspecting anything before Lynx can move on him."

"Can you get hold of Lynx tonight?"

"I don't know. He'll blow an artery because I called him on his cell, but oh well. I want the feds on this place fast."

Vic slid into the Hummer and immediately dialed Lynx.

"This better be good," a sleep-riddled Lynx said.

"Why? You getting laid?" Vic was hopeful for his old buddy.

Tiny snickered as he made a right turn, heading toward Vic's apartment. They drove through a brighter part of town, leaving behind the gloom of Conlin's neighborhood. Not to mention Vic's memories of his mother and his miserable time with her.

Lynx stayed silent.

"Because if you are," he said, "I could call back. You getting laid is a momentous occasion."

"Fuck you. Is there a reason for this call, or is it just to harass me about my lack of a social life?"

Good old, Lynx. So predictable.

"You're crabby when you wake up."

Tiny laughed out loud. "You are such an asshole."

Vic smiled.

"What the hell do you want?" Lynx hollered.

Yep. Lynx now had all pistons firing. Just where Vic needed him to be.

"I got a hot one for you, and I don't mean a woman. Although—never mind, you're not in the mood."

"You might be bigger than me, but I could still hurt you. I need to be up in a few hours. Can we get on with this?"

"You got a pen handy?"

He waited through the rustle of sheets and a drawer shutting. "Go," Lynx said, and Vic read off the address.

"What's the deal?" Lynx asked.

"Get a warrant and check out the second bedroom by the card table. There's a subfloor. Also, go five or six boards left. There's a present waiting for you."

"Does this have something to do with that Conlin guy you asked me about?"

"It's his house."

"How big is this?" Lynx sounded intrigued.

"I'm not sure. I told you what I know. I think it's worth having field guys check it out."

Tiny turned on Lake Shore Drive and Vic opened his window a bit, sucked in the clean moist air, hoping to rid himself of the layer of fifth. He'd still need a shower.

"How do you know about this?"

"I'm clairvoyant?"

Lynx laughed. A sneak and peek was nothing innovative, but Vic knew Lynx needed to cover his ass by asking. "You didn't screw this up before we even get in there, did you?"

"Not me, pal. I was thinking about doing an inventory on his trash, but decided not to risk it. The place is exactly the way Conlin left it."

"I'll get a hold of somebody at the FBI. We'll start with the trash and keep an eye on him for a few days. Maybe we'll get enough to secure a warrant. I'll let you know."

"Trust me," Vic said, "you need to get that warrant."

## 16

*Man Law: Always go for the sneak attack.*

THE NUMBERS ON THE SPREADSHEET SWAM TOGETHER, MAKING no sense. Gina swiveled from her computer and spotted Angie, the department assistant, carrying an overflowing vase of roses.

"Looks like Becca is getting flowers again," she said to Martha, who glanced up.

"Ooh, aren't they beautiful. *Orange* roses. That man broke the bank this time."

Gina went back to the blasted spreadsheet. "Lucky girl."

She didn't have time to be jealous. Monday of a payroll week and she couldn't figure out why a mail clerk suddenly got a thirty-thousand-dollar raise.

Angie placed the vase on the three-drawer filing cabinet behind Gina's chair. "Someone has an admirer."

Spinning her chair, Gina gawked at the flowers. "Me?"

"Yep."

A smile overtook her. She hadn't been sent flowers since Danny died. Longer than that really. And these flowers, their fiery orange color as deep as a western sunset, were exceptional.

"Are you holding out on me?" Martha asked, coming over and sniffing the flowers. "Who are they from?"

Gina reached for the card. She didn't dare hope they were from Vic. He was definitely not the flowers type. She opened it. *Thanks for a great weekend. Love, Vic.*

Still holding the card she put her hands over her eyes. Relief bubbled up. Had anyone else sent them, she'd have been disappointed. The man continually surprised her. He'd actually taken the time to order her flowers. Magnificent ones to boot.

"Well?" Martha asked, giggling at her reaction.

She couldn't tell her. They were good friends, but telling anyone would have the entire office gossiping about her and Wonder Butt.

"They're from a friend. I helped him with a problem."

"Must have been some problem."

"Must have been." She smiled and stuck her nose into the flowers.

"I know you're fibbing, but that's okay. I have a feeling I know who sent them. A certain vice president has been wandering through a lot more than usual."

"Behave," she said, neither confirming nor denying her cubemate's suspicions.

With a shrug, Martha went back to her desk. "I'm glad you're happy. Whoever they're from." Gina had no doubt she meant it.

Sticking the card into her pocket and away from prying eyes, she headed up to the executive offices.

Flowers. Unbelievable. Maybe there was hope for the man yet.

Vic sat back in his chair, feet on his desk, on speakerphone with some of the guys in Afghanistan, when Gina strode through the door. The sexy spike heels and tight black skirt didn't slow her down any. And what a skirt it was. Good Lord, she had miraculous curves.

She sped around the desk, grabbed his face in both hands and laid a smoking hot kiss on him that curled his toes. Well, okay. He could deal with this. At least he wasn't in trouble again.

He backed away and held his breath. Looking into those big brown eyes made him want to take a chance. To let her inside. The thought scared the shit out of him, and his chest squeezed. He let the breath out.

"Uh, guys," he said, "hold on a minute."

With jittery fingers, he hit the hold button and smiled at her. "Good morning to you too. What was that for?"

She pulled a card out of her pocket and waved it at him. "You know."

The flowers. How 'bout that service?

She leaned over, kissed him again, and he got a whiff of the lemon shampoo she used. She had to stop kissing him in his office. He didn't want anyone gossiping about her. He couldn't give a shit what they said about him, but not Gina.

"Thank you," she said. "I love them. What a wonderful surprise."

"I went with the orange. Red seemed too ordinary. The lady at the shop said they're called Firestorm roses." He shrugged, ran his hand over her hip. "For some reason they reminded me of you."

And he was damned proud he'd gone that way. Any schmo could send *red* roses.

"I'm going to take that as a compliment."

He laughed. "You should."

"You actually went to the store? You didn't call?"

"I wanted to pick them out myself."

And he was still wondering what the hell was up with that. Shocking enough he thought to send the flowers, never mind going to the store and picking them out. He should get double on the sex scorecard for that move.

The phone beeped. *Oh, shit.* He leaned forward, hit the button. "You still there?"

"Yeah. You jerking off or what?"

Gina's eyes went wider than bowling balls.

"Hey," Vic yelled into the phone. "There's a woman in my office."

"Oh, sorry," came the reply with some background laughter.

He shook his head. "Hold on, you imbecile." He hit the button again and tried not to laugh. "I'm sorry," he said to Gina. "My guys aren't housebroken yet."

She waved it off. "It's all right. Sorry I interrupted. I just wanted to say thanks. For everything."

Smiling, he said, "Anytime, darl—uh—anytime." Caught himself. He swore he'd never call her darlin' again.

"You're taking us to Jake's baseball practice tonight, right?" she asked.

"Yeah, I'll be by around six. Tiny's coming too."

"Okay. If you want, I'll save you some dinner."

A home-cooked meal? Again? This woman just might be perfect.

Before she got out the door, she turned back to him. "You know you've brought me back to life, don't you?"

Uh-oh. Getting into emotional territory here. The dread slithered around him. He stared at her a minute, his throat closing with every passing second. *Breathe.*

"You weren't dead," Vic said, because the idea of Gina dead became too much for him. "You were hibernating. And you're welcome."

The phone beeped again.

"Get back to work," she said. "I'll see you tonight."

Oh, he'd see her, all right.


"HEY," VIC CAME THROUGH GINA'S BACK DOOR AND FOUND her in a pair of cutoff shorts and a snug T-shirt, scrubbing the hell out of a pot.

She looked over her shoulder and smiled. "You're early."

"I stopped home to change and came right over."

"You hungry?"

"Oh, yeah. I want that meal you promised me."

He kept telling himself that's why he left the office early and rushed over here.

"I have meat loaf, mashed potatoes and peas on a plate in the fridge." She shut the faucet and grabbed a towel. "I just have to warm it."

"I got it. You need help cleaning up?"

"No, but thanks. This is a solitary thing for me."

He stuck the dish in the microwave and, through the doorway, spotted Lily sitting at the dining room table. "Hey, Lil. What's happening, sweet pea?"

"Hi, Vic. Doing my spelling words."

He made a face at Gina. "Spelling? What's that about? It's summer."

Gina grabbed the dirty plates off the table. "She's behind

in spelling, so I got her some workbooks to do over the summer."

*Yowzer. Poor kid.*

"Where are the boys?"

"Jake's getting ready for practice and Matt's at the movies. Roy went with him."

The microwave dinged. Food was ready. Using a potholder, Vic pulled the plate, but the kitchen table was cluttered with leftover dinner dishes. "Where do you want me to eat?"

"Take it in the dining room so I can finish in here."

He sat next to Lily at the end of the dining room table. "I got thrown out of the kitchen, Lil."

She shrugged one bony shoulder. "Me too. Mama doesn't like us in there when she's cleaning. She needs room. Do you want to help me? You could read me my words."

He popped a forkful of meat loaf in his mouth, savored the exploding flavor. Wow. That was good. And real mashed potatoes. Not from the box. Heaven.

"Sure," he said, swallowing the bite of food. "What have you got?"

She handed over the book and pointed. "Just read me these words."

"Okay. First word is *been.*"

"B-e-e-n."

"Good job. Next word is meant."

"Meant?" she asked.

"Yep."

She grabbed her pencil with the big strawberry eraser on it—again with the strawberries? This kid was obsessed—and wrote something down.

"I got it," she said. "M-e-n-t."

*Ooh, so close.*

"You left out a letter."

She studied the paper and shook her head. "How? M-e-n-t. I wrote it out. Men with a *T* on the end."

"Well, that's the way it sounds, but the *A* is silent."

Her squinty-eyed glare nearly impaled him. "There's an *A* in *meant*?"

"Yep."

"I don't understand," she said, sounding so much like her mother with that clipped tone.

Vic patted her hand. "It's M-e-a-n-t, but it's a hard word. Kind of a trick question." He waved his hand. "Let's skip it."

A minute later Gina coughed—loudly—from the kitchen doorway and gave him the same look Lily had given him. "Can I see you a minute?"

Not waiting for a response, she went back into the kitchen. Vic frowned. *This can't be good.*

"I think you're in trouble," Lily said.

He held out his hands. "What did I do?"

"I don't know, but you'd better get in there or it'll be worse."

He laughed. He couldn't help it. She made him smile in ways he never thought possible. He tugged on one of her springy curls. "If I'm not back in two minutes, come save me."


"What's up?" Vic asked, standing beside Gina at the sink.

She shut the water, wiped her hands on a dish towel and folded her arms. Oh, she'd tell him what was up.

"What are you doing?" She kept her voice low so Miss Big Ears in the other room wouldn't hear.

"I'm helping Lily while I eat. Why?"

"By telling her it's a trick question? Are you out of your mind?"

"It's a tough word," he griped.

She put her finger to her lips to quiet him down. "Of course it's tough. She has to learn. Do you have any idea the problems you could cause me?"

His blank stare gave Gina her answer. She rubbed her fingers over her forehead. "How would you know? You don't have children whose minds work overtime trying to figure out how to get out of schoolwork."

"Obviously."

"From now on," she said, "every time she gets stuck, she'll say 'it's a trick question. I can skip it.' Then she'll go to school, tell her teacher it's a trick question and she skipped it. The teacher will call me and I'll have to explain it."

"Oh. Didn't think of that."

She blew out a breath. "It's okay. Being around kids is like walking through a minefield."

"Yeah, no shit."

With stooped shoulders, he started back toward the dining room. Shoot. She'd been hard on him when all he wanted was to help her.

"Vic?" He angled back and she offered a genuine smile. "Thank you for helping. I do appreciate it."

His trademark crooked smile flashed and the tension melted away. "No problem."

"How'd it go?" Lily asked when he returned to the dining room.

Laughter bubbled in Gina's throat. She slapped at the faucet, until the water hit full blast, hoping they wouldn't hear her giggling.

"We're good, Lil. Just grown-up stuff."

"I'm glad," Lily said and then, "Are you going to be my daddy?"

Gina's body stiffened. Time stopped and the whooshing in her ears forced her to grab the edge of the sink for support.

"*Lileee*," Gina screamed, leaving the faucet running while she sprinted to the doorway. The pair of them were something else tonight.

Vic held up his hand. "We're fine. Go back to the dishes."

*Forget it, pal.* "Lily, you can't ask questions like that."

Vic, his back to Lily, stared at her with a wide-eyed, give-me-a-break face. "Gina, please. We're talking here."

"I was only asking, Mama."

"But—" she said.

Vic cleared his throat and nodded her back to the kitchen. *He* wanted to try to handle this one? She had to give him credit for it. Considering she'd just yelled at him about the homework.

Why did she ever teach her children to be so honest?

"Lil," he said, "your mom and I are dating. Do you know what that means?"

"Sort of like when two people go places together?"

Oh, Lord. Gina could not believe she was letting Vic, of all people, handle this situation. If she hadn't been paralyzed by her mortification, she'd have done it herself.

"You got it, squirt. Just because we're dating doesn't mean we'll get married. It doesn't mean we won't. We don't know what'll happen. Does that make sense?"

Gina smiled. Well, well, he handled that just fine.

"I guess so," Lily said. "But I think it would be cool to have you as my dad. Then you could help me with my words like Rachel's dad does."

Her body turned to stone. *Don't get upset.* But her knees

clearly didn't hear the order, because they wobbled and she shifted her weight against the counter. How the hell could she not get upset? Her daughter wanted a dad to help her with homework. Lily's pain struck Gina and she threw her hand over her mouth to smother a painful groan. The scream needed to come, but not here. Not now.

Every child deserved a dad to love her and spend time with her. Lily had it once. She deserved it now. Gina squeezed her eyes shut knowing she was seconds away from a full-blown tear fest.

"You know what, Lil? I don't know if I'm gonna be your dad or not, but I can still help you with your words. You call me up and I'll come over. How's that?"

That tore it. Gina shoved the dish towel to her face and let it absorb the sobs. The insane shattering, the coming apart bone by bone, that came when she allowed herself to wallow in what could have been, rocked her body.

"That sounds good," Lily said. "One other thing."

Vic laughed. "What's that?"

"How do you think you'd be at Daddy-Daughter Olympics? They have it every fall and I couldn't do it last year. That fat-face Misty Franklin teased me about it."

Gina tensed again. Misty Franklin. That little witch. No wonder. Considering her bitch of a mother constantly spurned Gina because she was a single working mother. It didn't matter to Dora Franklin that Danny had died rescuing three people from a burning building. Gina swatted at the tumbling tears.

"Daddy-Daughter Olympics?" Vic asked, sounding like he would actually consider it. But then, being a testos-terone-loaded, competitive male, of course he would. "I think I'd do pretty darn well with that."

"That would be awesome," Lily squealed.

"Okay, then. We'll give Misty Franklin something to talk about. I gotta heat up my meat loaf again. Be right back."

No. He was coming in here. Gina bent over the sink, splashed water on her face to clear the subsiding tears.

"Wait," she yelled, spinning toward the door and sucking in a breath. "I'll do it for you in a second. Just let me finish up in here."

*Please stay away.*

"No, it's okay," Vic said, entering the kitchen. "Whoa." He halted when he spotted her. She must look a mess, her face usually red and puffy after a crying jag.

She saw Vic's Adam's apple working. Poor guy. He wasn't used to this.

Crap. She gripped the edge of the sink, grappled with him seeing her in such a state.

"You okay?" he asked, the plate still in hand.

Gina picked up the dish towel, started working on the pot she'd just washed. "I'm fine. Go finish eating. I'll be done in a sec."

Please go away. *Please. Don't make me explain this.*

He waited a minute. Opened the microwave door and closed it. The chime of buttons being pressed filled the room. She could feel his eyes on her. The tactician working on his battle plan.

"Are you going to talk to me?"

She laughed. This was a switch. "Nope."

"You sure?"

"Yep."

"Later, then?"

Oh boy, she could love this man. He knew she needed space to sort out her emotions, and he'd give it to her.

"You bet," she said.

## 17

*Man Law: Always be prepared.*

"Jake's swing sucks," Tiny said, his Louisiana drawl stretching the last word for emphasis.

"You think?" Vic asked when Jake took strike one.

Vic cracked open a peanut shell, popped the peanut in his mouth and threw the shell in the upturned baseball cap in his lap. The evening air cooled and, with the cloud cover, made the heat bearable, but his long legs were stiff from being crammed between the damned bleacher seats. The barrel of the trusty Sig hidden under his T-shirt dug into his thigh.

He surveyed the area. Monk stood by the fence near first base and Billy patrolled the parking lot. Large oak trees dotted the outer edges of the ball field and Vic found himself wishing they weren't there. These large open parks were a bitch on protection details. Too many places for bad guys to hide.

Gina, on his left, propped her elbow on her knee and her chin in hand. Tiny, on his right, helped himself to the bag of peanuts. Lily sat in front of them reading a book and, with puckered lips, turned to Tiny.

"What?" he asked.

After spending so much time with her, Tiny recognized the Lily-thinking-too-much look.

"Is Tiny your real name?"

Gina snorted. "Of course not, honey,"

Vic spun toward her, his mouth agape. She made an *oops* face and whispered, "Is it?"

He waited a second, thinking he could torture her, but decided against it. "I'm busting your chops."

"My real name is Justin," Tiny told Lily.

She smiled a huge front-tooth-missing grin. "I like Justin. I'll call you that from now on. Is that okay?"

Tiny shrugged. "Sure."

"I haven't heard anyone but your mama and daddy call you Justin in years," Vic commented.

Tiny leaned over. "You should have been at my place a few nights ago. You would have heard it over and over and over again."

"You're a dog."

Gina's big brown eyes zeroed in on them. "Whatever you're saying, knock it off."

How the hell had she heard that? He'd barely heard it. "How do you *do* that?"

She elbowed him. "It's a gift you get when you become a parent. You were also whispering and that's always a clue. Oh, shoot. Jake struck out. Again." She slapped her hand on her thigh. "He hasn't had a hit all season."

"Gina, *what* is up with that swing?" Tiny asked.

"Talk to Michael. He taught him."

"That explains it," Vic shot. Jake threw his bat to the ground in frustration and Vic shook his head. This boy was destroying him. Nothing hurt more than being no good at something you enjoy.

"Did you talk to the coach?" he asked.

She glowered at him. "Of course. He's trying to correct him, but Michael keeps saying to do it his way, and I don't want to hurt my brother's feelings. I think the coach is afraid of Michael."

"Afraid of Mike?" What kind of bullshit was that? "What the hell for?"

Gina held her hands palms up. "See this coach. All five foot six of him? Compare him to my brother and you'll get it. Michael can be scary if you don't know him. Well, he can be scary if you do know him." She shook her head. "Anyway, I'm stuck."

"I'm done. I may suck at homework, but I'll nail this assignment." Vic rose from the bleachers and handed her the baseball cap filled with peanut shells. He brushed the crumbs from his jeans and stepped next to Lily. "Coming through, sweet pea."

"Where are you going?" Gina asked.

"To show him how to swing a bat. I seem to be the only one who doesn't care what Mike thinks."

He strode past the group of parents sitting in folding chairs and spotted a gorgeous blonde giving him the eye. They sure didn't make moms the way they used to. He smiled at her but made no prolonged eye contact and kept walking. *Where were you a few weeks ago, sister?*

"Hey," he said to a pouting Jake, who had dirt all over his formerly white baseball pants from a diving catch at short-stop. The kid always gave a hundred percent.

"Hi," Jake said, watching Vic grab a bat and a ball.

"Come over here. I wanna show you something."

He followed him to an open spot near third base. Vic handed him the bat. "Get into your batting stance."

Jake shrugged and struck up that piss-poor stance. Vic adjusted the bat.

"Spread your legs to shoulder width. Good. Shift your weight to the balls of your feet. Your feet should always be parallel with the plate. Got it?"

Jake nodded.

"Now, bend slightly at the waist and don't lock your knees. Just relax. Don't hunch your shoulders. Keep them level." He tapped Jake's right elbow. "What's happening with this elbow? Get it back and look where the bat is." Vic held the bat in place. "This is where the bat should be."

"But Uncle Mike said to do it the other way."

Vic should have rolled his eyes and said "Screw Uncle Mike" but, in an effort to not dis his buddy, said, "I know, and it's not working for you. Try this way and see what you think."

Jake nodded and Vic stepped back. "Okay. Now swing."

His right shoulder dipped, but otherwise he was level. "Not bad, but you dropped your shoulder. Get back into the stance."

Vic stayed with him, watching his practice swings until the inning ended and the coach called Jake to the field.

"You'll probably be up again." Vic slapped Jake on the shoulder. "Just relax and do it like I showed you."

Hopefully, Jake would have some success, because he wouldn't be able to stand watching him strike out time after time. Maybe he'd run him to the batting cages for some extra practice.

He spotted Gina heading toward him and his shoulders

tensed. Was he going to get yelled at again? Hadn't he ignored the blonde?

They met up behind the dugout and, hidden from spectators, she grabbed him by the shirt. "I'm so turned on right now, I could do you right here."

Holy shit. She pressed that great body of hers against him and planted a solid kiss on his lips. All his blood shot to his crotch, and he started counting backward from a hundred to get his mind focused on anything but his hard-on. Nope. Not working. At least he wore baggy jeans and a long T-shirt to hide it.

He pulled backed an inch. "Not that I'm complaining, but what brought this on?"

"Watching you with Jake. And earlier, with Lily and the Daddy-Daughter Olympics thing. You have no idea what it means to me."

He wiggled his eyebrows. "In that case, are there any other kid-related activities I might be able to assist with?"

She laughed. The sound bounced around in his head and made him smile. He slung an arm around her shoulders, and they started toward the bleachers. Then his phone buzzed.

Billy.

"What's up?"

"Your guy in the beat-up Chevy is out here."

"Are you kidding?"

This guy had a set of brass ones. Or maybe he was just fucking stupid, but Vic doubted it.

"Toward the back of the lot," Billy said. "He hid behind a minivan that just pulled out."

"Meet me by the bleachers."

Vic shoved his phone back into the belt clip. Time to have a little chat with this prick.

"Everything okay?" Gina asked.

Like he'd even admit this. "Yep. Billy needs a bathroom break. No worries. Go back to the game and I'll see you in a few."

"Unbelievable." Vic said, guiding Billy away from the bleachers. "He has to know I know his car."

"Yeah. What do you want to do?"

He scratched the back of his head. What *did* he want to do? He wanted to talk to this schmuck for sure, but there were people everywhere. Not to mention Gina and Lily sitting right there. He should let it go. Keep the peace.

Fuck that. "Let's go talk to him."

"Oh, yeah, right, we're just gonna march up to him."

"No. If he sees us, he'll take off. We'll ambush him. You go around the passenger side. I'll take the driver's side."

Billy looked skeptical. "The simplicity of your plan is a little fucked up. He could blow us both to hell."

The thought had some merit, but Conlin had done a shitty job of tailing Vic.

"Nah," Vic said. "If he wanted to cause trouble, he would have strapped a bomb to himself and walked onto the ball field. Conlin could be dispensable, though. Maybe he's Sirhan's cannon fodder du jour. Either way, he's trying to rattle me by being a pain in the ass."

"And I have to say, it appears to be working."

"Yeah, and I'm done. Let's do this before Gina starts getting antsy. I told her you needed a bathroom break. Tiny said he'd distract her."

They moved toward the parking lot.

"Company," Billy said.

Vic spotted a Chicago P.D. cruiser drive in and park next to the ball field. Now, this might get interesting. Sneaking up on Conlin would draw too much attention from the cop sitting a hundred yards away.

"Scrap the ambush," Vic said. "We're gonna walk right up to him."

"Okay." Billy sounded skeptical.

"Yes, the plan is seriously fucked up, but with a P.D. cruiser sitting in the lot, chances are Conlin won't do anything crazy."

Sirhan must not have given an order to complete this reign of terror, or he'd have made a more organized threat by now.

The sheikh still wanted to play.

The two of them crossed the parking lot like a couple of old buddies out for a stroll. Vic zeroed in on his target. Conlin spotted them, sat up in the seat and fired the engine. A familiar buzz streamed through Vic's body and his mouth watered. A preliminary action high.

"Gerard," he said cheerfully. "How you doing, buddy?"

He stepped up to the open driver's side window, took a quick survey of the backseat and casually leaned a hip against the door. Conlin looked up for a second but kept his hands at his sides.

*This* was the guy Sirhan sent? This guy had strawberry-blond hair and freckles all over his face. A memory slammed into Vic's brain and he ground his teeth together.

Son of a bitch.

Conlin was Howdy Doody, the fucker that had emailed him the video of Gina singing. Pissant.

"Put your hands on the wheel, asshole," Vic said. "Or do you prefer Howdy Doody? How very original, *Gerard*."

Billy stood on the other side of Vic, arms loose at his sides and ready in case he had to reach for a weapon. Conlin stayed focused on the P.D. cruiser and placed his hands on the steering wheel. Good boy.

"You're pissing me off," Vic said, "and I don't want to have to kill you. Tell your boss I'm losing faith in his ability to get shit done. He calls me and tells me he wants my ass in a sling and here I am, but no Sirhan." *Tsk-tsk.* "I'm losing patience, Gerard. Bodies start piling up when I lose patience, and I hate that."

Conlin shifted in his seat and sweat dribbled down his face.

"Go home, Gerard. Call your boss. Tell him I'm looking for him."

Vic and Billy stepped back, waving affectionately as he pulled out.

"What was all that bullshit?" Billy asked.

Vic shrugged. "Sirhan's got an ego. I need to draw him out, and he can't resist a direct challenge. I just need him to fuck up. Plus, I talked to Lynx on the way over here and they picked up Conlin's garbage."

Billy's face brightened with interest. "They find anything?"

"A bunch of money bands and some baggies with drug residue. They're going to keep an eye on Conlin for a while. Probably get a warrant for the house."

"Sirhan is going to be pissed when all that cash in the floor gets confiscated." Billy slapped him on the back.

Yeah, Vic thought, staring off toward the bleachers where Gina fiddled with Lily's hair. An annoying shard of panic pricked the back of his neck and he scratched at it.

Did he just fuck up by antagonizing Sirhan into coming after Gina and the kids instead of him?

.  .  .

GINA SET THE CHECKS MICHAEL NEEDED TO SIGN ON HIS chair. He'd never miss them there. His office, with its slick chrome desk and impeccable black leather chairs, was so buttoned up he'd spot a piece of dust out of place.

Where did he go? She checked her watch. He asked her to stay late and now he disappeared? On a Wednesday night? She still had to manage dinner for the kids before taking Jake to practice and Lily to dance. She didn't have time to wait. Maybe he went to Vic's office.

She walked toward Vic's office.

"Hey," she said.

He punched the button to disconnect from voicemail and sat back. "Hey to you."

His beautiful green eyes sparked and a little piece of her fell apart because she was simply crazy about him. It didn't help that he looked so darned good with his shaggy blond hair and rolled-up sleeves. And the damned goatee. He did messy-handsome better than any GQ model.

"Are you taking me home or is Michael?"

"I'd planned on it."

She nodded. "Okay. I'll be ready in ten minutes."

"Wait."

He reached into a drawer for a bag and dumped the contents onto his desk. A bunch of cell phones landed with a banging thud.

"I got you and the kids new cell phones," he said. "They have better...security options."

"Better security?"

"Just in case."

Her skin stung as if tiny rocks pelted her. "In case we're kidnapped?"

And wasn't this a lovely end to the day? A greater reminder that the man she'd fallen for had put her family in danger. God only knew what these phones were capable of. *Gina, you are so crabby tonight.*

Deep breath.

"It's only a precaution," he said. "Probably a good idea with a teenager anyway."

She ran her hands over her face, gently massaging her forehead. Too much emotional chaos. Too much. "Okay. I'll give them to the kids tonight, but I won't tell them about the *security*. I don't want them freaking out. What else?"

"This."

He held up one of those decorative shoe clips Lily liked. A strawberry. He'd taken the time to buy her daughter a gift she'd go crazy for. Part of the worry melted away. "She'll love it. Thank you."

"I didn't think she'd remember to carry the cell phone all the time so I had one of the techno geeks rig the clip as a backup. Gizmo has been experimenting with this tracking chip and it seems to work, but it's not foolproof."

So much for thinking he cared enough to buy her daughter a silly gift. Gina stared at him, tried to brush off the negative energy and reminded herself he cared enough to make sure they would always know where her children were.

He held up the clip. "The chip is inside the strawberry, so we'll always be able to locate her."

Why suddenly did they need GPS tracking? "Has something happened that you feel this is necessary?"

"It's a precaution."

"And there's nothing I should know?"

His body remained still; his eyes unwavering. "If I thought there was, I'd tell you."

Somehow, she didn't believe him.

## 18

*Man Law: Never blame a woman's hormones.*

ROXANN HANDED GINA A PLATTER OF ANTIPASTO TO TAKE OUT to the patio. A balmy Friday night and Gina and the kids rode to the lake house with Tiny to meet Michael and Roxann for the annual Fourth of July bash on Saturday.

Saturday's weather forecast sounded iffy, and Michael was outside supervising a tent installation over the patio. The younger kids enjoyed a pre-dinner swim and Matthew, as usual, was sacked out on his favorite chair with his iPod.

Gina brought the tray outside, placed it on the table and went back for plates.

"Where did you say Vic was?" Roxann asked, turning from the fridge. She wore a red T-shirt, a pair of gray running shorts and her hair piled in a Pebbles Flintstone ponytail. Her face, free of makeup, glowed under the bright kitchen lights, leaving Gina with a twinge of envy at Roxann's natural beauty.

"He said he had a client meeting." Gina took care to keep her tone even.

Roxann set her hands on the breakfast bar and leaned in. "I'm guessing you don't think he's at a client meeting?"

Gathering up the plates and utensils, Gina shrugged. "I didn't say that."

"You didn't have to. I guessed it the minute you walked in here."

Nothing got past her. This was why she ran a huge newspaper.

While Gina separated the forks and knives, Roxann came around the breakfast bar and slid onto the stool next to her. She dropped the forks. "I mean, who has a client meeting on the Friday night of a holiday weekend?"

"Vic does. Do you honestly think he pays attention to whether it's a holiday weekend or not? He's not that structured. If he has an opening, he fills it."

Made sense. Or did she just want to believe it made sense? "You think he's at a meeting?"

"He's not a liar. And you're making yourself crazy over nothing. And what's worse is he probably senses it."

Gina nodded. "We've never talked about being exclusive. And I've been out of the dating game a long time. How do I ask him something like that?"

Roxann looped an arm over Gina's shoulder. "You wear your heart on your sleeve, and he's trained to read people. Talk to him. Settle it for yourself. At the very least, you need to know where your relationship stands."

Gina leaned forward, put her hands over her face. "I hate this. I wasn't prepared to care so much. I just wanted to get laid."

Roxann burst out laughing and Gina, giving up on her foul mood, joined her.

After the gigglefest, Gina swiveled to Roxann. "I don't know if I can do this. I can't be a good mother with all this emotional stuff spewing. My kids deserve better."

Before Rox could speak, Michael stepped through the patio doorway. "Grill's ready. Are we gonna eat tonight or what?"

"Such a charmer." Roxann went to him and threw her arms around his neck. "Have I ever mentioned what a charmer you are?"

He slapped his hand over her ass with a loud *thwack*. "Once. Maybe."

He moved his hands to her face, and they stared at each other for a moment. Everything in the room expanded, smothered. Or maybe Gina had become the third wheel, but either way, Roxi and Michael were in their own world when he finally kissed her.

They loved each other in a way that, day by day, became more of what they needed, and to see them grow into it was a blessing.

Could Gina get that lucky?

With Vic?

AT TWENTY-THREE HUNDRED HOURS, VIC PULLED INTO MIKE'S driveway and parked behind Tiny's Hummer. The place resembled an upscale used-car lot. Everyone must be here. His shoulders sagged. All he wanted was a shower and sleep. Dog-assed tired and he didn't even know if he'd get a bed. The floor wouldn't do it tonight. Normally, he could rack out anywhere, but the exhaustion had slipped into his bones and he knew he was close to his limit. Staring at the house, he debated on reclining his seat and sleeping in the car.

The four two-story white columns that served as the entryway were illuminated by strategically spaced ground lights. The house had been painted a bright, clean white with green shutters and trim. Even the lush green shrubs had been meticulously picked. Mike had poured big bucks into this house, and it had been worth every penny.

Unfortunately, all five bedrooms would be full. Roy said he'd come up tonight to help them map out security for the party. By tomorrow afternoon there'd be over a hundred people here, and these things always went long. Roy had been told to bring his wife and two kids with him, and the lucky pups were probably sleeping in Vic's room.

That was okay.

He guessed.

After all, Roy wouldn't get to spend much time with his family this weekend, but at least they'd be in the same place and the kids could enjoy the pool.

Maybe he could crash on one of the pullout couches in the basement? Tiny and Monk probably snagged those already. Hell, if worse came to worse, he would sneak in with Gina for a while and get out before anyone woke up. He needed a good three hours of slumber. Problem was, if he got in bed with Gina, he wouldn't want to sleep.

Then again, she'd been an iceberg all day and he had no idea why. He shook his head, climbed out of the car and started for the front door. Women confused the hell out of him.

Monk marched around the side of the house in his typical uniform of combat boots, black cargo shorts and a T-shirt. The red do-rag on his head was a nice touch.

"Hey," Vic said. "Everything okay?"

"Yeah. Just checking the grounds. Everything is quiet. I'll be out here for a few hours, then Tiny is up. Roy's got the back. Billy should be here any time now. By tomorrow we'll have enough guys here, the president would be safe."

No lie there. This would be the safest place for Gina and the kids. Sirhan would be a total dumb-ass to try a breach. "I'm gonna rack out for a while and take a shift later."

"Roger that." Monk went on his way.

Vic lumbered through the front door, glanced left and right. Lamp lights were on in the living room, but the formal dining room remained dark. He reached in and flipped on the light. The oak table and china cabinet had been polished to a gleam and he wondered the last time Mike and Roxi had actually used it.

Leaving the light on—he wasn't about to give any bad guys an opportunity to hide in a darkened room—he moved down the hallway toward the kitchen and heard the television on low volume in the great room.

"What's happening?" he asked Mike, who wore shorts and a Go Army T-shirt.

Mike pointed to the gallon of rocky road he had just covered. "You wanna hit this?"

"Nah." He dropped his overnight bag on the floor. "Everyone in bed?"

"Yeah." Mike put the ice-cream scoop in the dishwasher. "Tiny's downstairs sleeping. Gina and the kids are in bed. Roxi is out like a light. She wants to get up early for a run before everything gets crazy tomorrow."

Roxann could run a good ten miles in one shot. "You going with her?"

"Unless you volunteer."

"Forget that."

"Why is my sister a grouch?" Mike asked, taking the bowl of ice cream to the couch with him.

Vic scratched his head, ran his hand through the too-long strands. *Dammit.* He forgot to get his haircut. Again. "Couldn't tell ya. I've asked her three times. She's driving me bat-shit."

Mike grunted. "Welcome to my world, pal."

"Thanks." An idea flashed. "Maybe it's hormones?"

"Hey now," Mike laughed. "Don't be saying that to her. I said that to my ex-wife once and she nearly ripped my nuts off. Women get pissed when men talk about their hormones."

Good to know. This would be why Vic didn't do relationships, but he wasn't about to say that out loud. They were still trying to find level ground when it came to Gina.

"I'm gonna hit the shower and grab a nap," Vic said.

"Your bed is taken. You can try one of the pullouts downstairs or this one. I'm going up after the ice cream."

Vic grabbed his bag and headed upstairs. He'd kicked his dirty sneakers off at the front door and his feet sank into the soft carpet. He passed the boys' room and laughed because one of them was snoring like a linebacker. Nearly three steps from the bathroom Gina's door opened and she stuck her head out.

"Hi." She stepped into the hallway and the sight of her gave him a warm feeling in his gut. She'd shoved her wild hair into a clip and had the Michelin Man bathrobe on again. That bathrobe needed to find a home elsewhere.

He tossed his bag in the bathroom, walked to her and leaned against the doorjamb. "Did I wake you up?"

"I heard you pull in."

"Sorry."

She shrugged. "I wasn't really sleeping anyway. Come in, let's not talk out here. We'll wake everyone."

Stepping into the room he said, "Your brother is still downstairs."

Not knowing what Gina had in mind he wanted to make sure she had all the information. Somehow, he didn't think Mike would appreciate the chorus of moaning that accompanied sex with his sister.

"I'll try to control myself," she cracked, flipping the lamp on and sitting on the bed. She held a hand out to the wingback chair in the corner. "Have a seat."

"I wanna hit the shower first."

"You need a shower that bad?"

"Actually, yeah. My jeans are covered in farm dust and I don't want to sit on the furniture."

She drew her eyebrows together. "Farm dust? Why?"

Given his current state of exhaustion he wondered why they needed to do the how-was-your-day-dear routine now.

"That's where I was tonight."

She gave her head a good shake. What the hell? Maybe she was groggy from sleep or something.

"You said you had a business meeting."

*Earth to Gina.* "I did."

"At the farm? With a client?"

*Whoa.* The harsh voice reminded him of his mother when she got whacked out on heroin, and it felt like a brick falling on his head. What was this about? He'd never known Gina to be bipolar.

"Yes," he said, trying not to sound like the sarcastic prick he was. "At the farm. With a—" He stopped. Hold it. Back the truck up. "Where'd you think I was?"

"All I know is what you told me."

His girl was a little pissy tonight. Maybe she figured him for an idiot? That was what he'd have to be to not catch her insinuation. "You think I *lied* to you?"

Silence. She actually thought he was with another woman? Pressure exploded behind his eyes.

Even when he did the right thing he got into trouble. This was total horse shit. He took a deep breath, fought the fury gushing inside him. Way too tired for this, but he'd deal with it and then he would take his fucking shower and grab a combat nap.

"I met with the floating-palace guy. He asked me to teach him how to shoot his new nine-millimeter, and I parlayed it into getting you another cruise on the yacht. We drove out to the farm and we've been running through cornfields all night."

Silence again.

He made a knocking gesture. "Hello?"

"Oh. My. God." She covered her mouth with her hand. "I'm such a bitch."

"At the moment, I'm inclined to agree with you."

"I'm so sorry."

What the hell was going on with her?

He stared at her for a second and rubbed his gritty eyes, hoping they wouldn't bleed. He hadn't felt this kind of torment in years, and it took every bit of his already depleted energy not to rail on her. He'd screwed up by letting his guard down. He'd let the machine take a break. And wound up with this mess.

"How the *hell* could you think, after what has happened these past weeks, I'd lie to you?"

She rocketed toward him, but he held his hand up. "I may be a screwup when it comes to the kids, but I've been honest with you."

He paced the room. What a fucked-up scenario. His own damned fault for letting his emotions get in the way. The machine would never have let this happen.

Gina grabbed his wrist. "Please let me explain."

"No." He snapped his arm away. "I need a shower and

some sleep and then I'll listen. I'm so pissed at you right now; I'll say something I'll regret."

He stepped back, jerked the door open and headed for the much-needed shower.

Damn her. He should have just left things the way they were. Should have stuck with his miserable, broken life, but no, he'd given in and let himself come out of his emotional prison and for what? For this? For this fucking torture that felt like he was being eaten alive. No fucking thank you.

His phone buzzed and he ripped it off his belt. "What?"

"We got activity out here," Monk said, his voice barely a whisper.

## 19

---

*Man Law: Never let the enemy close to home.*

THE HEIGHTENED STATE OF BATTLE CALM TOOK OVER AND VIC concentrated on Monk's words while hauling ass to the first floor. "What is it?"

"Guy in the trees next to the house. Right side. Can't see him yet, but he's out there. I caught a shadow."

"What?" Mike said when he saw Vic flying down the stairs.

"Activity, side of the house." He went back to Monk. "I'm coming out the back and around the far side. Don't shoot me. No guns unless you have to. Gunshots bring cops and there's nothing we can tell them. Let's just grab this guy."

He hung up and held a hand to Mike already moving toward the door. "No. Wake Tiny up and stay in the house. Somebody has to be with the kids."

Fuck battle calm. If this was that fucking Conlin again, he'd snap his neck. Vic was done with this asshole.

He tore around the house, his adrenaline howling after his fight with Gina. He needed to blow off some steam, and this couldn't have come at a more perfect time.

He slowed as he reached the side of the house and took three deep breaths to contain his swarming anger. He needed to mentally sweep it into a pile. Take thirty seconds to get his head straight before he got his ass shot off doing something stupid.

A long, surveilling look around the side of the house only yielded parked cars. He moved a couple of feet to hide behind the Weeping Cherry tree. No movement, just the sound of the evening wind coming off the lake. He waited a minute. *I know you're out there, you little fucker.* Come out and play.

The soft snap of a twig gave him a direction and he shifted his head toward it. He'd wait another minute. Which way was the asshole moving? A second later leaves rustled to his right and he squinted into the trees. Gotcha. Sneaking along the tree line not twenty feet away.

Vic's body moved into the hypersensitive state of alert where everything went quiet and he absorbed all sound around him. He squeezed his eyes tight and released them. His system hummed.

*Don't move, don't move. Let him come closer.* At any second the asshole would see him huddled behind the tree.

The guy came closer. One more step. One more. Yes. The adrenaline charge propelled Vic from his hiding spot and he dove for the intruder. At the last second, the enemy leaped sideways and Vic hit the ground hard. Missed. He popped to his feet, flipping a roundhouse kick in the guy's direction, tagging him on the hip, but the son of a bitch stayed on his feet.

The sharp gleam of metal caught Vic's attention. Knife!

A full roar rang in his ears and he stepped in, leading with an elbow to the nose. *Crunch.* Blood streaming.

A knee to the midsection, and the asshole bent over and let out a whoosh of air.

*Don't let him recover.*

Vic blasted him with an elbow to the back of the shoulders and the guy went down, moaning as he hit the ground face-first. Monk flew around the corner and jumped in to secure the bad guy.

"He's got a knife," Vic said.

Monk ran a penlight over the ground and stopped. "Got it. Shit."

"What?" Vic, out of breath—*what the fuck?*—bent over. *Ow.*

Stinging sensation. Just below his ribs.

Monk shined the light at him. "Did he get you?"

Vic straightened and glanced down at his suddenly wet and illuminated golf shirt. Blood.

*Fuck.* "You son of a bitch. You cut me."

He stepped to his assailant, already knowing it wasn't Conlin, and flipped the hulking fucker over. Blood oozed from his nose and mouth, but there was no denying this was the asshole from the bar. *Dammit.* These guys were persistent, not to mention sneaky, little bastards. They'd been able to penetrate Vic's security and take pictures, shoot video and get onto Mike's property.

He'd like to put a bullet in this fucker and be done with him, but he was associated with a terrorist and might have useful information. Maybe he'd lead them to Sirhan, the big ticket. Taking him out was the goal.

Vic gave the guy a not so light nudge with his foot. "You again. You're really making me regret not tossing you off the roof of that club. You and Conlin are pissing me off."

The guy moaned, half-unconscious. Tiny walked up, shook his head at the guy and smirked.

"Sweet," he said.

"Keep an eye on our friend here." Monk gestured to the bad guy. "Vic's wounded and I want to check him out."

"I'm fine," he said. "I'll need a few stitches."

Monk waved the penlight at him. "Let's see."

On a huff, Vic pulled up his shirt and Monk shined the light on his upper abs. "He gave you a nice slice there. I'm guessing twenty-three stitches. No more, no less."

"Thank you for the expert analysis. Watch him. I gotta talk to Mike a minute."

"What do you want to do with him?"

"That's what I'm gonna talk to Mike about."

"Hey," Tiny called. "Gina's in the kitchen."

Oh, fucking great. She'd take one look at him in a bloody shirt and freak. He'd deal with that next. Right now, he needed to talk to Mike without Gina around. He unclipped his phone and dialed Mike's cell, hoping he had it on him.

"What's up?"

*Thank you.* Finally a break.

"We're secure. Meet me out back. Leave Gina in the house."

The floodlights lit up the yard and Vic spotted Roy standing by a clump of trees. The boat knocked gently against the dock while the cool night air rustled the trees along the property. Vic inhaled the moist air, let his body come down from the rush. He waited by the edge of the house until Mike came out. Tried to ignore his stinging belly.

"What the hell?" Mike asked, taking a gander at Vic's bloody shirt.

"Knife wound. Not a puncture. A few stitches is all."

"Did you get him?"

"Yeah. He's by the side of the house."

"Do you recognize him?"

Vic had to tread carefully here. He hadn't told Mike about the guy hassling Gina in the bar, and Mikey would go ape shit if he found out now. What with the scumbag on his property and all.

"He's one of Sirhan's guys." Not necessarily a lie.

Mike stepped around Vic to see the guy and came back. "What are you doing with him?"

"We'll take him to the farm and work on him. See if he has anything to say."

The look Mike gave him could have euthanized the entire town.

He shrugged. "What?"

Mike laughed, but it was an annoying, sarcastic laugh. "You're so focused on the kill you're not thinking straight."

"*I'm* not thinking straight? This fucker was marching around your property intending to do who knows what, and you don't want me to have a go at him?"

Mike gritted his teeth and stepped closer. "This is my house and my family is in it. You want to take this person to another piece of property that I own and 'work on him'?" Mike stalked around for a minute. "What if he doesn't tell you anything? Are you going to let him go? What if he squeals to the cops? You're not the only one at stake here."

Over Mike's shoulder, he spotted the asshole sitting up and did not want to be wasting time arguing. He wanted to load this fucker into his car and haul ass to the farm.

"He won't talk to the cops."

Again with the sarcastic laugh. "How do you know? Are you going to *neutralize* him? Because then you've got a body to dump. We're not in some third-world country where you can go in, take a guy out and head home. We're on our own here. The government won't help us."

A boiling fit of rage went up Vic's arms and he fisted his hands in Mike's T-shirt. It took every stinking ounce of effort to keep his voice low. "Don't you think I know that? I've hit every kind of roadblock with this situation, I'm worried I underestimated these assholes and now *you're* being a problem? I'm trying to keep your sister and her family safe, and I don't need this bullshit from you."

"Guys," Tiny said, stepping between them and giving them both a shove. "Take a break."

Vic leaned against the house, stared out at the quiet lake. They needed to get this show on the road because they could only stand out here so long without attracting some sort of attention.

"All I'm saying," Mike said, sounding calmer, "is we need to think this through. I've got a lot to lose here and, unless I'm going blind, you do too. My sister is in the kitchen wondering what's going on. If you disappear after just arriving, she'll know something's up, and she'll become a lunatic. I don't want her going through that. And neither should you."

A guilt trip. Fucking great.

Vic turned to Tiny. "Did you find anything on our intruder?"

"A car key." Tiny said. "No ID. The key is for a Honda."

"He probably left his ID in the car, in case he got caught." Vic angled back to Mike. "What do *you* want to do?"

Mike held out his hands. "I'd love for you to beat the crap out of this guy, but the risk is too high. The only thing we can do is call the cops. Tell them we caught a prowler."

Vic's head lopped forward. The weight of it suddenly too much for him to hold up. "The P.D.? That's a new one."

Mike shrugged. "Maybe they can lock him up?"

"For what? Walking across the lawn? Last I checked that wasn't a crime."

Even in the shadows, Vic could see the venom in Mike's eyes. "He was carrying a weapon. One he attacked you with."

No fucking way. "You want me to admit to the P.D. this fucker got me?"

Sure his ego was in the way, but admitting this prick had hurt him made Vic boil. Getting even didn't involve the police.

"It's a holiday," Mike said. "Maybe they'll keep him locked up for the weekend. Meantime, you call Lynx, tell him we got a suspected terrorist behind bars, and he sends the feds in to scoop the guy up." He paused. "Maybe this asshole will give them something on Sirhan, and you'll get your opportunity to take care of him."

Vic scratched his head. Not what he wanted to hear, but Mikey and his sister were a lot alike when they dug in. Vic would need a fucking bulldozer to move Mike from this line of thinking. "You know anybody at the P.D. that could help us in keeping him locked up all weekend?"

All Vic really needed was the guy's identity. He didn't give a shit about the asshole being locked up. If Lynx could make a case, that would be fine, but it wasn't going to happen in a few days, and the asshole would probably post bond anyway. Whether the guy was in jail or not, Vic would find a way to get satisfaction.

"Rox knows the police chief," Mike said, "but I'm not sure how I feel about her being involved."

"All she'd have to do is make a call, but I see your point. Maybe there's another way."

"Let me talk to her. Knowing her, she'll want to help."

Vic heard a car pull in and the sound had his ears pounding. He whirled around ready for battle again but saw Duck and Billy getting out of a truck. He bent over, hands on his thighs, laughing at himself for being so fucking strung out he'd turned into a pussy. Despite that, a plan took shape.

He straightened and whapped Tiny's arm. "I wanna know who this guy is. I'm betting he parked his car around the neighborhood and walked up. You and Duck locate that Honda. It's probably a beater like Conlin's. It shouldn't be hard to find in this neighborhood. Leave the key so our friend doesn't tell the cops we took it. Take the slim-jim from my truck." He looked at Mike. "Can we give them a ten-minute head start before we call the cops?"

A vision of Tiny and Duck breaking into thirty Hondas parked on the street went through Vic's mind. It would be his luck.

"Take fifteen," Mike said, trying to lighten the mood. "I'll tell the P.D. to come in quietly. Let's not scare the shit out of everybody."

"Good idea," Vic said, hoping they'd find some sort of ID for this pain in the ass.

Mike gestured toward the house. "Gina's having fits in there. She saw you barrel down the stairs and interrogated me."

"I'll talk to her."

Seeming to be satisfied with that lame answer, Mike nodded. "Who's got a suture kit to stitch you up?"

"I don't know. Billy's our best bet."

"Well, that'll suck."

"Not as much as facing your sister."


"My God!" Gina said when Vic came through the patio door, his shirt soaked in blood.

They'd been out there long enough for her to guess something went wrong. Now she knew it to be true.

Vic held up his hands. "Don't spaz."

*Don't spaz?* He had to be kidding. She went to him and reached for his shirt, but he stopped her. "What happened?"

Not knowing what else to do with her hands, she shoved them in the pockets of the shorts she'd thrown on before coming downstairs.

"It's just a cut. No big deal. Billy will stitch me up."

Michael stepped into the house behind Vic and raised his eyebrows. Someone better tell her what the hell was going on.

"Who's outside?"

Vic sighed, rubbed his hands over his face. "We caught a prowler. He's one of Sirhan's men. The cops are on their way."

Prowler. Sirhan. A wave of panic seized her and she inched to the arm of the couch. Sirhan getting this close meant he was good. He almost got to her children.

Michael grabbed her arm. "You okay?"

She yanked her arm free. "Of course I'm not okay. My children are upstairs sleeping and Vic walks in here all bloody. Am I supposed to be okay?"

Michael, clearly out of patience with the situation, growled. "All yours, Vic. I have to tell Roxann what's going on. It's her house too."

She pointed at Vic. "You need to go to the hospital."

"Uh, that's a big negative. Hospitals ask questions."

Monk opened the patio door and stuck his head in. "Where's Mike? Cops just pulled in."

"Upstairs," Vic said. "I'll send him out." He turned back to Gina. "We have to talk to the cops for a few minutes, and then Billy will stitch me up."

"The police will send you to the hospital."

Vic nodded. "They'll try and I'll refuse. I don't like hospitals. They take too long and people die there. Besides, it's just a scrape."

"Were you *stabbed*?"

"Not exactly."

The couch shifted and the whooshing came back. Seeing him wounded paralyzed her. Another man she cared about had gotten hurt. She swallowed the bile building in her throat. Throwing up was not an option. "Where's the knife?"

"Monk's keeping an eye on it outside." Vic walked to the bottom of the stairs. "Cops are here," he said to Michael as he came downstairs.

"Fine." Michael glanced at her as he strode by. "Stay inside."

Great. She'd just sit here and stew until they came back. Who the hell was out there? She folded her arms, quite sure her ears would pop off from the steam whistling through them.

Thirty minutes later, Vic came in, slid her a sideways glimpse and walked right past. Ignoring her? What the *hell*?

She followed him, doing double time to keep up with his long strides to the basement. "If you were stabbed, you need to go the hospital."

"I wasn't stabbed. He sliced me. I knocked the knife out of his hand before he could do any real damage. Please calm down."

Calm down? "Don't tell me to calm down."

He reached the bottom of the stairs and spun toward her. His eyes sparked with malice.

"Tell me what I can say to make you feel better about this."

She jerked back and he began prowling the basement.

"I can't fight with you anymore tonight," he yelled. "I'm trying to manage this and *you* are in the way."

The harsh words blasted her. No. No. No. She would *not* let herself get involved with him and this crazy life. It could get worse and that was a movie she'd seen before.

She poked him in the chest. "You don't get to talk to me that way. Not when I care what happens to you. And frankly, I'm beginning to wonder why I *do* care. Damn you."

"Hey." Billy tore down the steps with a canvas bag in his hand. "Take it easy. You'll wake everyone up."

"You got a suture kit in there?" Vic asked. He fisted and released his hands. The usual time-out thing he did when mad.

"Of course." Billy glanced around the room. "Where do you want to do this?"

"The floor. I don't want to get blood on anything. Let me get a blanket so we don't mess up the carpet."

"I'll get it." Gina needed her own time-out from this suffocating environment.

She went upstairs, grabbed a blanket off the couch and headed back down. How did she get herself into this? Had she learned nothing from Danny's death? She'd let herself believe Vic not being on the road kept him safe, but this was his life. The dark side followed him. Stupid, stupid woman. And the worst of it was she'd fallen in love with him.

When she returned, the two of them were speaking in low voices. Billy, on his knees, pulled medical supplies from his bag. Good God. He really intended on doing this in Michael's basement.

She set the blanket over the thick beige carpet. "He needs to go to the hospital."

Billy pulled his shoulder-length hair into a ponytail. "Nah. It's only the skin and subcutaneous tissue."

When Vic pulled off his shirt, Gina got a glimpse of the nasty wound. Dried blood had already formed around it as fresh blood continued to spill over.

"Why don't you go upstairs?" Vic asked, clearly wanting to be rid of her.

She squared her shoulders. Screw him being mad. He had no idea the go around they'd have. "You could get an infection."

"Yeah, at the hospital."

Anger rocketed through her. He could be such a bastard. "Damn you."

They glared at each other for a long minute. Two stubborn people battling it out. Vic finally jerked his head at Billy. "Give us a minute."

"No problem. I'll get some ice to numb you up."

They waited for the basement door to close and Vic stepped in front of her. "You gotta help me here. I'm trying to see this from your perspective, and it must look bad, but it's not. This is what we do. Billy has stitched me up plenty of times."

At his business-as-usual demeanor, she began to wonder if she'd overreacted to the situation. No. Uh-uh. He might have been accustomed to this, but she wasn't. Trying to breathe in some of his calm energy, she reached out and ran a finger down the side of his rock-hard stomach. "It's bad. A doctor should check it."

Then he did it. He smiled that crooked player smile. The

devastating one. He cupped her cheeks in his big hands and kissed her. Just a slow, gliding kiss that made her heart hammer.

Distracting her.

No. She stiffened against the warmth of the kiss.

"Trust me this time," he said backing away an inch.

Ouch. That hurt. Particularly after their earlier argument. Boy, oh, boy, this man knew how to manipulate a situation.

Something ripped in her chest and she blinked back the tears forming in her eyes.

He swiped at the tears with his thumb. "I know what this is about. I'm not going to die on you. *You'll* probably kill me before my job does."

She couldn't resist laughing. "Most likely."

He leaned down, kissed her again. "I'm fine. The kids are fine. The bad guy is going to jail, and we've got a plan. We're a lot better off than we were a few hours ago."

From the top of the stairs, Billy asked, "Can I come back?"

Vic tilted his head at her and she nodded. "Yeah, we're good," he said.

Had she just allowed herself to be talked down? Without a fight? Pathetic. And knowing how much she wanted Vic in her life, she'd probably let it happen again.

No. She couldn't let herself get used to life with him. Not with his dangerous job. The risk would be too high.

For this to work out, one of them would have to make major changes and it couldn't be her. Not with the kids involved. Vic would have to do it.

What a disaster.

.   .   .

"So, how did you learn to do this?" Gina asked as Billy finished off a stitch.

They knelt on either side of him in Mike's fancy basement with the slick television and collectible movie posters. Gina, the sexy, able-bodied assistant, scrutinized the procedure while snapping on a pair of latex gloves. She'd gone from insisting he go to the hospital to being completely engaged in the process. Go figure. Women.

"I was a medic in the army," Billy said. "I've done thousands of these. Vic's been my patient a few times."

"Shut up, Billy." All he needed on this already fucked-up night was the telling of war stories.

"You're very good with a needle," she said.

Talk about a weird scenario. Someday he'd find it amusing, but right now, with Gina watching, it made him damned uncomfortable.

"Ow," he complained when Billy started another stitch.

Billy sat back. "I can give you Lidocaine."

As if. "Save it for something big. Put more ice on it, though."

Gina set the ice bag on his stomach. "Are you okay?"

"He's fine," Billy said. "He's not usually a baby about this stuff."

"Finish up and then fuck off." Vic shot Gina a glance. "I'm not done with you either. Don't think I forgot about our little discussion earlier this evening."

"Ooh, this sounds good. You kids have a fight?"

They both ignored the question, but Gina shifted to her right a few inches and leaned toward Vic's face. The lemon scent of her soap did wonders to ease his discomfort.

"I didn't think you'd forgotten about it," she said. "I know I have to explain."

Billy stopped suturing. "Whoa. Hold on. You screwed up?"

Oh, Jee-*zus*.

"I sure did," she said.

Vic—God help him—laughed. "Gina, shut the hell up. You have no idea what you're doing to me. I'll never live this down."

"Do tell," Billy said.

"Keep suturing."

They both shushed him.

"I'm done stitching. All I need to do is cover it."

When Vic heard the snapping of latex, he lifted his head. "You done?"

"Yep."

Vic rolled to his side to avoid tearing a stitch and got to his feet. "Go away. I'll clean this up."

Billy laughed. "What? No thank-you for twenty-three of my best knots?"

"Twenty-three," Vic said. "Son of a bitch."

"Monk?" Billy asked.

"Nailed it."

"My man is good."

Gina's gaze bounced between them. "I don't understand."

"Never mind," Vic said. "It's a guy thing." He pulled on the clean T-shirt he'd brought down with him as his pain-in-the-ass friend marched upstairs.

Bending over with the stitches proved to be a little harder than he thought, so he knelt and started gathering the discarded supplies. Gina, still on her knees across from him, took off her gloves.

"I'm sorry about earlier."

He glanced at her, saw the mixture of confusion and

sadness on her face. "I don't get it. Why would you think I was with someone else?"

Her big brown eyes wandered to the floor. "Well, I didn't want to believe it, but we've never talked about dating exclusively. My mind worked me over and the more I thought about it, the more I worried."

He scooted over, put his hands on her legs. "You should have said something."

"I didn't know how to bring it up."

"I'll never lie to you. Even if it hurts. I'll never lie."

Gina held her hands in front of her face to shut him up. "I don't care. Not anymore. I'm just pissed at myself for not speaking up. I always speak up, but this hit a nerve and I was scared."

"You're scared? I just admitted I was in a relationship for the first time in my thirty-six years."

She laughed and tugged on his T-shirt. "I'm sorry. I should have trusted you. I *do* trust you. I went temporarily insane."

He grunted. "I understand. I'm usually the insane one."

When she leaned forward the bottom edge of her tank top brushed his arm, and he had a sudden urge to slide his hand under it. Nope. Not going there with the guys right upstairs. He kissed her and the chaos in his mind quieted. Finally, a moment of peace.

He backed away an inch. "So, to clarify, we're not seeing other people, right? That's what I want. If that's not what you want, we need to talk about it. And can I just say all this talking about talking is giving me hives?"

Gina did that loud belly laugh of hers, and some of the tension in him faded. She squeezed his cheeks between her hands. "I do love you."

*Oh, shit.* He swallowed hard. The dreaded *L* word. The

word he had never spoken to anyone. Sure he said it as a joke, but he'd never said it and meant it. How pathetic. He loved his aunt, he loved Mike and Roxann.

He even loved Gina. Probably more than he wanted to, but to verbalize it? No way. That would mean opening himself up to the eventual agony of losing her. Losing all of them. And who needed that?

He buckled Billy's field kit shut and got to his feet. "That's what they all say."

Reaching for his outstretched hand, Gina stood and gripped his hand tighter. "Hearing me say it makes you want to jump out a window, doesn't it?"

"Oh, yeah."

She sighed, rubbed her free hand across her forehead. "There are all kinds of love. It doesn't necessarily mean happily-ever-after love. Maybe it just means you're someone special in my life, and I wanted to tell you."

He nodded, looked at the stairs leading to freedom. "Okay. Got it."

She stepped closer, touched his face and laughed. "You want to run screaming from this room. And I'll let you. All I'll say is I don't count on anything anymore, and seeing you with blood all over you tonight reminded me of it. So, I do love you. I love you because you're my friend, you're good to my kids and you make me laugh. Don't get me wrong, you're a challenge, but it doesn't make you unlovable. Live with it."

"It's easier for you."

That got him the massive eye roll.

"That's bullshit and you know it."

He shook his head. "I *don't* know it. What I know is I've never said it to anyone. Not my aunt, certainly not my mother, so for me, it means changing something that I've hung on to my whole life. They're not just words and I don't know if I can handle the commitment that goes with them."

Somebody get the shrink in here. What the hell was he talking about? All this introspection and the inadequacy it made him feel was making him psycho. He needed to get back to killing people. At least he was good at that.

Gina took a deep breath, squeezed his hand. "I don't know what to say, except you sell yourself short, but that's for you to figure out." She marched toward the steps. "I'm going to bed. If you need a place to crash for a couple of hours, you can sleep in my bed, but you'll need to relocate before everyone wakes up."

A month ago, he would have ignored the invitation and slept on the couch. It would have been the beginning of his extraction. A woman telling him she loved him always forced him to implement an extraction plan. He couldn't think about an extraction plan right now, though. His head hurt too fucking much.

When Gina opened the basement door, he heard Tiny's voice from upstairs. *They're back.* A little buzz whipped through him as he double-timed the stairs.

"How'd you do?" Vic asked when he reached the kitchen.

Duck stood behind Tiny at the breakfast bar while he busied himself on a laptop.

"Found the car three blocks away," Duck said.

Vic pumped his fist. "Nice."

Duck swung toward him. He wore a bandanna wrapped around his head, a la Monk style, and his beard needed a trim. "The piece of shit was the only one parked on the street. It's registered to some woman in Florida. We didn't find any ID. He must have left it somewhere in case he got caught."

Vic scowled. "Crap."

"I did find a dry-cleaning slip dated two months ago under the seat. The name on the slip is Benson and there's a phone number. Tiny's doing a reverse lookup."

"What have we got?" Mike asked, coming down the stairs.

No Roxann in sight. She must have gone back to bed. Vic checked his watch. One-thirty. So much for getting sleep tonight.

"Got it." Tiny spun the stool to face them. "23 Franklin. Oak Park. I love the internet. The phone number is a cell, so I couldn't get it through the regular listings, but I did a people search and got a match."

"How accurate is it?" Mike asked.

"It says it's matched against public utilities, so it's the best we'll get tonight. I already left Janet a message."

Vic ran his fingers over his chin. "Let's check it out. Duck, stay here. Tiny and I will go."

Mike's eyes popped. "You're going?"

Nobody moved and the air suddenly left the room. Shit. Gina was upstairs. After the invitation to crash in her bed, if he didn't show up, she'd get whacky. But dammit, he wanted to do this. He *needed* to do this. The job offered him a sense of purpose.

He stepped back, leaned against the wall and glowered at Mike. "Tiny and Duck will go. I'll stay here. We'll sweep the house. Make sure this Benson asshole didn't leave us any gift-wrapped explosives."

"Cool," Duck said, obviously pleased to be doing the sneak and peek.

"Thank you," Mike said. "I won't have to listen to Gina and Roxann harping at me. You need help searching?"

"Nah," Vic said.

"Yell if you need me. Otherwise, I'm exhausted and going to bed."

Mike made his way to the stairs.

"Oh, and you're welcome," Vic said, snickering. He turned to Duck and Tiny. "Call me when you're done. If there's a computer, grab it. As soon as Conlin gets wind this guy got pinched, they're going to clean the place out. I called Lynx, but we can't count on the feds to move that quick."

"Roger that," Tiny said before the two of them hauled ass out the door.

EASING INTO GINA'S BED WAS AN UNEXPECTED AND WELCOME pleasure, but he made sure to keep his back to her. No sense tempting himself by touching her and sparking the inevitable explosion. Besides, he'd kept her awake enough tonight and just wanted to be close to her these next few hours. With the kids around, sleeping in the same room with her didn't happen much, but he didn't have a problem with it. He knew the angst that came with men coming and going out of his own mother's bedroom.

A yawn sneaked up on him. Damn, he needed shut-eye. The constant mental pandemonium was new to him. He could deal with the physical end of fatigue, but throw in outmaneuvering a crazy-assed terrorist, and it was a different ball game.

He inhaled through his nose and tried to quiet his mind by concentrating on Gina's soft breathing. She rolled over, rubbed her hand over his bare back and let it settle on his hip. Her warm fingers made his body hum. She'd better watch where that hand landed or they wouldn't be getting much sleep tonight. And he needed the rest. Fatigue left an inch of grit building up in his eyes.

Sleep. Please.

Part of him was still pissy about the sneak and peek. He didn't want to miss the fun. And yes, he was definitely hacked off about dumping that asshole on the cops. Once the cops had left, Monk checked all the cars and, lo and behold, found C-4 on the Tahoe.

Rat fucking bastard. And he'd gifted him to the cops. Son of a bitch.

It took two hours to check the foundation of the house before they cleared it. Two hours of second-guessing whether he should wake everyone up and get them the hell out of there, but Monk swore either he or Roy would have seen the fucker roaming near the house.

Of course, his brain might blow to bits all over Mike's fancy walls from all this thinking, but life sucked that way.

Sickness swirled in his belly. Guilt. He preferred anger. At least he could do something with it. He should have pumped a couple of bullets into that fucker.

An agonizing burn settled in his shoulders and he ground his fist into the pillow.

Gina scooted next to him, spooning that delectable little body against him and offering a nice distraction. Not too much was wrong with climbing into a warm bed with her.

*Don't go there.*

He had to sleep. But sex would definitely help get him there.

"Stop thinking so loud," she mumbled.

"What?"

"You're grumbling."

"Sorry. I'm thinking about thrashing you."

She snorted. "You're tired. So am I. Thrash me tomorrow."

"If I have to, I guess. Go back to sleep."

"I'm glad you're here."

"Yeah. Me too."

Gina would never know how glad, because he wouldn't tell her about that bomb. No way. He'd just have to step up security. No problem. Everything would be fine.

And his next job would be as a Rockette.

## 20

*Man Law: Always avoid emotional clutter.*

"GOT A SEC?" MIKE ASKED, JERKING HIS HEAD TOWARD THE side of the house and away from the partygoers.

Crap. What now? Maybe Mike had gotten wind of the C-4 they found on the Tahoe.

He couldn't know about that. Monk wouldn't squeal. Vic shook off the thought.

The rain, as predicted, had stopped and the sun burned through the abundant clouds. Everyone had cheerfully joined in to dry the chairs. Once the job was complete, guests scattered all over Mike's sopping wet lawn.

"What's up?" Vic asked when they'd reached a quiet spot. He tried to ignore the squishing water soaking his sandaled feet.

"Roxi called the police chief."

His ears tingled at the hardened, tight look on Mike's face. Worried. This would be bad.

"Let's hear it."

"Your guy has a warrant in Virginia for failure to appear. Joel Benson is an alias. His real name is Joel Baldridge. He fled on a rape and sodomy charge."

Vic's legs wobbled and he backed against the house before he crashed to the ground. A rape charge. This was the guy that shoved Gina against a wall. What would have happened if he hadn't walked up? A vision of that fucker slamming himself into Gina had Vic bending over and sucking air into his failing lungs.

No air.

Mike touched his shoulder. "Just breathe, buddy. Concentrate on small breaths. You'll be all right. You need a chair?"

A fucking chair? Was he a geriatric patient now? Oh, man, he had to get it together. He bolted up and leaned against the house. He counted to three, thought about a good sail and let his heart rate settle. A minute later, his breathing leveled off.

"What the hell was that?" Mike asked.

To justify his reaction, Vic wanted to tell Mike the truth. That he showed up in time to haul a fugitive rapist off Gina. But he wouldn't do that. This secret would stay with him.

"Maybe I'm getting sick. What else did the chief say?"

"They'll probably ship his ass back to Virginia. I know you wanted a shot at him, but at least you got him off the street."

"Hold on," Vic said. "Tiny told me the Honda Benson was driving had Florida plates. Whose car is it?"

Mike nodded. "The P.D. impounded the car this morning. It's Benson's—Baldridge, whatever his name is. It's his mother's car."

"Michael," someone yelled from under the tent and they

both turned. Mike's father, Frank, waved him over. No telling what Frank had going on. Mike held up a hand.

"Gotta go. We'll talk later." He wandered to his father, leaving Vic alone with thoughts of killing a fugitive rapist.

His cell phone buzzed and he rolled his eyes. Could he get five seconds to put a thought together? He checked the ID. Janet. Finally.

He hit the connect button. "It's almost four o'clock. Where've you been?"

"I've been getting the wheels moving on our terrorist," she fired back. "I'm not James Bond. It takes time to go through all these files."

Tiny had snagged Baldridge's computer last night and Janet was in the process of hacking into it.

"Blah, blah, blah. What have you got?"

"One interesting thing so far. It appears that Benson—"

"His real name is Baldridge. The P.D. ran his prints. He's a rapist from Virginia."

"Baldridge," Janet said, probably writing the name down. "Wow. I'll check him out. Anyway, I found a copy of a file someone emailed him with his work schedule. He works at the same market as Gerard Conlin."

That held Vic's interest. "Really?"

"Maybe they're friends and Conlin got him the job?"

Nah. That wasn't sitting right. An absurd thought penetrated his brain. "Find out who owns the market."

"Hang on," Janet said and he heard her tapping her keyboard. "Nope. Nothing. I need to make a couple of calls. I'll get back to you."

"Don't be surprised if it's the shell company that owns Conlin's house."

"Speaking of which," she said, "the same company owns Benson slash Baldridge's house. It has to be Sirhan."

"Yep. While you're at it, see if you can get a list of everything under the shell company's umbrella. Let's see what this guy is up to."

And if his instincts were at their best, he'd bet the market was a laundering facility. He had to get a hold of Lynx.

"I gotta run. Let me know as soon as you find anything."

He disconnected and immediately called Lynx. Voicemail. He left him a message regarding the market. Every piece of this slow puzzle seemed to simultaneously thrill and suck more life out of him. Bizarre. He wanted this done and the pace was sapping his energy.

This job sat like a bulldozer on his chest. Literally too close to home. A home he didn't even realize he had until the initial threat against Lily. Who couldn't seem to remember to keep her damned phone on. He'd just have to hound her about it until she understood how important it was that they be able to reach her. He let out a breath and everything inside him dropped to his heels.

He scanned the crowded yard, spotted Gina in a devastating red bikini surveying the food table and swinging her hips to the old disco song plowing through the speakers.

Suddenly, every ounce of him needed to be near her. To touch her and assure himself she was safe. He started toward her, doing a quick assessment of the yard as he went along. Matt on the lawn talking to Roy's wife. Tiny hovering over Lily and two other girls. Jake in the pool. All kids accounted for by the time he got to Gina.

He moved behind her, slid his arm around her waist and hugged her to him. Inhaling the warm scent of her settled his raw nerves.

She shifted back and grinned. "I like that greeting. Are you hungry?"

*There's a loaded question.* He leaned in close. "There are a lot of people here."

*And everyone is outside.* He half scolded himself for his triple-X thoughts.

She popped a blueberry in her mouth. "How very observant of you."

"The kids are distracted."

When he began running his thumb over her stomach, she narrowed her eyes. It took her a second, but she finally got it.

"You devil," she whispered.

She checked the yard, making sure the kids were supervised.

"I'll meet you upstairs in five minutes," he said.


"THIS IS SO BAD." GINA LAUGHED AND DOVE ON TOP OF HIM when she came into the bedroom.

"Ow! Watch the stitches."

"I'm so sorry." She tugged up his T-shirt to inspect the wound and dropped a kiss there.

"Forget it. Door locked?" He pulled the shirt the rest of the way off.

"Yep. I feel like a sneaky teenager with my parents downstairs."

Vic shook his head. Holy hell. He'd have to look Frank in the face when this was over. "You had to bring that up?"

She laughed and raked her hands through his newly shortened hair. "You are a major hottie with short hair. I've been lusting after you all afternoon."

He had needed some quiet time this morning to clear his mind and, using the excuse of an overdue haircut, sneaked out to the town's barber. On a whim, he'd gone back to a modified military cut and was still getting used to it himself, but Gina definitely liked it. She'd been walking by him all day and casually sliding her fingers through it. Now he knew what he'd been missing when he'd seen women do that to men they'd been intimate with. The heated connection made his system fire.

"Lily said I look like Tiny." He untied the bottom strap of her bikini top.

Gina laughed. "We have to hurry."

"That won't be a problem."

For sure. They may have slept in the same bed for a while the night before, but that was all they'd done, and after five days of not having his hands on that body of hers, he was about to explode.

Not bothering to untie the top strap of her bathing suit, she whipped it over her head and slung it across the room. Without hesitation, she pulled the bottoms off, tossed them over her shoulder. No being-naked-in-broad-daylight phobia there. His kind of woman.

She waited for him to get a condom on, but scooted behind him and ran her hands over his arms. The sensation of her bare breasts against his back made him groan. The instant he had the condom on, he lay back on the bed and she straddled him. He'd discovered Gina liked to be on top and he wasn't about to argue since he had a great view.

"I love being like this with you," she said, sliding herself onto him.

Rolling his eyes back, he savored that initial feeling of being inside her. Heaven. Right here. He laid his hands on her thighs, moved them up and down, the heat of her skin warming his hands.

Her dark hair, still damp from her swim, was a riot of curls falling around her face, and he pushed it back. Grabbing his hands, she moved them over her body and gave him the sex-kitten smile. She loved being touched and made sure he always knew it. Gina took sexy to another universe. All these years he'd lived without this, and she was right there.

His muscles tensed and he wondered how this woman had the ability to shatter every ounce of his emotional control.

She rocked her hips and he hauled her down, held her face in his hands and kissed her. Smothered her really, and when he shifted his hips, she moaned. The moaning had tension coiling in him. Oh, baby.

"I can't do it. I can't hang on." He stared into her eyes and concentrated on not flying apart.

She wiggled her eyebrows. "It's okay. You'll make it up to me later."

Somehow, she always knew what he needed. Always made him feel like he wasn't a screwup. He grabbed a pillow, threw it over his face and growled into it, his body bucking and convulsing under her.

"Well," Gina said, bending over and kissing his stitched-up stomach again, "that was fun."

"I'll say."

She peeked at the nightstand clock. "Fifteen minutes. Time to go." She arched her back and stretched her arms. The sight of her, completely at ease in her nakedness, heated him up again. There'd never be enough. Then she slid off of him. Damn.

"Oh, come on." He grabbed her arm. "You know you don't want to leave. We're just getting started here."

It made her laugh, but she tossed his shorts to him and sauntered toward the adjoining bathroom. "Get dressed, big boy. This mission is over."

Feeling like he could run a marathon, he rolled to his side and stood. Nothing like a good spin with Gina to boost his energy. A minute later, she came back dressed in the killer bikini.

"I'll see you downstairs."

She smacked him on his bare ass, but he grabbed her hand, pulled her close and brushed a soft kiss over her lips. The quiet indulgence, the standing still and her ability make his world a happy place let him savor the peace for a minute.

"I love you."

Whoa. His body froze. What the *hell*? He said it. He'd always imagined it to be monumentally difficult, but it just slipped out. He had even practiced it a few times over the years, but the words had never felt quite right, and now they just rolled off his tongue with no warning.

The stillness snapped him to reality and he realized Gina was trying hard not to smile. She would understand what an important step this was for him, but would she push him on it? Would she make him talk about it? Please, no. No talking.

"I knew you loved me," she cracked. "I just didn't want to say anything."

She spun and headed toward the door. She knew not to make a big deal of it. To play it cool and not make him *explore* it. He smiled as the bedroom door shut. Gina just might be the direction he'd been heading all these years.

.  .  .

THE HECTIC SCHEDULE OF THE LAST TWO DAYS HUNG ON GINA like an extra hundred pounds. On Sunday afternoon, she marched out Michael's back door wearing her new blue bikini, made her way to her favorite lounge chair and plopped onto it.

The French doors lining the back of the house were covered by the red-and-white striped awning Roxann had just opened and offered shade to anyone who chose to partake. Not her. She wanted the warm sun.

Jake and Lily splashed happily in the pool while Michael, Vic and Matt fiddled with the boat. The better of it being they didn't need to rush home tonight due to the long holiday weekend.

Yesterday's rain left behind a cloudless blue sky. She closed her eyes and blocked out the half dozen men scattered around the house on guard duty. She refused to let it get to her. The goal for today would be total relaxation.

Gina opened her eyes as Roxann, in a black one-piece bathing suit, handed her one of two Bloody Marys.

"I figured we could use these." She took the chair next to Gina's.

"Thank you. Do you have ten more?"

Roxann laughed and brushed something off her leg. "What is with Vic today?"

"Ha. What's with him any day? He's our own version of the man of mystery."

After glimpsing toward the dock to see what the boys were doing, Roxann swung her legs to the side to face Gina. "Michael's worried about him."

The nudge of alarm slithered up Gina's back. "Why?"

Roxann sipped her Bloody Mary, gave a thumbs-up. "I did good with this batch. Anyway, Vic came downstairs this morning and announced he loved us. Personally, I found it adorable, but your brother doesn't know what to make of it."

Gina clapped her hands together and laughed. Yes, she would joyfully take credit for getting this man out of his own head and making him think about what was important in life. "I love it."

"Well, Michael doesn't. He thinks the pressure of the last few weeks is getting to him, and wants to send him for a drug test."

Gina's euphoria went south and she shot up to face Roxann. "He can't do that. Please, Rox, talk him out of it. It's not drugs. I swear to you."

"*What* is going on around here? I feel like I'm living someone else's life. And for a control freak, that's not good. The three of you are acting completely out of character and it's confusing me."

She was confused? She didn't know the half of it. "Vic saying he loves you is a good thing, right?"

Roxann did the legendary eye roll. "Of course."

"It wasn't easy for him to do. I think it terrifies him because he feels vulnerable. Him saying it out loud is major progress."

"And if Michael makes him go for a drug test, he'll be mortified."

"You know how Vic is. He'll tell himself he shouldn't have done it and he'll close himself off. He already thinks his emotions get him in trouble. It'll set him back again."

Roxann snickered. "And you're working too hard to have him set back."

There would be no sense denying it. At this point, getting Vic to talk about his feelings was almost a science project.

"He's going through something," Gina said. "I don't

understand it. None of us could, but I think he's trying to figure out what makes him happy."

Male voices drifted their way and she twisted to see the men making their way up the lawn.

Roxann waved. "Here they come. I'll talk to Michael. Tell him to leave it alone. Given his penchant for interfering, it should make him deliriously happy. Don't you think?"

"We all know how much he loves to be told to butt out."

Roxann took a healthy gulp of her Bloody Mary. "And how awful he is at doing it."

For the millionth time, Gina tilted her head skyward and said thanks for Roxann. She was the ice to Michael's fire and always managed to help her deal with him. "Thanks, Rox. I know I'm sending you into battle and I appreciate it."

She waved her off. "As crazy as these weeks have been, you seem happy. I like seeing you this way. And I always thought Vic was happy, but now I realize something was missing. Maybe you're helping him figure out what it is."

"Hey," Vic said stepping up to where they sat. "What are we talking about?"

He straddled Gina's chair, sat behind her and kissed the top of her head. The warmth of his skin made her tingle, and she snuggled into him, enjoying the ease of it.

"Actually, we're talking about you and how much we love you."

With a suspicious glance at Roxann, he hesitated a minute. "I love you guys too."

"Oh, boy. I think I've unleashed a monster."

"Yeah," Vic laughed. "And now he's out of control. What will you do?"

Gina ran her hand along his cheek. "I'm not worried. I think he needs to be out of control awhile."

"I don't know," he said, clearly teasing her. "What if you get stuck with him?"

Forget that. What if she *wanted* to be stuck with him? What if she got used to this easy banter and affection? Would it be so wrong?

She shouldn't even be contemplating it.

---

## 21

*Man Law: Always have a good wingman.*

"HEY, Y'ALL," VIC SAID WHEN DUCK AND JANET HUSTLED INTO the executive board room at Taylor Security.

They sat next to each other at the table, laughing over something Duck said. They'd been circling each other for months and Vic wondered if it had moved to the next stage. Not that he cared, but he'd have to make sure they didn't work together. He was currently experiencing the emotional chaos of working with someone he cared about, and he couldn't have two of his best operators getting distracted.

"Sorry to call you in on a holiday," he said, "but I need to take stock of what we have. Feels like crap is flying everywhere."

After a wild weekend, one that included some great time with Gina and the kids, this was the last place he wanted to be, and he felt sure Bobby, Billy, Monk, Janet and Duck felt the same.

"No problem," Bobby said. He hadn't bothered changing out of his ratty T-shirt and denim shorts, but Vic couldn't blame him. Fourth of July, and they all should be finishing up a nice dinner after a day on the water.

"Where's Tiny?" Monk asked from his spot on the windowsill, where he enjoyed the warmth from the waning sun.

Vic snorted a laugh. "He's at the house with Gina and the kids. Roy and the new guy are there too. Lily said something about painting Tiny's toenails, and I couldn't get out of there fast enough."

"It sucks to be Tiny these days." Monk shook his do-rag adorned head.

"Amen, brother," Vic said.

Janet booted up her laptop. "Ready, boss."

"Go."

She passed out a report. "I looked into the market. It does *really* well."

Vic skimmed the report. Financials. Damn, she was good. "In comparison to what?"

"Flip the page and look at the spreadsheet. My guy at the IRS helped me with tax returns for three other similar businesses in the area. Our market has triple the revenue."

"Whoosh," Monk said.

"That's impossible." Bobby perked up, not necessarily questioning the report.

The team liked to poke holes in a theory and they had all learned to take it in stride.

"Why?" Vic asked.

Bobby shrugged. "I've been on Conlin almost every day. He works different shifts and I see who comes and goes from the market. It gets about five customers a day and half of them don't come out with any bags."

A lot of eyebrows went up. "I've been thinking it's a front," Vic said. "Maybe drugs. Do we have anything on the owners? Anything leading to Sirhan?"

Please. Let her have something. Sirhan had to have a piece of the market. Janet flipped through her notes, passed a sheet of paper over.

"It's definitely a shell company. Sirhan isn't listed on any paperwork, but it doesn't mean he's not the owner. One of his underlings could have signed the papers. The shell has eleven other businesses across the country." Janet read from her notes. "San Francisco, New York, Dallas, Minneapolis and Boston. Four of them are markets and the remainder are check-cashing businesses."

"They must be dumping all the money into the shell company," Vic said.

"Any offshore accounts?" Duck asked.

Janet tapped the tip of her nose with her index finger. "Bingo. The company is headquartered in Dubai, and I'm guessing that's where all the money goes. Dubai has relaxed reporting standards. People walk into the bank with a bag full of cash and deposit it with no questions asked."

"Makes sense," Vic said. "The launderers report higher earnings and wash the dirty money through the bank in Dubai."

"Something is screwed up here," Bobby said.

Vic jerked his head. "Go."

"Last week, I followed Conlin to work, but he didn't park in his usual spot. He pulled in front of the store. I figured he was picking up his check or something. He came out a few minutes later carrying a bag."

He stopped and Vic recognized his hesitation. That moment when a thought crash lands and it takes a few seconds to sort through the debris.

"And what?" Billy asked, getting impatient.

"Son of a gun."

"*What?*" They all asked in unison.

Bobby thumped himself on the head. "Conlin stopped at some ATMs that morning."

ATMs. Hot damn. Vic tapped a foot. Maybe they were finally on to something with this asshole.

"They're smurfing," Bobby said. "I totally missed that."

"Yep," Monk replied. "They're cleaning the money through the ATMs. They deposit small increments into several accounts so they don't go over the limit."

"The bank has to report any deposits over ten grand, right?" Vic asked Janet.

She nodded. "It's called a SAR—suspicious activity report. What do you think they're running?"

Vic sat back, propped his feet on the table. Lynx would love this. And there was no getting around the truckload of harassment he'd get when they, a handful of ex-special ops people, cracked a Chicago-based terrorist ring the government didn't even have on radar. True, they'd broken a few laws to get the job done, but it was all part of the greater good.

Yep, Lynx would take a good, long whipping on this one.

"Vic?" Janet snapped her fingers at him.

He bolted to attention. "Huh?" She'd asked a question. Right. "I was thinking drugs, but now I'm betting it's a hawala. Could be both."

"A hawala?" Billy asked.

"It's an unregulated system for transferring money to areas that are underserved by banks. They usually run them out of small rooms off of a store. I had to use one in Afghanistan once to get cash."

"How do they work?" Billy asked.

"Say you were in Afghanistan or Somalia. Pakistan even. They're all over." Vic waved his hand. "If you needed funds right away, I would take cash into the hawala and they'd charge me a fee to send the money. Once I pay, they call their contact in Afghanistan. Their contact makes sure you get the cash and they keep the fee. It's faster than traditional wiring and there's no paperwork. Terrorists love it because they can use the profits from the transaction fees to fund their activities. Innocent people use them as a way to send money to their families."

"No money actually changes hands?" Billy sounded skeptical.

Vic shook his head. "Not a dime. They keep a running tally of what was sent and work it out later. They might settle up with goods rather than cash. If I'm the sender and I have some electronics they can't get on the other end, maybe I'll send the electronics to settle the tab. The receiver sells the electronics to recoup their money."

"Pretty slick," Duck said.

Vic sat up, scratched his head. "It's actually simplistic, but it's been going on for years and the government has trouble tracking it. There's no paper trail to know how much money actually gets passed around."

The more Vic thought about it, the more he was sure Sirhan had set up a hawala in that damned market. A rather large hum of excitement sang in his ears.

"Does the shell company own any other property in Chicago?" he asked Janet.

She flipped through her notes again. "A warehouse on the far south side. Here's the address."

She wrote the address down and slid it over.

Well, well. What, pray tell, would they find there? They might be having a bitch of a time finding Sirhan, but even putting a crimp in the fucker's operation would give partial satisfaction.

"Let's go check out a warehouse, boys."

"No fucking way." Vic stared at the metal sign hanging on the crappy chain-link fence surrounding the warehouse.

Monk grunted out a laugh while Vic dialed Janet. The night air hung hot and humid and Vic wiped sweat from the side of his face.

After doing a drive-by of this dump of a warehouse, they'd parked two blocks away and walked back. The building, an old brick deal with a few windows along the front, one of them boarded up, sat at the end of a dead-end street. Large trees and weeds grew against the far side of the building. A few spotlights here and there left most of the building in shadows. Good for them, bad for Sirhan.

The back of the building housed the loading dock and one entry door. Probably an office where drivers could check in when making deliveries. Vic had his eye on that door but stopped dead when they approached the fence and he spotted the "Premises protected by DSI Security" sign.

DSI Security.

The company Taylor Security had acquired fifteen months ago. There was some fucking irony. He might own a piece of the security company protecting Sirhan's illegal operation.

"What's up?" Janet asked, finally answering.

"Are you near your computer?"

"You bet. What do you need?"

A car turned down the street and Vic, Billy and Monk ducked into the shadows behind a clump of trees. The car pulled into one of the long row of warehouse lots, turned around and headed back the way it came.

"I need you to log into the office database and check this address. There's a sign on the fence that says DSI handles this building."

The clacking of a computer keyboard seemed inordinately loud in Vic's ear. Damn, he needed a break here. He needed this building to not have an active alarm. Not to mention cameras. If there were cameras, he was fucked. He couldn't risk getting caught on video and tipping Sirhan off.

They needed Sirhan thinking they knew nothing about his Chicago operation. They *needed* to buy time for Lynx to get his precious probable cause and Vic didn't want to jeopardize that. Freakin' probable cause always took too damn long. It could take weeks, months even, for the feds to get enough evidence to secure a warrant.

"They were a DSI client," Janet said. "They canceled the contract. They had an alarm system and cameras."

"How long has the shell company been leasing this building?"

"Hang on." Janet shuffled some papers. "Just over a year."

"Got it. Thanks." Vic disconnected.

"What do you think?" Billy asked from his spot against the large oak tree.

"They killed the contract. If they had hired another company, the DSI sign would have been replaced." He tapped the phone against his bottom lip while he absorbed the quiet and let his mind and instincts work. "I say we go in."

They worked their way through the trees to the back of the building, their feet occasionally landing on trash in the tall grass they trudged through.

"I guess the landscapers don't visit much," Billy whispered.

Vic stepped up to the gate. Locked. "I guess we're going over."

His stitched-up belly would love this.

"Upsy-daisy," Monk said, doing his Spidey thing and hauling ass over the top.

Vic followed and swung himself over, making sure to keep the stitched side of his stomach away from the top of the fence.

After spending some time with a complicated lock on the back door, they stood in the middle of a musty-smelling hallway. The place stunk like an ashtray.

Vic pulled his penlight from the side pocket of his cargo shorts and led Monk and Billy down the darkened hallway to an office on the left. The miniscule office contained way too much furniture and stacks and stacks of paper. Yellowing newspapers sat on top of a five-drawer vertical filing cabinet and the grimy window above probably hadn't been opened in years. Talk about a Feng Shui nightmare. No positive energy here.

"Total shit hole," Billy said.

Vic shrugged. "Rent's probably cheap."

They crept single file into the storage area of the warehouse. The space, maybe thirty or forty thousand square feet, contained boxes stacked to the second level catwalk. Grocery boxes. Cereal, soup, pasta. Great. Too bad he didn't need to stock up.

Monk moved to the catwalk and stared down over the darkened warehouse while running his penlight over the boxes. "Hey, check out these crates. Far right side."

"On it." Vic strode to where he shined the light.

The large, rectangular wooden crates, maybe four feet

long, had Fragile stamped on the sides in big red lettering. Vic lifted the lid and Billy held it with one arm while he shined light into the box with his free hand.

Vic pushed aside the shreds of packing material and let out a soft whistle. A burst of adrenaline whipped through him and his stomach churned from the sudden attack.

"MP5s," Billy said, wide eyed and almost drooling.

"The king of close-quarters combat," Vic said. "What, dare I ask, would a grocery store be doing storing a machine gun?"

He stepped back, ran his flashlight over the area. "Must be forty crates here."

"Check the other ones," Monk, still on the catwalk, said.

Vic moved three rows over and opened another crate. Billy replaced the lid on the first crate and jogged over to shine his light into the next box.

"RPGs. Son of a bitch. This fucker is running guns through our fair city."

A clanging noise came from the loading dock. *Fuck.*

"We got company."

---

## 22

*Man Law: Always find a way out.*

"LET'S BOLT." VIC KEPT HIS VOICE LOW, ALREADY PLANNING his call to Lynx. He replaced the crate lid as disappointment settled on him.

He so did not want to leave this warehouse right now.

Monk crept toward the door they'd entered through.

Maybe he'd lay eyes on the people coming in. Would it be too much to ask for it to be Sirhan himself? He could take him out right here and put an end to this fucked-up game.

Before stepping into the hallway, he swiveled and saw a white cargo van back into the warehouse. His heart hammered. Something was coming or going.

Two men exited the van, but the darkness hid their identities. One of them jogged to the side wall and flipped on the lights. The warehouse flooded with bright light, and Vic ducked back and shut his eyes for a second to let them adjust.

He sneaked to the entry door. Surveying the loading dock from the doorway, Monk gave a thumbs-up. No one outside. Unable to resist, Vic stole a glance around the wall but didn't recognize either man. Probably a couple of lackeys. Damn.

The first guy, dark haired, maybe around thirty, moved to the back of the van and opened the doors.

"Help me with this," he said to his partner in a voice so flat and indistinct Vic didn't even try to place an accent.

The two men hefted a large crate, similar to the ones stacked in the warehouse, from the cargo area of the van. More guns?

Vic's adrenaline surged again. He flexed his fingers, tried to release some of the anger raging inside him. Where the hell were all these weapons going?

He'd like to hang out until these pricks were done unloading. Maybe they'd leave and he and the boys could finish the search. He didn't want to risk getting caught, though. Not that they couldn't handle these two mopes, but staying under Sirhan's radar would be the most important thing.

Monk gave him a silent what-the-fuck shrug. Vic slowly swung his head back to the cargo van.

"Hey," the second, gray-haired man said, "when we're done here, why don't you run and get some sandwiches? Who knows when they'll be here with the next load?"

"Got it," the other responded.

Shit. These two were going to be here awhile. Waiting on another shipment.

Holy hell.

But Vic couldn't risk staying. As much as his body

yearned for action, his mind overrode him. The smart thing would be to wait for the big score and bring down the whole operation.

He took one last glance around the corner and watched another crate come out of the van. That had to be it. The van couldn't hold much more.

Vic shifted toward the door and hustled out after Monk. Damn. They'd get these guys, just not tonight.

Forty-five flippin' minutes later Vic stomped through Gina's back door. Traffic at eleven o'clock at night. Go figure some drunk would wrap his car around a pole when he wanted to get to Gina's for a quick visit.

"I'm sorry I'm late," he said when she came into the kitchen still wearing the khaki shorts and tank top she wore earlier in the day.

She went up on tiptoes, kissed him quick. She'd started doing that lately and he didn't mind one bit. Mike did it with Roxann all the time, and Vic always wondered how two people got to that comfort level. He didn't know how he and Gina had gotten there, but he liked it. Who knew a simple kiss could mean so much?

He pulled one of the kitchen chairs out, winced at the loud scraping noise and the vibration shot up his arm. She needed felt on the bottoms of these chairs. Maybe he'd do that for her.

Spying the nail polish remover on the table, he said, "Do I want to know who needed that?"

She laughed. "Probably not."

She grabbed the hand he held out to her and let him pull her on to his lap.

"Tiny really let her paint his toenails?"

Gina gave an emphatic nod. "I set him up with a bowl of popcorn and SportsCenter and he endured it. She gave him alternating toes of pink and red."

Oh, man, what Vic would have paid to see that. "I suppose you didn't take pictures."

Her mouth fell open. "Tiny said you'd say that."

Tiny knew him too well. He shrugged. "He's family. We spent our formative years living together. He knows my hot buttons."

"Well, please don't tease him. He wanted to make Lily happy. He's a good man."

Vic slid an errant curl off her cheek. "He is that. He and Mike are the only two guys I really trust."

She leaned back and stared at him a second. "Really?"

"My men are all good guys, but Tiny and Mike are the ones I know, without a doubt, will stand up when everyone else sits down."

"Have you told Tiny you love him?"

He smiled, proud of himself. "Yep. I think he thinks I'm losing it."

"Men," Gina huffed. "I'll never understand how your minds work."

"We pretty much feel the same about women."

Warmth blasted through him when she ran her hand over his shortened hair. "You like it short, huh?"

"It feels like velvet." She grinned and leaned into him. The movement had all his blood moving to the wrong places and...yep...hard-on. She obviously felt the bulge digging into her and, with a wicked smile, wiggled her butt against him. Jeezalou.

"Really, not funny," Vic said.

Her laughter filled the room and he lightly pinched her leg.

"I'm sorry," she said. "You're easy to torment that way."

He tapped his fingers against the table. "Kids asleep?"

"Matthew's awake. Sorry." Just to torture him, she ran her tongue behind his ear. She then snorted in said ear. Nice. Wasn't she quite the seductress?

"Have you ever noticed," he said, "when you purposely try to be sexy you blow it by laughing?"

She smacked his arm. "I know. I can't help it."

"I'm not complaining. I think it's cute." He dragged his hands over her bare legs. "Besides, you're sexy without trying."

That earned him a smoker of a kiss. Tongue and all, and he tried to squelch the frustration of not being able to strip her naked.

"I guess that was my goodnight kiss. I need some sleep. I want to get to the gym before I pick you up for work in the morning."

She grabbed his hand and walked him to the door. "Thanks for coming by. You gave me the attention I needed."

Gina needy? Never. Even so, if a visit from him cured her, she was most definitely perfect.

He cupped his hands over her cheeks, let them rest there a second in anticipation of the spine melting that would come when he kissed her. He'd gotten used to the feeling and suddenly craved it on a daily basis.

"Good night," she said.

"Yep. Tomorrow will be a good day."

He knew this because he had a legal pad filled with notes about Sirhan he'd pass on to Lynx. Soon this nightmare would be over and he and Gina could figure out what they were doing with each other.

And didn't that just scare the crap out of him?

.  .  .

Vic gave up on his emails and checked his cell phone for at least the tenth time. Where the hell was Lynx? He'd left him a message at nine o'clock this morning. Six freakin' hours ago. He tossed his cell on top of a stack of reports Mike wanted him to read and picked up the prepaid phone he called Lynx on. Maybe King of the Paranoids called back on that one. Nope.

*Crap.*

He stood, unbuttoned his sleeves and rolled them to his elbows. A quick inspection of his khakis confirmed he succeeded in wiping away the coffee spill. Not bad for an amateur. He marched to the outer office. The assistant sat at her pristine desk—no wonder Mike liked her—typing like a banshee.

"Any calls for me?"

"Nope." She turned back to her computer.

His cell phone rang and he darted back to the desk, scooped up the phone and checked the ID. A D.C. number he didn't recognize. He punched the button. "Vic Andrews."

"You rang?" Lynx said, trying to talk above the sounds of traffic.

"Finally. Where've you been?"

"As a reminder, I do have a full-time job with the United States government. One that keeps me pretty damned busy without your screwed-up scenario added to it. I'm on my way back from a meeting on the Hill. I have five minutes."

"Are you done whining so I can tell you what I've got?"

"Fire away. You pain in the ass. I really should beat the hell out of you."

Vic laughed. Lynx was one tough son of a bitch.

"Sirhan has definitely set up shop here. I think he's running a hawala out of the market I told you about. Plus, that guy I nabbed at Mike's house the other night is wanted on a rape charge in Virginia."

"No shit?"

"Yeah. Also, one of my guys saw Gerard Conlin making ATM deposits all over the city. I think they're smurfing."

"Hang on. Let me get my notepad."

Vic heard the shuffling of paper through the phone line.

"What else?" Lynx asked.

"There's a warehouse on the south side. It's owned by the same shell company that owns the market. You'll want to have someone check that out."

"Why?"

This was where things got sticky. Vic couldn't necessarily say there were guns in the place because technically he shouldn't know. "I believe there is illegal activity happening there."

Lynx sighed. "I hesitate to ask, but why do you think that?"

Vic blew out a breath and sat back in his chair. Propped his feet up. "You don't want me to answer that."

The line went quiet. Five. Four. Three. Two...

"Don't tell me you broke into that building."

"Okay. I won't tell you."

The fact that he didn't deny it would set Lynx off. At least he hadn't called him a stupid, fucking redneck yet.

"You have to stop doing that," he hollered. "You could be screwing up evidence. We need probable cause. We *need* warrants. You know all this. I've explained it a hundred times, you stupid, fucking redneck."

"Hey," Vic put his feet on the floor and sat straight. "Don't bitch at me. If you federal boys were on top of this shit, I wouldn't have a problem here."

The call waiting beeped and he pulled the phone from his ear, checked the ID. Tiny. He'd have to wait.

"What's the address of the warehouse?"

Vic read it off.

"I'll run it by a few people, see if anything pops. What else?"

He smiled. "Hell, I should be on the damn payroll considering I'm doing your job."

"Not *my* job, asshole. Somebody's, but not mine."

The assistant knocked on the open door. "Tiny is holding for you," she said.

"Tell him I'll call him back. Two minutes."

"He said it's an emergency."

An icy panic zipped up his spine. Tiny wouldn't say emergency if it weren't true.

"Gotta, go, Lynx. Call me later."

Vic disconnected and picked up his desk phone.

"Goddamn you," Tiny screamed at someone. "You should have checked the door."

Vic jerked the phone from his ear. Uh-oh. Something was seriously haywire. All the spit in his mouth dried up. Beads of sweat broke out on his upper lip and he swiped at them.

"Whoa. Hey, bud," Vic said loud enough to get Tiny's attention. "What's going on?"

"Fucking new guy," Tiny raged, then stopped, took an audible breath. "Forget it. Shit."

"What happened?"

"Lily's gone."

## 23

*Man Law: Never get attached.*

LILY. GONE.

The words hit Vic like a gunshot from a .45. The shock left him numb at first, and then searing pain ripped through his midsection.

Everything spun. He tried to focus. The voice in his head shouted commands, but nothing connected. When the howling in his ears started, he sucked in air, tensed his forearms and released them. The spinning and the howling stopped.

Finally, the warrior in him came to life and he shot out of his chair, sending it crashing against the wall. "Gone how?"

"I had to run an errand and I called the new guy, Freddie, to watch Lily here at the school. The kids were all playing outside, she went in to go to the bathroom and never came out. We've scoured the place and she's not here. I think she must have gone out the back door."

Vic squared his shoulders. "Not alone she didn't. She wouldn't do that." He dug his fist into his forehead. Lily. Gone. He had to get her back.

The GPS.

"Hold on," he said and put the phone down.

He grabbed his phone, punched the button to get him to the internet. The screen's message said Opening and he tapped his finger against the side. "Come on, come on."

It finally connected and he went to the website Gizmo instructed him on. A map popped up. Lily's location, if she had her phone on, should be a green blinking arrow on the screen. Nothing. Shit.

He went to the other website. The one for the shoe clip. Please be there. The map popped up. Nothing blinking.

*Fuck.* He slammed his hands on the desk, leaned into them, felt the boiling-hot rage move through him. Control. He begged for it. *Think. Work the problem.* He held a breath until his lungs cried mercy, released it slowly through his mouth.

They got Lily.

What would he tell Gina?

He picked up the phone again. "You still there?"

"Yeah."

"Stay at the school. Check the building again. Make sure she's not there."

"The lady in charge of the daycare wants to call the cops."

Cops. Great. He didn't need cops getting in his way. But wait...

"Let her call them," Vic said.

"*What?*"

"Yeah. They'll put out an Amber Alert. Sirhan won't be able to move her around too much."

"Won't that add to Gina's stress? She's going to have to act like we're not involved. What if we find her first?"

There was an angle Vic hadn't thought of. Gina was strong. She could handle the stress if it meant getting Lily back safe. The memory of her crazy curls the night they watched *Dirty Dancing* together popped into his head, and the pain in his midsection came roaring back. Sweet girl must be terrified.

"Get the cops over there. Keep me posted."

He hung up and called Gizmo.

"I need you in my office, pronto. Lily is missing."

He jammed the phone into the cradle, grabbed his cell phone and ran to Mike's office.

For the first time, Vic didn't want to face his closest friend. He didn't want to deliver this devastating news. And he really didn't want to be the one responsible for dragging Mike's family into this mess. But that guilt lay squarely with him and he'd have to live with it if something happened to that beautiful little girl.

Mike must have seen the misery on his face. "What's up?"

Vic stood in front of the desk in a modified parade rest, waiting for Mike to start screaming at him. To his credit, he stayed calm. His face, however, spoke volumes. The skin hardened over his cheekbones and a storm brewed behind his eyes.

"How long has she been gone?" Mike asked.

"About half an hour."

"The GPS?"

Vic shook his head. "She must not have the phone on,

and I don't know what's up with the clip. Gizmo is on his way up."

"Does Gina know?"

Vic shook his head again. "I'll tell her. I wanted to get a line on Lily first, but with the cops coming in, we'll have to tell her before they do."

"Good idea." Mike's voice finally cracked; a sound Vic had never experienced. Mike cleared his throat. "We have to get her back and kill this fucker. They'd better not touch one curl on her head."

"I don't think they will. She's the bargaining chip and Sirhan knows if they hurt her, I'll come at him with everything I've got."

"Why now?"

Vic shrugged. "He's probably tired of the game. Particularly after we nabbed his guy at your house the other night. By now he knows we've got that laptop. He wants me to suffer and grabbing Lily is the start. Hell, I half expected a call already. I think he'll suggest a trade. Me for her." What a fucking life.

"No."

"If it'll get Lily home safe, I'll do it."

Mike threw up his hands. "Let's not get too far ahead of this thing. We have to tell Gina and we can't do it here. She's going to freak and I want her to be able to do that at home where she doesn't have to face people."

Mike put his hands over his face and sat a minute. Vic knew he wanted to fall apart. They both did, but neither would. They'd work this out instead.

"I'm here." Gizmo stood in the doorway breathing a little heavy in his jeans and Pink Floyd T-shirt.

"I can't get a signal from her cell or the clip." Vic shoved his phone at him.

Giz took it, punched a couple of buttons and shook his head. "Mike, can I use your computer?"

He logged into the system and, with his hands moving at light speed, got into some kind of database. "You didn't get anything on the phone?"

"No."

"She probably doesn't have it on. If she did, you should have gotten something before she went indoors. If she doesn't have a clear view of open sky the clip might not work."

"And?" Mike asked, his voice harsh.

Gizmo glanced at Mike, then at Vic. "I told you I was still working out the kinks. It's not perfect yet. Still, we should be getting something."

He turned back to the computer. "The last reading I got from the clip was at the school at 1:56 p.m."

The muscles in Vic's neck curled and he rolled his head side to side to loosen them. "I need some answers."

Giz suddenly squeezed his eyes shut.

"What?" Mike asked.

"It rained last night."

"Big fucking deal," Vic said.

"If the unit got wet, soaking wet, it probably won't work. Maybe she stepped in a puddle or something."

The last morsel of GPS hope fizzled from his body. Vic stalked the office, willing his brain to work. "If this thing got wet, is there any hope it'll dry and then work?"

Giz shrugged. "I don't know. I haven't tested it after getting wet. I guess it's possible."

"Fuck," Vic shouted. "We'll have to fucking wait. We'll sit around with our thumbs up our asses and wait for a call. This is exactly what he wants. He wants me sweating this shit."

Fucking Sirhan. No way this asshole would get away with this. No way. He needed to be ripped apart an inch at a time.

Mike held up his hands. "Settle down. You blowing a gasket won't get Lily back. Let's get Gina home and tell her before the cops or the school track her down."

Listening to Mike's calm reasoning brought Vic back to sanity. Forget this emotional crap. It got in the way. He needed to become a machine again. He could do it. He could go back to his old way of thinking.

He had to.

"I'll get Gina and drive her to the house." Vic hauled ass toward the door.

"I'll meet you there. Make sure she doesn't answer her cell if it rings. It might be the cops and I want her to hear it from us."


GINA DROPPED HER PURSE ON HER KITCHEN TABLE AND KICKED off her high heels, freeing her aching feet. She eyed Vic. "What's going on?"

She'd peppered him with questions on the ride home, and he'd been doing a good job of stalling, but she wanted to know why he'd hauled her out of work early. And, given his sour mood, it obviously wasn't for a quickie.

He swallowed a couple of times. "Let's wait for Mike."

The immediate burst of panic flooded her brain and her thoughts moved at hyper speed. Michael was coming. Something bad had to have happened. Why else would Michael be coming?

The kids.

She shoved away from Vic, turned and ran to the base of the stairs leading to the second floor. "Matthew, Jake, Lily!"

No answer.

From the corner of her eye she could see Vic approaching, his long strides eating up the floor as he got closer. A man with a purpose. Banging in her head drowned out any coherent thought.

With one hand on the banister, she focused on his sad eyes. She slid to the steps because a mother always knew when something happened to one of her children. After Danny, how much more could she possibly take? "Where are they?"

He knelt in front of her, grabbed both her hands and squeezed. "The boys are fine. They're with Roy at Mike's. I wanted a few minutes alone with you."

*The boys are fine.* The words rolled around inside her, but instead of making her feel better, the realization hit. She pulled her hands free, put them over her eyes. A groan started deep in her throat.

"Lily?"

Vic blinked a couple of times.

Oh no.

The back door opened and she bolted from the step, pushed past Vic and headed for the kitchen. "Lily."

"It's me," Michael said and the moment of hope faded into the black hole it had come from.

Michael stepped into the dining room, and he and Vic barely exchanged a glance. If either of them carried an ounce of joy, they were keeping it hidden. *What happened to my baby?*

"Stop this," Gina screamed. "Just tell me where she is."

She spun to her big brother, the one who'd always protected her. He'd tell her. Vic was afraid. She saw that clearly enough, but Michael would do it. "Please. Just tell me."

"We think Sirhan grabbed her from school," Vic said from behind her.

It took a second to sink in, and she stiffened against the onslaught. She whirled to him. "She's not dead?"

"No."

What did he expect her to think after her daughter had been kidnapped? "You know that for sure?"

He scrubbed his hands over his face and sighed. "Do I have proof? No. But I don't think he'd hurt her. Not yet. I'm figuring he'll call me and tell me what he wants."

*She's not dead.* A sliver of hope came up from the darkness. With it came a twirling sensation and she closed her eyes. Too fast. Spinning, spinning, spinning. Her knees gave way and she hit the hardwood floor. Resting on all fours, her hair hanging in front of her face, she focused on a groove in the wood. *Stay calm. Hysterics won't help.* She'd learned this when Danny died. Panic could make her a lunatic.

She tried to steady her quivering body. At some point she'd started crying and tears tumbled down her cheeks. Her baby had been taken. A familiar hand ran over her back, up and down, up and down, and she shifted her eyes to the right. Vic's tasseled black shoes. He stood next to her, bent over, rubbing her back.

"I'm okay," she croaked. "I just need a minute and then I need you to tell me what happened."

Vic crouched next to her, shoved some hair from her face and held it. "I'm sorry. I can't tell you how sorry, but we'll get her back safe. I swear to you."

It sounded good, but could they do it? Then she remembered the cell phone and lifted her head. "What about her phone or the shoe clip? Can't we find her that way?"

"She doesn't have the phone on and the clip isn't working."

The phone wasn't on. It seemed ridiculous. Funny even, in some grotesque way.

"G," Michael said, "I know we're throwing a lot at you, but the cops will probably be by anytime to talk to you. You need to act as if this was a random abduction."

Random abduction? She gave her head a shake. "What are you talking about?"

"The school called the police. It's important you tell them you don't know anything. We need to get the guys out searching, and if the cops know we're involved, they're going to want to interview everyone and it'll eat up time."

Vic's phone rang and he snatched it from his belt. Shook his head. "It's Billy. He's out front." He hit the button and street noises came through the speaker. "What's up?"

"Cops pulling up."

"Thanks." He turned to Gina. "Showtime. You ready for this?"

"Do I have a choice?"

He gave her a half-pitying smile. "Not really."

AT SEVEN O'CLOCK, VIC STRODE INTO HIS OFFICE, DROPPED into his desk chair and booted up his laptop. The team would be here in a few minutes and they were scheduled to meet in the executive conference room. He had guys all over the street asking questions, but his team, Tiny, Roy, Monk, Billy, Bobby, Janet and Duck, would be coming in for a quick brainstorming meeting. Lily was gone and they needed to find her. That was all he knew.

Things were fucked up.

He shoved aside a stack of folders on the cluttered desk and set his cell phone down.

Lily had been gone five hours and her picture was all

over the news. Radio stations made announcements as well. Not a peep from Sirhan, though. The fucker was making him wait. He had to kill this asshole. Make him suffer. He'd do the government a favor and make it a freebie.

And then, as if he'd willed it to happen, the phone rang. He stared at the screen.

Lily.

Adrenaline surged and he fumbled the phone when he tried to pick it up. *Calm. Slow down.* It might not be her. Maybe they took the phone from her.

He cleared the clog in his throat. "Vic Andrews," he said as if it were any other mundane call.

"Where's Mommy?" Lily asked.

He nearly pissed himself. The stone-cold anger he'd been carrying around for the past hours evaporated. Holy hell, he'd never been so happy to hear someone speak.

"Honey, where are you?"

"Can you come get me please?"

He almost laughed. She made it sound like a playdate that had gotten old.

"The man you sent is very mean," she said. "I told him I couldn't go with him, but he picked me up and put his hand over my mouth so no one could hear me scream. I don't understand."

When she started crying Vic's intestines sank. He'd done this to her.

"It's going to be okay, baby. I'm sorry he was mean to you. I didn't send him. Are you hurt?"

"No," she said, sniffling.

He pumped his fist in the air. "Where are you? I'll come get you, but I need to know where you are."

And why were they letting her call him? This had to be a trap.

"I'm in an office in one of those buildings where they store stuff."

The warehouse. They took her to the fucking warehouse with all those weapons? Son of a bitch.

"A warehouse?" Vic asked, just to be sure.

"Mmm-hmm. He locked me in this office and told me to shut up. He's very mean. He told me Mommy would come, but she hasn't. I'm tired of waiting."

"So you're alone in the office?"

"Yes."

"Does the man know you have a phone?"

Say no, Lily. Say no.

"I don't think so. I keep it in the side pocket of my shorts, like Justin does."

They hadn't searched her. *Score one for our side.* None of those assholes had put their hands on her. She must be wearing cargo shorts. Gina had said Lily developed a case of hero worship and started dressing like Tiny.

"Lily, you are such a smart girl. I love you for that. It's good that he doesn't know. Don't tell him you have it."

"Okay, but I want to go home now. This place stinks like cigarettes. It's not good for my lungs."

Vic snorted. He couldn't help it. The kid had no idea how funny she was. "Okay, sweetheart, but I need you to do me a favor. Can you do that?"

"I guess."

"Is there a small window in the office you're in? Just above the filing cabinet?"

Please be the same warehouse. She waited a minute. "Yes, but it's high up."

*Yes!* "I know it is. Can you stand on the chair and hold the phone near the window?"

She needed to get that phone as close to open sky as she could.

"Okay. I'll try."

Bingo. "Good girl. You're so brave. Just hold the phone to the window. Okay?"

"Got it."

"Good. After that, I'll tell you how to shut the ringer off. I want you to keep the phone on, but I don't want the man with you to hear the phone ringing."

"All right."

And then the line went dead. Oh, crap. Did she hang up? Did someone hear her? Bile climbed into his throat. What if she didn't call back? What if her captors heard her on the phone? What if the fucking battery went dead? What was he doing?

Totally friggin' losing it. *Get it together.* He tightened his forearms until they ached and released. He closed his eyes, let the breaths come. The machine had to take over. He imagined sweeping the emotional chaos into a pile and tucking it away. He'd deal with it later.

*Okay.*

*Get to work.*

He shifted to his laptop, connected to the internet. *Come on, come on.* He clicked on the GPS website and—lo and behold—green blinking arrows.

"Tiny," he yelled. "Bring everyone in here."

Tiny rushed in. "What's up?"

"The GPS is working. Lily called me. She's at that warehouse."

Tiny stared at him, his mouth slightly open. "The one from last night?"

"Yeah. Get Mike on the horn, tell him she called me and she's fine. Gina needs to know she's okay, but if I call her, she'll bombard me with questions and we don't need the distraction. Just make sure she knows Lily is okay."

Monk stormed in with the others behind him. "Hang on. What's happening?"

Vic started to speak, but his phone rang. Lily. He punched the speaker button. "Hi, honey. You did good. We know exactly where you are. Will you keep your phone on for me?"

"Are you coming to get me?"

"You bet. Tiny's here. He'll come with me."

"Hi, Justin."

Tiny smiled. "Hey, squirt. You doing okay?"

"I'm tired. I want to come home now. This man was mean to me."

Vic rolled his eyes. Cripes. All he needed was her going on and on and in walks the bad guy. The phone would get deep sixed and they'd move her. Nope. Couldn't let her get caught with the phone. "Lil, there's a button on the side of your phone. Press the bottom part and it'll turn off the ringer. Keep pressing that button until the phone vibrates. Can you do that?"

"Yes."

"And let's not waste your battery. How about you call me every fifteen minutes so I know you're okay?"

"All right. But hurry. I want Mommy."

"We'll hurry, honey."

She hung up.

His finger wandered over the button before he finally pressed it. What if she didn't call back?

Vic bolted from his chair. "Let's go get her."

Monk threw his hands up. "Hold up here, boys. What are you thinking?"

"*Excuse* me?"

"Did someone hit you with a two-by-four?"

"Hey," Vic hollered.

"First of all—" Monk held up a finger, "—you and Tiny are too close to this situation, and you're not thinking straight. You don't know shit about that setup. Lily said there was one man. How does she know there aren't ten guys in that warehouse?"

Vic nodded. Monk had a point. Nothing like letting emotions dictate. That had been happening way too much lately. Freakin' Gina.

"Second." He held up another finger. "Tiny has never even seen this warehouse. He doesn't know how many entry doors or windows there are, whether it's one floor or two. And third—" another finger went up, "—it's broad daylight. Are you just going to drive up and bust in there? Come on, man. We all want her out of there, but let's do this right. Map it out. Plan for the unexpected and nobody gets hurt."

*Dammit.* The little bastard was right.

"Okay. But let's get someone over there to keep an eye on the place. If they move her and the GPS goes bat-shit, we'll lose her again."

He pointed at Billy leaning against the door frame. "Run over there and hang out in that clump of trees by the back door. You'll be able to see the garage doors and the door by the office."

"Got it."

"Conference room," Vic said, hustling toward the door. "We'll call Mike and work out a plan. Lily should be calling again in a few minutes."

He checked his watch. What if she didn't call back?

He had to get her out of there.

Fast.

.   .   .

GINA SAT AT HER KITCHEN TABLE WATCHING MICHAEL, IN A rumpled dress shirt, analyze his dish of cold pasta. She couldn't eat either. She'd already vomited twice. She rubbed her hand across her T-shirt and her aching stomach. All she wanted was sleep. She'd probably never sleep again. Not after this. Could there be anything worse than not knowing where her child was? Not even wondering if her husband was alive had topped this.

Michael's phone rang and she straightened. "It's Tiny," he said.

He put the phone to his ear. No speakerphone this time. Jerk.

"Yeah," he said. "Okay. That's good."

But he wasn't smiling and his eyes stayed focused on the dish in front of him. Michael became unreadable. What did that mean?

"What's he saying?" Gina asked.

He held up a finger. Damn him.

"Right. Keep me posted."

He hung up, slid the phone onto the table and raised his eyebrows. "Lily called."

Lily.

Gina sat back, all the air rushing from her body, and blinked back tears. Her baby, alive. Oh, to hell with it. She slapped her hands over her face and let the fierce, racking sobs take over until she nearly broke apart.

After a few seconds, Michael rested his hand on her shoulder and squeezed. "She's all right. She turned her phone on and they have her location. She's in a warehouse on the South Side. The guys will get her."

"Are they going now?" Gina asked, hopeful the nightmare would soon end.

"In a little while. Vic told her to call every fifteen minutes."

She reached for Michael's phone. "I need to talk to her."

"No." He snatched the phone away and an agonizing anger shot up Gina's neck.

She grabbed for it again. "She is *my* child and she needs me. Imagine how terrified she must be."

Michael nodded. "I know, but what if she didn't silence the ringer and someone hears it? Let me talk to Vic and I'll have her call you."

Talk to Vic? Who the hell did these two think they were telling her when she could speak with her own daughter? And what about Vic? Why the hell didn't he call her with this news?

"Where *is* he? I want to talk to him too."

That earned her an eye roll *and* a huff. Mr. Dramatic.

"He can't talk right now. That's why Tiny called. They're working on how to get Lily out."

Gina stood. "Fine. I'll go to the office. I want to know what they're planning."

Michael jumped out of the chair and blocked her. "Not a chance."

They squared off, each measuring the level of resolve, but Michael had that stony-eyed look that told her she wouldn't win.

Gina balked. "I don't understand why I can't talk to him about Lily. Why make Tiny call? Unless he's not telling us something."

That had to be it. She stalked the kitchen to get her runaway thoughts together. What would Vic not be telling her? *Think.*

Michael shook his head. "Don't start."

She halted. "What does that mean?"

"It means they called to let us know she is unharmed and they're working out a plan. Nothing else to tell."

"Then why didn't Vic call me? I think, given the circumstances, he could have contacted me himself."

Lord, she sounded like a crazy brat. It had to be the stress. She put her ice-cold fingers over her eyes, tried to focus on Lily being alive.

"Michael, I feel like the only reason he wouldn't have called would be if something were wrong and he didn't want to alarm me. Maybe Lily is injured and he wants to get her back before he tells me."

Could that be it? She reached for the counter to steady the swirling room. Deep breath.

"Gina—"

She waved her hands in front of her. No. No. No talking.

Michael scrunched his eyes closed and she recognized his steely resolve, the monumental effort to control his temper. "She is *fine*."

"I don't believe you." She steadied herself and pushed away from the counter.

He grunted. "Go ahead. Drive yourself crazy. You always do."

A hot, searing rage muscled into her rioting thoughts. "Screw you. My daughter is missing. When you walk this path, then you have the right to lecture me."

"You distract him," he yelled, the venom in his tone forcing her to step back. She pushed too hard, as usual. Not that she cared right now.

It had been a long time since Michael's famous temper, and the blast of fury that came with it, targeted her.

"Dammit." He kicked a chair and sent it crashing into the cabinets. "You never know when to stop."

"I'm not even there. How can I distract him?"

Michael rubbed his fingers above his eyes until his nail beds turned pink. "This is the fucking problem. Always has been, but you didn't want to listen."

"Oh, shut up!"

"When he's on a job, that's what he needs to concentrate on. He can't get emotional or he'll screw up."

"So, if he gets emotional, it's my fault?"

He scoffed. "I didn't say that."

"Maybe not, but it's what you meant."

Before he could say anything, she held up her hand. "I can't worry about it now. I need my daughter to come home. The rest is bullshit anyway."

This had been the issue all along. Mr. Anti-Emotion liked being a robot. He *liked* not having to feel anything. It gave him an excuse to live his solitary life and run off to play super-agent somewhere.

She breathed deep. She needed her daughter home.

That was all she needed. Her family intact.

Which included Vic.

And here she was, all over again, worrying about a man in a dangerous profession.

Had she learned nothing the first time around?

*Man Law: Never leave a man behind.*

THE SKY APPEARED A BLANK CANVAS DUE TO CLOUD COVER. No moonlight tonight. In Vic's opinion, the perfect night for an op.

He stood behind the clump of trees where Billy had been holed up for the last three hours. A twig cracked as Monk and Tiny made their way up the small hill with Duck and Roy in tow, all suited up in Kevlar vests. They'd come in two cars. Vic had driven out to the farm and loaded up on weapons for everyone.

At this moment most of what they carried would literally blow a man's head off. He had his Sig Sauer .45 strapped to his thigh. An MP5 hung around his shoulder over his custom-made vest, the pockets stuffed full of extra rounds of ammo and flash bangs. He shifted the vest for a more comfortable fit and studied the warehouse through the trees.

Lily would be inside. Waiting. He visualized the hallway just inside the door. Long and narrow. He and Monk could not go in side by side. They'd have to scatter. Overall, though, they should be in and out quick.

If all went well, the good guys would come out unscathed. He didn't know or care about the bad guys. Snatching a seven-year-old girl earned them whatever they might get.

"Hey," Tiny said. Even in the darkness, their eyes met for a second.

"You okay?" He wanted Tiny's head on straight or he'd make him sit out. Tiny was part of the team, but more than that, they were family and Vic wanted him firing on all cylinders.

They didn't need to blow the place to bits because they were pissed about Lily. Particularly when they weren't sure what kind of explosives might be in all those crates.

Tiny nodded. "I'm good. I wouldn't risk Lily because I'm hacked off."

Vic pulled out his headset, put it on and adjusted the microphone so it sat just below his lip.

The guys did the same and Vic clucked his tongue to check his mic. Everyone nodded. The radios worked and the boys were ready for action.

Vic circled his index finger in the air. "Let's go."

When they emerged from the trees, He flipped the safety on the MP5, crouched, and ran to the side of the building. Monk followed, while the rest of the team split up to access the other entrances. Not knowing the thickness of the other entry doors, they would use C-4 to blow them off. Monk assembled the explosives necessary to do the job.

The familiar adrenaline buzz streamed through Vic's system and he took in a breath. For years he'd lived on that rush, but now, knowing Lily was inside a building loaded with weapons and who knew what else, it felt like a curse.

They moved to the door. Monk placed the C-4 around the hinges and the lock. He set the detonators and waited for the signal the other teams were ready.

"One set," Monk whispered.

"Two set," Tiny responded.

And finally. "Three set."

They'd do this all at once to increase the confusion on the inside. Poor Lily would be scared shitless. *Don't go there. Don't think about it. She'll be safe in a couple of minutes.*

"One, two, three," Vic whispered, and...

*Boom!*

The door crashed off the hinges, and Vic and Monk rushed through. Yelling from inside drew Vic's attention, the MP5 at the ready. If anyone came through that doorway, they'd better duck and cover.

He and Monk, on opposite walls, moved in sync down the hallway. A bare bulb illuminated the area and the closed door of the office where Lily should be. A prickle pinched at Vic's neck. Something was not right in this place. But what? Was Lily gone? They'd just checked on her twenty minutes ago.

Monk hustled to the side of the hallway.

Something was...off. Vic controlled his breathing, slowed his system and faced the office. He gave the handle a turn. A double key lock. No time to mess with it. He stepped back and, with a good kick, walloped it just below the handle. The frame splintered and the door flew inward.

Lily let out a painful, howling scream from inside the office and it drowned out the yelling in the warehouse. Crap. He didn't see her.

*Follow the screaming.*

He moved into the office with the MP5 up and stepped behind the desk where she cowered, her hands entwined behind her head.

"Lily," he said in a stern voice. "It's me."

Still screaming, she peered up. Tears dragged down her cheeks and she shoved the curly mass of hair from her face. Her eyes widened and she launched herself at him. When he scooped her up, something in his chest exploded and he hugged her to him as she locked her arms and legs around him. The kid had a hell of a grip. Monk had better be alert out there, because Vic was useless at the moment.

"*Shhh,* honey. We'll get you home, *shhh.*"

But she continued the banshee screaming and his head hammered from the sound.

A frantic round of automatic weapon fire thundered through the warehouse, followed by the controlled three-shot bursts of his team. Vic spun toward the door. He needed to get Lily out.

"Who's firing?" he said into his mic.

No answer. Monk, still standing in the hallway, had backed up a step and nodded. He hadn't fired.

*Fuck.* All went quiet.

"Check in," Vic said, holding his MP5 with his free hand while a howling Lily clung to him. He blocked out the screaming, concentrated on the entry to the warehouse. *Control the breathing, slow it down. Slow. Deep breaths.* Monk nudged up for a look.

"Three clear," Duck said, indicating he and Billy were fine.

"Two?" Vic asked.

*Come on, come on. Be there.*

"Area clear. Tango down. Tiny is down," Roy said, his voice like gravel.

Tiny down? Is that what he said? Couldn't be.

Monk hauled ass through the hallway. Vic followed but stopped short, afraid to take Lily into the main part of the warehouse. *Shit. Shit. Shit.*

"Only one tango? Nobody else hiding?"

"We did a quick check. Area clear," Duck said.

"You're sure? I've got Lily here."

He should get Lily the fuck out of here and let the guys handle Tiny. He couldn't leave Tiny, though. The agony of indecision tore at him.

Fucking Tiny. He should have made him sit out. He knew it.

"I'll check again," Roy said.

Duck materialized from the warehouse and tried to take the still-screaming Lily, but she wouldn't let go.

The more Duck pulled at her, the harder she squeezed.

"Forget it," Vic said, unwilling to traumatize her further.

Duck backed up a step and waited.

"Lily," Vic said in as gentle a voice as he could summon. "I need you to stop, honey. I know you're scared, but I have to talk to you."

The screaming stopped in an abrupt and almost eerie manner.

"Good, girl. Can you look at me?"

She lifted her head from his shoulder and stared into his eyes. Excellent.

"Good. We're taking you out of here, but I can't leave just yet. Duck is here, though, and you know him. He won't hurt you. He'll get you outside and I'll be right behind you, okay? I just have to take care of something."

She stared at him but didn't move. Was any of this registering? Shock. She had to be in shock. "Lily? Did you hear me?"

She nodded.

"Okay. I'm going to hand you over to Duck. Is that all right?"

After giving Duck a sideways glance, she slid her arms from Vic's shoulders.

"That's my girl." Vic handed her off. "I'll be right out."

He jerked his head toward the entrance and Duck marched away, Lily's head on his shoulder. It would take her a long time to recover from this.

*No.*

*Focus.*

Vic moved into the main part of the warehouse and found it lit up like a runway at night. The familiar stacks of crates remained in their places and he stepped around one of them. Roy and Monk stood at the ready in case anyone new jumped out. Gerard Conlin's bloody body lay a few feet away, and Vic assumed he was dead. *Fucker.*

From the corner of his eye he spotted a boot and turned to see Tiny's six-foot-three form sprawled on the floor, Billy checking for a pulse. "Oh, Jesus."

Tiny's skull had blown apart from gunfire. The side of his head was gone. Brain matter lay exposed from the gaping wound and blood pooled on the cement floor. *Oh, Tiny. Son of a bitch. Don't do this.*

Vic staggered back, slammed his eyes shut. A cold burst shot up his back and his knees buckled. He knelt a few feet from Tiny.

"A pulse?" he asked.

Billy stayed silent.

"Do CPR," Vic roared.

Billy shook his head. "No one could survive this. You know it."

No. Vic scooted forward. Felt for a pulse. Nothing. "Come on, Justin. Don't do this."

His throat started to close. No air. He opened his mouth and a guttural groan escaped. He tensed his forearms. Closed his eyes. Think of something else. Gina's face when she saw Lily. Yes. Gina's face.

No falling apart.

"What the hell happened?" Vic asked Roy, who had been partnered with Tiny.

"Conlin spotted us, saw Tiny and started firing."

*Oh, crap.* With his newly shorn hair, he and Tiny resembled each other. Conlin must have thought he was firing at Vic. A razor-sharp pain hit him square in the chest, and Vic hoped he wouldn't puke. Tiny was dead because of him.

"I took him out the second after Tiny got hit," Roy said.

"Sirens," Monk said, moving toward Tiny's body. "We need to get out of here."

"Get his head wrapped," Vic croaked, levering off the floor and concentrating on breathing. "And we'll carry him out."

By the time they'd reached the cars, Lily had quieted, but upon seeing Vic, immediately reached for him. He shoved her head to his shoulder. He didn't want her seeing Tiny's body while they loaded him into the SUV. Once Tiny was safely in the back, he'd let Lily raise her head.

"Cover him with the blanket that's in the emergency kit," Vic said, his voice still hoarse.

"On it," Monk said.

The blanket wouldn't be big enough to cover all of him, but it would do the job. The pounding in Vic's head started again and he blinked. He took a breath, concentrated on pulling himself back together. No emotional crap. Just get through it like every other time he'd lost a friend. He'd never lost anyone like Tiny, though. Not family. Not someone he considered a brother.

"Billy, take him to Foyle's. I'll call and let them know you're coming. Take Roy and Duck. Monk and I will go in the other car."

"That's the funeral parlor on Chestnut, right?" Billy asked.

"Yeah. Mike's buddy is related to the guy who owns it. We've used him a couple of times."

The sound of approaching sirens drove Vic's spine straight. They parked behind a neighboring warehouse and could exit on the opposite street, but he wanted to get out fast. "Let's get moving. Billy, whatever you do, don't get pulled over. Monk and I will take Lily home and meet you. Don't let them touch him until I get there. Someone call Mike and let him know."

"Got it."

"Nobody touches him," Vic said and stalked to the other car.

Fucking Sirhan. He just earned himself a slow death.

Vic shifted in his seat just as Monk hit Cicero and headed north. Lily sat wide-eyed, staring at nothing in particular. She hadn't moved since Vic strapped her into the middle backseat next to him. Her head suddenly lolled against his left arm, her curls soft against his bare skin, and he pushed the hair from her face.

Poor thing. She'd never be the same. This he knew for sure.

The sound of her breathing filled the otherwise silent car. Monk wouldn't say anything. Neither would Vic. They had both been close to Tiny and would suffer the loss differently, but they'd grieve hard.

Vic grabbed his phone from the seat pocket and dialed

Lynx. No answer. Tried the other numbers. He picked up on the third.

"Tiny is...gone," Vic said, not wanting to say *dead* in front of Lily.

"Shit." Lynx went quiet for a minute then asked, "Did you find Lily?"

"Yeah. She's right here. She's wiped. They held her at that location I told you about."

He didn't want to say too much on the phone. Lynx had probably already figured out that Tiny died during the op.

"Anyway," Vic said, "the locals are going to beat you there, but it'll be worth your effort."

Vic should have garnered some satisfaction over the warehouse discovery, but with Tiny dead, Lily traumatized and Sirhan walking around, this whole fucking thing was a mess that had detonated in his face.

He clicked off. Lily's warm breath hit his arm and he rested his head back. The weight of the grief settled on him. His body had gone numb, but the ache burrowed deep in his bones, snickering at him, letting him know the numbness would wear off. And then what? He'd have to deal with it. That was all. Just deal with it. Sweep it into a pile. Think of other things. He stared out the window. He'd have to tell his aunt about Tiny, something he'd always hoped he'd never have to do.

## 25

*Man Law: Always avoid the "talk to me" trap.*

"LILY," GINA SQUEALED WHEN VIC WALKED THROUGH THE front door with her baby in his arms.

Euphoria zipped through her as Lily bolted up, swiveled her head and spotted her.

"Mommy," she yelled and reached for her.

The scent of strawberry shampoo lingered, and Gina inhaled. Not a dream.

Sparing a glimpse toward the couch, she moved to it.

"I think she's in shock," Vic said to Michael, standing by the steps. "Get the doc to take a look at her. She's not hurt. She did great. She got scared when I kicked in the door."

"Hey, Lil," Michael said, claiming the spot next to Gina.

Lily gazed up at him and scooted onto his lap. She wanted love from everyone and she'd get it.

An audible breath came from Vic, and Gina peered up at him. He wore navy cargo pants, a matching T-shirt and battered boots. She'd never seen him dressed this way. Battle clothes? She didn't know. Didn't want to know. That was part of his *other* life.

The one that had crashed into hers.

He cleared his throat, and his sad eyes left her wondering what bothered him.

"I have to go," he said.

Michael stared at him from his spot on the couch. A silent message drifted between them, and the air became stagnant. Something went wrong.

"Mike, call the cops, make sure they know she's home. Tell them she wandered off and fell asleep under a tree. I don't know, make something up." He started for the door. "I'll talk to you both later."

Gina smiled at Lily, safe and dozing in Michael's arms. "I'll be right back." She headed after Vic. He reached the porch by the time she'd caught up with him.

She grabbed Vic's hand. "What happened?"

He focused on their joined hands a minute; his expression still sullen. "Lily's home. Enjoy her. I'll talk to you later."

What kind of answer was that? And why wouldn't he look at her?

"Tell me why you're upset."

He sighed. "I need you to leave me alone. Please."

An edge of annoyance slipped through her, but she tamped it down. "Why won't you tell me what happened?"

He narrowed his eyes—at least she had his attention— and took a step closer. She sensed the contained fury and threw her shoulders back.

"Why can't you leave me be?" he asked in that quiet voice she'd termed the mad voice. "You always want me to talk when what I really need is to *not* talk."

"I don't understand. You got her home safe. You should be happy and I want you to tell me why you're not."

He grunted and waved toward the SUV idling in front of the house. "I have to go."

When he stepped off the porch something snapped in her. She'd had it. All this secrecy had to stop. She wanted some damned answers. "Why? What's so important that you have to leave now?"

He halted, stood for a minute, then slowly turned. Even in the dark, the rage in his eyes flashed. "My cousin is dead. His head is being held together with Monk's do-rag and you want to know where I'm going? I'm *going* to get him cleaned up so his mother doesn't have to see him this way."

He spun around, headed for the truck. "Happy now?"

The words sunk in. Tiny. *Dead.* No. She clamped her eyes closed. The misery exploded inside her and crawled up inch by inch. She swallowed back the sob moving into her throat.

*Stop him.*

She opened her eyes just as Vic got to the curb. "Wait. Please."

"Get off my back." He jumped into the passenger's seat of the truck.

She should leave him alone. Like he asked. She couldn't, though. She understood grief and he'd need her.

By the time she'd gotten off the porch, the truck pulled away. She should get back to her daughter. Lily needed her, but the sadness pushed her to the step. Maybe she could sit for a minute and get her emotions under control. She put her head in her hands, closed her eyes against the tears. To hell with it. She let them fall.

For Tiny.

.    .    .

GINA DRAGGED HER EYES OPEN AND STARED AT THE BACK OF Lily's curl-snarled head. They had both fallen asleep in her single bed, and Gina's side throbbed from balancing on the edge of the mattress.

A shred of moonlight slanted through the blinds and shone on the strawberry wallpaper Lily loved so much. Gina smiled a sad smile. Life wouldn't be so simple anymore.

Again.

How much could one child take? First losing her father and now this? Unbelievable.

After a minute of absorbing the silence within the room, Gina heard Lily's soft, easy breaths. A good sign, but nightmares would come. She'd have to find a way to keep her baby from suffering their wrath. And wouldn't that discovery make millions of moms worldwide happy?

She slid her arm from under Lily's tiny body and waited. No movement. In one quick motion she angled off the bed and glanced at the clock. Two-thirty. Late. She'd only slept a few hours, but the rumbling in her stomach brought her awake. When had she eaten last?

She needed to eat, if for no other reason than to keep her strength up. For the kids. They didn't deserve a crabby mom.

Shuffling through the dark, she left the door open and made her way down the creaking steps into the lit living room. Out of the corner of her eye, she caught a flash of movement from the sofa.

Her heart slamming against her rib cage, she gasped but focused on the man in her house.

Michael.

"You scared the hell out of me."

The sudden blood rush created a dizzy spell and she grabbed on to the armchair and sat down.

"I'm sorry," he said, rubbing his palms against sleepy eyes. "I fell asleep. When I heard the stairs creak, I jumped up. You scared the shit of me too."

"Sorry," she muttered. "Why are you still here? Go home. Roxann shouldn't have to sit with the boys alone."

"She's not alone. I sent a couple guys over there. Besides, *she* told me to stay with *you*. And, for the record, I'm more afraid of her than I am you."

Gina snorted.

"How's Lily?"

"She fell asleep. I don't know for how long, but I woke up hungry. I need to eat something. If nothing else, I'll keep my strength up."

"What does that mean?"

Suddenly she didn't know. At first, she really did believe she needed fuel to keep her body moving, but maybe it was more than that.

"Maybe it means that I've been utterly helpless these past few weeks."

"Oh, please," Michael said.

She began pacing. "No. It's true. My brother and my supposed boyfriend are involved with criminals. My daughter was kidnapped and held in a warehouse full of weapons and explosives. She's been traumatized by shooting all around her, not to mention Tiny, a man she adored—a man *I* adored—is dead."

He shook his head. Leaned back on the sofa.

"It's like Danny all over again," she said. "Those hours of waiting for the phone to ring. Waiting and praying for someone to tell me they found my husband alive. That same panic bubbling. Maybe it's the anticipation of more bad news that may or may not come."

Before she'd let herself fall in love with Vic, she didn't

have this feeling. This angst. And now she had a look into her future. Him on his little trips, gone for undetermined amounts of time. Her wondering where he was. All this frustration and worrying and bargaining with herself would be her life. And could she spend the rest of her days in this state?

Absolutely not.

"I'm sorry," Michael said.

And didn't that just work her last nerve? He was *sorry*. Weren't they all?

"I don't want to hear you're sorry. Or Vic's sorry. I'm sick of sorry. I want my life back. I've worked hard to give my kids a stable environment. Really hard, and I'm pissed off that it was taken from me. Just because Vic likes to live on the edge, doesn't mean I deserve the repercussions."

"I—"

She spun around, pointed at him. "And don't you *freaking* dare tell me you warned me about this." She stopped, felt the burst of hysteria crawl up her throat and threw her hands over her face.

The racking sobs came, making her chest want to burst, but she stood there, taking the punishment, letting herself fall apart.

How did she let her family get involved in this mess? She'd failed as a parent. All to make herself happy. So she could feel that rush of excitement that had been gone for so long. She'd risked her children's safety for great sex?

Heaven help her.

She flinched when Michael put his arms around her. Déjà vu. How many times had he talked her off a ledge?

"It's just the stress," he whispered. "Let it out and then we'll get you something to eat. We'll fix this. I wasn't going to say I told you so. I wasn't."

"I'm so sorry," she sobbed, wrapping her arms around his waist, just needing something to hold on to.

"It's all right."

They stood a minute in the quiet of the house, and all she wished for was the silence to remain. She needed a break.

With one last deep breath she took a step back.

She would have to find a way to privately grieve for Tiny, a man who gave his life to save Lily's. What a tragic sacrifice. She'd never, ever get over this loss.

And then there would be Vic.

What to do about *that* situation?

He had his own agenda right now, and where she and the kids fit in, she had no idea.

Maybe they didn't fit in at all.

# 26

*Man Law: Always hide the pain.*

SUNNY SUMMER DAYS AND BLUE SKIES WERE MEANT FOR sailing and baseball. Hot dogs and watermelon.

Not funerals.

The Louisiana humidity hung thick and Vic's shirt stuck to him, confined him. He'd long since taken off his suit jacket but experienced little relief from the stifling heat. He leaned against a tree in the cemetery where Tiny's body would soon be lowered into the ground. Mourners stepped to the casket, one by one, tossing blood-red roses as a final farewell.

Vic had already tossed his flower and walked his aunt and uncle to the car. Somehow, he wound up leaning against this fucking tree in this fucking place where he didn't want to be. Saying goodbye to a man he didn't want to say goodbye to.

He drove his heel into the ground, steadied himself

against the wave of emotion that had been threatening all morning. *Goddammit.*

"Hi," Gina said, coming to stand beside him.

She and Mike had flown in this morning for the funeral and would be heading back to Chicago tonight. The kids were with Roxann, all of them under guard.

*Think about something else.* Gina, so pretty in her blue dress, but her puffy, tired eyes told of the sadness. As much as he'd missed her these past few days, she distracted him, made him feel things he didn't want to feel, and he wished she had stayed home. The turmoil felt too real, too willing to swallow him whole, and he'd taken care to check his emotions.

He slid his hand under her hair, rested it on the back of her neck. Skin to skin. "Hi."

She smiled but stayed quiet. *Thank you.* Talking he did not need. She stepped closer, shifted into him, and he kissed the top of her head. A warm wind blew and he breathed in.

"Thanks for being here."

She nodded, her gaze on the casket. "They're almost done."

A slender woman with dark blond hair and a short black dress moved to the casket. She looked familiar, but from the back... *Oh, shit.* His body morphed to steel.

Nuh-uh. Not today.

"She must be joking," he said.

"What?"

"My mother is here." He inclined his head. "That's her. The black dress. Her hair is darker now and I almost didn't recognize her."

Gina swiveled her head so fast it should have spun off her shoulders. He almost laughed.

"How long has it been since you've seen her?"

"Five short years."

"Oh boy." Gina jumped in front of him, grabbed his chin and forced him to focus on her. "She's coming over here. This is Tiny's funeral and you need to behave."

He nodded once. Cripes. He knew how to act at funerals. He'd been to enough of them.

"Should I leave?" Gina asked.

"Nah. Might as well stay for the show."

"Hey, sugar," his mother said in that deep drawl of hers.

"Mama." He didn't move from his spot against the tree, but he touched Gina's shoulder. "This is Gina. Gina, my mother."

The crackhead.

"Gloria Andrews," she said, holding her hand to Gina. "Nice to meet you."

He had to admit Gloria's appearance was different. Her skin not as leathered, her hair not as blond and her frame not as thin. The eyes, though. They had a sharpness to them he didn't remember.

"Mama, are you clean?"

Gina breathed in hard. "Vic."

"It's all right," his mother said, not taking her eyes off him. "He's entitled." She straightened and lifted her chin. "Yes. Going on six months now."

Six months. Not bad. Her own personal record. "Congratulations. I think."

Her shoulders sagged and she faced Gina. "He's angry and I don't blame him."

How generous of her. Did she want a teary reunion? She wouldn't get it. Not from him. She had turned him into a machine and that was what she'd get. "You walked out on me. That I could have lived with, but the coming around asking for money?"

He stopped, shook his head and remembered where he was. "Thank you for coming. I'm sure everyone appreciates it."

She looked at the ground and nodded. Maybe acting like a cold-hearted prick wasn't right, but he didn't need this today. Or any day. He'd done right by supporting her and now he wanted to be left alone.

"At the time," his mother said, "I did the only decent thing I knew how to do. I'm sorry."

With that she faced Gina. "I hope to see you again."

His mother walked away, and that piece of his heart she still owned got chiseled down further. He couldn't count how many times he'd watched her walk away and each time, no matter how old he was, it still hurt.

"Wow," Gina said.

"Welcome to my world, babe."

"She's prettier than I thought. Younger too. How old was she when you were born?"

"Seventeen," Vic said.

"Ugh. So young."

And what? Sure, she'd been young. Did that give her the right to throw her life away for drugs?

"Not that what she did was right," Gina said, "but did you ever think maybe she did you a favor by leaving you with your aunt? I know you don't think she loved you enough to stay, but maybe she loved you enough to go. *Maybe* she knew you'd have a better life with Tiny's family."

He pushed away from the tree. "Can we talk about this later?"

She shrugged. "Whenever you're ready."

Yeah. How about never?

The last of the mourners stepped away from the casket.

Gina didn't look happy and that made two miserable people.

"I need a minute with Tiny," he said. "I'll meet you back at the house."

That got him the lips-sealed-tight, wounded look. Batting a thousand today. He'd been pushing her away for five days now. Not returning her calls, giving her one-word answers when he did call. Shitty, yes, but he needed room and she didn't want to give it to him.

"I have my cell if you need something. Michael and I are flying back tonight. Lily isn't sleeping well and I want to be home before she goes to bed. Just so you know."

He should say something. Every fiber told him so, but he'd never make her understand his grief manifested itself differently. She wouldn't understand his working out until every muscle ached, or shooting until his hands blistered. Expending the energy had become his way of coping. This time, though, it wasn't working. He felt beat up, his body pushed beyond its limits, and the fierce corrosion of his insides continued without relief. He couldn't get rid of it. Couldn't shut his mind off and free himself of Tiny with his head blown apart.

"Got it," he said, making no attempt to stop her from walking away.

His mother.

His aunt.

Gina.

For sure, his world had gone to hell. Vic loved them all in ways he couldn't define because, after all, his mother had rejected him, Gina had *not* rejected him, and his aunt put up with his rebellious ways when it had hardly been her responsibility.

And all three of them stood chatting by the old oak bookcase, not twenty feet from him.

*Kill me now.*

The late-afternoon sun warmed his legs and he rested his head against the wingback chair in his aunt's living room. He closed his eyes to shut out the twenty people wandering around, reluctant to leave. He understood. He didn't want to let go of Tiny either.

He opened his eyes, caught Gina analyzing him, and turned to the window.

"Hey," Mike said, copping a squat in the opposite chair. He wore one of his slick designer suits, black, with a crisp white shirt and a tie. Mike hated ties and only did them when the occasion demanded it.

"Well, this sucks."

Vic laughed for the first time all day. No wonder he and Mike got along.

"I checked on the kids a while ago," he said. "Everyone is at your place with Roxann. The kids are bored so the guys took them up to the pool."

"Gina's been calling every hour, but thanks." Mike brushed fuzz off his pants. "I met your mother. She seems like she's gotten her act together."

His stomach twisted like scrap metal and he slid a sideways glance toward the three musketeers by the bookcase. "It's too early to tell."

No way he'd let himself believe in her and wind up disappointed. He'd been around that block too many times already.

"I need air." He stood, but Mike held up a hand.

"I know the timing stinks, and I'm sorry."

What could be worse than Tiny's funeral?

Vic settled into his chair again. "What's up?"

"I got a call from our neighbor at the farm. He got an offer on the property we talked about."

The training-center property. Vic's dream. He hadn't made a decision yet.

"An offer already?"

Mike held out his hands.

"Is he jerking us around? Trying to jack up the price?" Vic didn't want to be forced into a decision.

"I don't think so. He said he wanted to let us know since we had inquired first. He's giving us first shot. Like I said, the timing stinks, but have you thought about this?"

Vic slouched in the chair, stared out the window. "Yeah, I thought about it. How could I not? But I'm not there yet. It's a huge change. I figured I had more time."

"It's a nice piece of property."

"Damn nice." Vic's mind moved at warp speed.

He could say yes and have a life with Gina. He could say no and possibly lose Gina, but hang on to the life he knew. The life he'd been building for years and had become comfortable with.

Mike leaned forward, rested his elbows on his knees. "If you're not ready to do it yet but think down the road it's a definite, we should buy the property and hang on to it. We could use it for our own guys until you're ready to do a full-blown training center. If we pass on this, we may not get another opportunity to grab that much acreage so close to our existing facility."

Vic stared at him, not sure what to say. Mike had just told him he'd be willing to spend almost seven million bucks on a not sure. "You'd do that for me?"

Mike grinned. "My sister *is* making you a sissy."

"Fuck you."

"Seriously, yes, I'd do that for you. Call it a long-term investment."

Vic stood, held his hand to Mike. "Make the deal. I'll go on the hook for half the cash if you want. If we lose money, it'll be both of ours."

"I'm not worried about it. It's a smart move."

A smart move. Vic snorted. So why did it feel like everything that brought him comfort was being washed away? He rubbed a hand over his head. "I really need air."

Mike slapped him on the back. "You're stressed. It'll be fine."

"We'll see."

He stepped onto the wide porch that spanned the length of the house and wrapped around the side. He eyeballed the swing, now painted a shocking red. When had that happened? The change hit him like a gut punch. So many fucking changes.

He'd barely flopped down when the door opened. Couldn't these people leave him alone?

Aunt May. Oh no. Bad enough he'd gotten her son killed, now he had to look at her and know he'd caused that sadness. Guilt was a new and fucked-up thing in his world, and he wished he'd never allowed his emotions to run amok.

Aunt May smiled in spite of herself. She'd made a special effort to dress nice in a dark green dress and heels, her hair pulled back into a knot. She wore pearl earrings and a necklace. She'd done her son proud today. He blinked a few times, cleared his vision and tried to think about anything but suffocating.

She sat next to him. "Are you hiding?"

"It's not working."

He pushed off with one foot and set the swing in motion while she laughed at him.

"You could never hide from me."

"True enough."

He shifted to her, stared at her long perfect nose and green eyes similar to his. Green eyes like his mother's. He opened his mouth, shut it again.

"He wouldn't want you doing this to yourself." She reached for his hand. "Justin was a grown man. He knew the danger."

Vic shrugged. "I sensed something wasn't right with him that night. He cared about Lily. He shouldn't have even been there."

"You care about Lily and you were there. Would anyone have been able to convince you not to go?"

She had a point there. Smart-ass. "Not a chance."

Aunt May nodded. "Okay, then. Stop blaming yourself. We have enough to deal with around here with him being —" she stopped, put a hand over her eyes, sucked in a ragged breath, "—with him being gone, so let's help each other through it."

Vic stared straight ahead. Avoiding his aunt's pain would be easier than trying to live with it. *Sweep it into a pile, manage it.*

"You know," she said, "the only way to the other side is through it. All your life you've been hiding your feelings, hardening them into something you could control. It won't work this time. Let yourself hurt for a while. It'll never go away, but it'll get better."

He nodded and blinked back his sissy tears. Crying? Seriously? "I'm sorry."

She smiled a tight-lipped smile, ran her hand down the

back of his head the way she'd done when he was twelve. "Me too."

A warm breeze fluttered the trees and Vic put his head back. "So. My mother?"

Aunt May sighed. "I didn't tell you she was coming. I knew it would upset you and I didn't see any reason for you to know until you absolutely had to. My intentions were good and I'd do it again."

"I'm not mad at you, although I would have liked a warning. She's actually clean?"

"She is. It's hard to believe, but she went to rehab and goes to meetings every day. Your uncle got her a job as a desk clerk in a motel. The money isn't great, but she's working. She's trying, Vic."

He stared off, enjoyed the bright blue sky while his mind went ape-shit.

"Do you think," he asked, "she did the right thing by leaving me?"

Aunt May sat back and thought about it. "I can't say she did the right thing, but I can't say she did wrong either. It's never right to abandon a child, but we were afraid you'd wind up in the system. You were so close to Justin and Tiffany, and I didn't want my children to grow up without their cousin. I talked her into it."

This was the equivalent of setting C-4 off in front of him. His ears clanged. "*You* did? She didn't just up and leave?"

Aunt May shook her head. "She and I talked about it for a couple of months. I told you that when you came to live with us. You don't remember?"

The weight of his head pushed him forward. Holy shit. Had he done this to himself? Created this scenario where his mother dumped him without thinking twice when, in actuality, she'd given it a lot of thought? Oh, damn. The years he'd spent hating her and loving her at the same time and never talking to anyone about it.

He wandered across the porch, needing to get rid of the whooshing in his ears. He alone had created the emotionally bankrupt man he'd become.

"Holy hell," he said, stacking his hands on his head.

Aunt May walked to him, put a hand on his back. "Talk to her. She doesn't want anything but a conversation. Maybe the two of you can find a place to begin again."

His heels fused to the porch. All he could do was stare at the quiet, tree-lined street where he'd played football and baseball. The only place he'd known as home.

"Do you want me to leave you alone?"

*Yes. Everyone. Please. Leave me alone.*

He nodded.

"All right, but I want you to think about something for me."

At the soft sound of her voice the tension in his body uncoiled. "Anything."

"I want you to think about giving up your job."

"But—"

She held up her hands. "You may not be my biological child, but you are the child of my heart," she said, her voice fracturing. She took a minute, focused on the porch rail and looked back to him, tears rimming her eyes. "I've just lost one of my children. Please don't make me go through this again."

He shrugged. "It's all I know."

"I realize that, but I suspect you have more at stake now."

"You mean Gina and the kids?"

She nodded. "They must be important to you or we wouldn't have buried my son today."

"It's complicated."

"I'm sure it is. But I have faith in you and I think you'll do what's best. The children I raised generally do."

Yeah. No pressure there.


AIRPORT LOUNGE AREAS SUCKED. VIC HAD AN HOUR BEFORE his flight and he slouched in a crappy way-too-small-for-his-body plastic chair.

A smattering of people wandered aimlessly at the news-stand or snack bar. He made calls and checked his emails. Nothing urgent, but it had been a busy week in Chicago. In the seven days he'd been gone, the feds had raided Sirhan's warehouse and market and had confiscated everything. Guns, money, drugs. All of it. Gerard Conlin's dead body remained a mystery, but the authorities assumed the death was a result of a gun sale gone bad.

*Lucky me.*

All in all, Vic and his team helped bust a multi-city terrorist ring filtering millions of dollars into illegal activities. They'd never be able to take credit, but the result was good.

Still, Sirhan stayed free. Hiding. The fucking rat bastard. The feds couldn't tie him to anything. No paper trail. They knew it was him, though.

His phone chirped. An unrecognizable D.C. number. Must be Lynx on his Maxwell Smart shoe phone.

Vic hit the button, grabbed his duffel and stepped away from the crowd. "What's up?"

"I thought you might want to know we got a read on your friend."

His friend? Had to be Sirhan. Otherwise he'd have said his name. Adrenaline packed into his veins. "Where is he?"

"We got some chatter that he's in a small village in Pakistan. Suleiman Mountain region."

Vic leaned against a support pole at one of the vacant gates and stared at the tarmac. Planes rolled by ready to launch into the early morning sky. "Are you telling me my contact is going to call me with an assignment?"

"Not yet. We're short on plausible deniability. I thought you'd want to know."

O-*kay*. Translation: the government thought things were too hot to take Sirhan out. But Lynx had added the "not yet." He never said anything he didn't intend to.

"Would anyone be averse to the problem going away?" Vic tapped his foot, anticipating the answer he hoped for.

"I don't think anyone would mind if you managed this one on your own."

Yes. His system roared to life like one of those big-engine planes sitting on the runway.

"Send me what you've got and I'll take care of it."

"No problem."

"And, hey, thanks."

"You got it," Lynx said and hung up.

Lynx had taken a risk by passing this info along and Vic would always appreciate it. They'd been friends over ten years and Lynx understood the grief burning a hole in him. Vic would do everyone a favor and take Sirhan out. Gina and the kids would be safe, not to mention the world would be rid of this scumbag and they would all get on with their lives.

"Going to Pakistan," he muttered to himself.

"YOU'RE BACK," GINA SAID FROM THE DOORWAY OF VIC'S office.

Damn, she was quick. He'd only been in the building thirty minutes. He sat back in his chair, let himself enjoy the sight of her in the tight black skirt he'd come to love. Shadows darkened her eyes. The result of Lily's nightmares, he surmised. The poor girl had lost a good friend in Tiny and she was too young to be dealing with it all.

Even more reason to take Sirhan out. He'd just keep telling himself that.

"I was going to call you in a few minutes. I got caught up in my messages."

She waved him off. "That's all right. I brought some paperwork up for Michael, and he told me you were back."

Vic nodded. A weeklong gulf had landed between them and he wasn't sure how to fix it. Going to Pakistan wouldn't do it. He should sit her down and talk to her about his guilt over putting her family in danger. About Tiny dying and the grief eating him alive. That was what she wanted. And what he couldn't give. Not now anyway. He needed to stick to his routine and close off for a while. Deal with the anger on his own. Go dormant.

"How's Lily?" he asked.

Gina curled her lip. "Hanging in there. She misses Tiny. I took her to that therapist Michael recommended. The one that deals with post-traumatic stress disorder. He's a nice man and very patient with her. She seems to be responding."

"I'm glad for that, at least."

Then she stepped closer to the desk and leaned in. "She misses *you* too. I miss you."

He tapped his fingers on the desk. If ever he heard a call to action, it was now. "Me too."

Lame. Very lame.

Silence widened the gulf and she folded her arms. "What's this about?"

*Uh-oh.*

*Play dumb.*

"What do you mean?"

"Don't give me that bullshit. I get you're hurting. I *know* how that feels, but why am I being treated like a leper? I've given you all the space you wanted, so I'm not real clear on what the hell it is *I* did to *you*."

He walked around the desk to stand in front of her. "Nothing. You did nothing. You have to know that."

She sighed. "So stop shutting me out. A lot has happened and I'm trying not to push you, but give me something to hang on to."

"I'm going out of town," he blurted.

Not much to hang on to, but the truth.

She gawked at him; eyes razor sharp. "You're leaving again?"

"Duty calls."

Being a smart woman, she knew that meant he had an assignment. He'd given her a piss-poor answer and, prick that he was, he'd done it on purpose. He knew it would put her over the edge.

"Duty. *Calls.* That's all you're telling me?"

He kept quiet. Saying anything right now would be the wrong thing.

She gave a sarcastic laugh. "When will you be back?"

"Hopefully, a few days. Not sure."

The moment drifted between them in silence. She was pissed. He could see it in the harsh lines in her face. The tight lips. Hell, he could feel all that anger channeling right to him. Didn't blame her, but there wasn't a whole lot he could do about it.

"I won't do this, Vic. I won't spend my life wondering when and if you'll come back. I can't live in standby mode. My kids and I deserve better."

The words hit him like cannon fire. He stepped back, reached behind him for the desk and propped himself on the edge of it. Gina waited. He should say something to cancel out everything she'd just said, but he couldn't. Maybe he wanted her to walk away. Then he wouldn't have to change his life and give up the only comfortable thing he'd known.

Only, he hadn't imagined the gutted feeling that came with hearing the words. Tiny's death started the vacant feelings and now, with Gina walking away, nothing but loss surrounded him. And he'd caused it.

"I understand, but can we talk about it when I get back?"

"Will anything change between now and then?"

Jesus H. Christ, he needed a break. He scrubbed his hands over his face. "I don't know. I wish I did."

"Then there's nothing to talk about. I can compromise, but not on this."

He needed to say something worthwhile. Honest. She liked honesty. He levered off the desk and went to her. "I do love you. I love you in a way I never expected, and, honestly, I never wanted. I never wanted the constant agony of wondering if you're okay and the kids are okay and hoping I don't screw up. I never worried about screwing up before. I never cared. It's much easier than the mental chaos I've got now."

"Sure, but what about the good stuff? All the laughs. The fun. The love. Doesn't that count for something?"

"You bet it does. It makes me realize what I've missed all these years and that's something else I'll have to contend with, but I can't do it now. I have one more job to do and it'll end this madness. It'll free me from the guilt over Tiny. I know you'll never understand, but I have to do this."

She clamped on to his forearms. "Please don't go after Sirhan. Let someone else do it."

He didn't say anything. Why bother? They both knew he'd finish it. She threw her hands over her face and after a minute her shoulders began to shake. Crap. Crying.

*Think. Do something, asshole. Fix this.*

After a moment, she pulled her hands away, swiped at the tears. "I knew this would happen. The dark side will always win with you. You just can't help it."

She hustled out of the office. He took a step to go after her and stopped. No. His way would be better.

## 27

*Man Law: Always wait it out.*

"DADDY'S HOME," VIC SAID, EDGING BETWEEN TWO BOULDERS while adjusting his binoculars. The late-afternoon wind offered little relief from the heat.

He shifted right and examined the valley three hundred feet below. Odd shades of red, brown and tan boulders lay strewn over the valley floor.

A quarter mile away, and directly across the desolate lowland, sat a cabin on the other side of the valley. The obscure structure was nestled in a recess at the base of the towering Sulaiman Mountain range. Two armed guards watched from their stations on the cabin's front porch.

Hopefully, it was *the* cabin.

Vic glanced to his left at Monk, his unwelcome cohort on this op. Mike, sneaky bastard that he was, offered the corporate jet for the trip, and Vic gladly accepted but stepped on the plane to find Monk buckled up and ready to fly. Then the traitorous pilot informed him that Mr. Taylor gave orders he couldn't take off if Monk wasn't on board.

Well, what the fuck?

At the time, Vic had been royally pissed and wanted to give *Mr. Taylor* an ass-whooping for forcing a babysitter on him when he normally worked alone, but with this layout, Monk's presence would be a benefit.

Besides, the guy was a world-class operator. Maybe the old adage about safety in numbers had something to it.

"You think that's the right cabin?" Monk asked, dragging Vic from his thoughts.

"It fits the description."

They had been schlepping around this lawless, remote mountain area of Pakistan for three days and, with the help of some friends in the region, Vic was certain they'd found Sirhan's hideout. After a quick search of the area, they'd parked their asses behind these large boulders and waited.

Movement. To the right. Across the valley. A car barreled down a narrow road, throwing dust, and Vic pulled Monk into a squat. Vic zeroed in on the older-model pale green Volvo.

The car halted in front of two armed guards. The driver's door opened and out stepped Sirhan dressed in green camouflage. As if that made him tough? Green camouflage. Please.

"It's him," Monk muttered.

"Yep."

A woman exited the car wearing a burka. She had to be roasting.

"Probably the mistress," Vic said.

He lowered his binoculars and, using his arm, wiped sweat from his forehead. Must have been a hundred degrees. Pakistan in July was a fucking furnace. A headache nagged at him, but at three thousand feet, he couldn't attribute it to an acclimatizing problem. He checked his watch while Monk kept his sight trained on their prey and the cabin.

Nineteen hundred hours. Damn. They still had two hours before nightfall.

"Another guard just came from the back," Monk said.

Vic lifted his binoculars. Three guards assisted Sirhan and his mistress onto the cabin's porch. The guards scanned the area while Sirhan and his guest entered the cabin and shut the door behind them. The single guard went back toward the rear, while his buddies took up their original positions on the porch.

"Three guards," Monk said. "Two in front and one in back."

"That we know of."

Vic lowered his binoculars and stared down into the valley. Long shadows dragged over the craggy boulders, and the descending sun hung just above the razor-edged mountaintops. It glimmered as if shining a warning light.

The odds weren't good.

The cabin's position made it almost unapproachable. The small brick structure was pressed deep into a recess of the mountain, the rear protected by a sheer wall of rock that shot hundreds of feet straight up.

Three guards. Maybe more. Automatic weapons. *Fuck.* The last meal Vic ate tumbled in his belly. Screw the odds. They sucked. Really sucked.

Monk lowered his binoculars and his eyes glowed with an inner fire that came from years on the battlefield.

"This isn't going to be easy," Vic said, taking a deep breath.

"Then let it be hard. You suddenly afraid of hard?"

That earned Monk a flip of the bird, and he smiled. "What's the plan?"

Vic raised his binoculars and focused on the cabin. The slab roof, probably eight or nine feet high, tilted to the right as a result of the structure being built on uneven ground. It hadn't taken an engineering expert to slap that sucker up.

"What's that?" Vic adjusted the focus knob again.

"What?"

"That beam sticking out of the mountainside. Maybe ten or fifteen feet above the roof. It might be part of an old lookout platform."

Monk raised his binoculars. "Got it."

"And that dark line running along the side of the mountain about five feet below the level of the beam. See that?"

"Yep."

"I think there's a ridgeline running along the mountain. It leads right up to the beam. I can't tell if the ridge is wide enough to walk on."

Using his index finger, Vic tried adjusting the lenses again, but he'd already adjusted the hell out of them. *Dammit*. He needed a better view of that ridgeline.

He lowered the binoculars, turned to Monk. "If the ridge is wide enough, it might be our way in. Looks like the wall of the mountain curves just enough to hide someone moving along that line."

"If it is a ridgeline."

Vic brought his gaze back to the valley where, off to the right, an avalanche of boulders had fallen and formed a wall.

"The wall," he began, "doesn't span the entire valley and won't hide us completely from the guard's view, but if we wait until dark, just a couple more hours, we'll be damned hard to see crossing in the lowland. And once we make it to the boulders, we'll be invisible."

"Hello, boys!" Monk replied.

Two hours later, under a clear night sky sparkling with glowing stars and the wan light of a quarter moon, the temperature still hovering above ninety, they inched their way down into the valley toward the wall of boulders.

Vic gave his shirt a good tug to free it from his perspiring body.

The sound of their boots crunched on loose gravel as they inched their way into the valley, but unless they caused a rockslide, the noise wouldn't be detectable from this distance.

Minutes later, they reached the boulders that would provide cover as they crossed the valley. They headed toward the sharp curve of mountain road hidden from the cabin—and the guard's view.

"Let's go over it again," Vic said.

Monk nodded. "You're going to climb up the ridgeline, drop to the roof of the cabin and take out the guards in front."

"Right. And you'll be where?"

Monk jerked a thumb in the direction they just came. "Across the road, behind a boulder, so I can see the cabin."

"After I take out the two in front, you're going to have to haul ass to get to the guy in back."

"Got it."

"And who knows if there are any others inside? We'll have to wing that one."

Monk grinned. "I love a challenge."

Yeah, but Vic was about done with freaking challenges for a while. He stared at the gravel under his battered boots, took a breath and counted ten to clear his mind and get focused. He jerked his head at Monk. "See you on the flip side."

"Yep." He worked his way back to his cover.

Vic, hands on hips, stared up at the ridgeline wondering just how wide it was and if his size thirteen hoof would fit on it.

Only one way to find out.

Under darkening skies, his heart beat a loud, pounding rhythm as he surveyed the ridgeline fifteen feet above his head. The ridge appeared about six inches wide—too narrow to walk on—but would it retain that width all the way to the cabin? And in the darkness, he couldn't see that far to know the answer. He'd have to figure it out when he got there.

And hopefully not fall off.

Sweat slipped down his cheek and he swiped at it. Freakin' heat.

*Okay. Settle down.* What was up with all the drama? He'd done missions like this how many times?

Maybe too many. Thus, his problem. He couldn't just back away like Gina wanted. He'd spent years doing this work. Important work for a country he loved, and abandoning his commitment to freedom seemed flat-out wrong.

But he had to choose. Gina or the job? It should have been a no-brainer. Should have been.

Screw this. Enough with the emotional clutter.

With a solid shake of his head, he unbuttoned his military-grade long-sleeved shirt and stripped it off, leaving only his T-shirt. He flung the shirt over his shoulder. The belt came next and he tied it to the sleeve of his shirt. His eyes settled on the ridgeline one last time while he got his thoughts straight on what he had to do.

*Do it and get home.*

Vic stood on the edge of the ridgeline, one foot in front of the other and one hand clinging to the mountain for balance. Yep. The ridge definitely would not be wide enough to walk on. He glanced down at the cabin roughly sixty yards away. He'd have to inch his way that far.

Son of a bitch.

With his free hand, he grabbed a protruding rock and swung so his belly faced the mountain and his heels hung off the ridge. He'd just work his way down the line. No problem.

*Slow and steady. Watch the rocks under foot. Don't kick any.*

Step.

Step.

Step.

The lone guard stood just below him under the ridge. He needed to get by without a sound.

Step.

No movement from below. Nice.

Five more steps and he'd be there. Slow and steady.

Yes.

Sweat poured down his neck from the effort, his muscles straining as he hung on, but each tiny step brought him closer. Now, directly over the cabin's roof, he reached the iron beam he'd spied earlier and stopped to catch his breath. Quiet the hammering in his head.

His eyes swept the distance to the roof. This could work. The beam sat just at his waist. If he tied his shirt and belt together, they would measure roughly five feet and, with his six-foot-five frame, he could make it to just above the roof and lightly drop down.

If luck was with him.

Which hadn't been happening much lately.

He gave an inaudible grunt.

More fucking emotional clutter. *Get it together. Focus.*

He grasped the beam with his left hand. Using the other hand, he draped one end of his shirt around it and, holding the shirt in place with his thumb, tied it around the beam. Gave it a tug. Good and tight.

He knelt, grabbed the edge of the ridgeline and eased off the side. His fingers bit into the rocky terrain, and the searing pressure of hanging there sliced through his fingertips. Gravel slipped under his grip, tearing into his skin, and he squeezed harder. Momentary panic fired through his bloodstream. *Hang on. Just fucking hang on.*

Crashing to the roof would not give him the approach he wanted, but hell, two hundred and ten pounds felt a lot heavier when dangling by fingertips.

*Concentrate. Grab the belt.* No problem. He'd just let go with his right hand and hang by his left.

One, two, three. He let go. His left shoulder exploded with pain and he tightened his grasp. Let his fingers dig further into the biting ground.

*Don't fall.*

He reached to his right, grasped the belt swaying in the warm night wind and gave it another yank to ensure it would hold his weight. Nothing moved. He grabbed it with both hands and the throbbing in his shoulder eased.

Good God. He let out a breath and the heavy material of his shirt made a slight tearing sound.

He closed his eyes.

Watch the fucker rip. He'd go hurtling down screaming "Honey, I'm home!"

The shirt held.

Hoo-ah.

Hand over hand, his muscles aching, he lowered himself until his hands came to the bottom of the belt and his feet hung barely six inches from the roof. He'd just release the shirt and drop. Landing on his feet was imperative to keep his approach quiet.

Now or never.

He let go.

---

## 28

*Man Law: Never walk away from a fight.*

VIC'S BODY FELL FREE FOR A SECOND UNTIL HE LANDED SQUARE on his feet. Yes. Surrounded by darkness, he waited for any movement from the guards. Could they have heard him? Unlikely.

Before padding across the roof, he double-checked the toys he'd brought with him. Gun, holstered. Check. Piano wire, front pants pocket. Check. Good to go.

From the roof, he spotted a sliver of light through the crack at the bottom of the front door. The two guards stood three feet apart speaking Arabic. Someone had food poisoning. *You boys are gonna have a lot worse than that.*

If they'd just step a foot closer, he'd be all set. Hopefully, it wouldn't take too long. He didn't want to be sitting on this fucking roof, in this fucking heat, sweating his ass off. With any luck, in a few minutes the whole nightmare would end and he could go home.

*Concentrate.* Jeez. Dying tonight was not in the plan.

He surveyed the area where Monk would be hiding, but saw nothing. No surprise there. Monk would be ready though. No doubt about it.

Vic pulled the length of piano wire from his pocket and pulled it taut.

Guard number two stepped closer to his buddy.

Now.

He launched himself off the roof, his right boot landing square on number two's head. *Crack.* Snapped neck. Nasty shit.

He wrapped the wire around number one's neck and pulled with all his strength. His muscles quivered with exhaustion, but all he needed was six seconds for the blood supply to the brain to stop and this fucker would be dead.

Four, five, six. The guard's hands fell limp and Vic dropped him.

Movement in the distance drew his gaze to the right. He sensed Monk fly past him on his way to the back door.

*Get inside.*

*Now.*

He grabbed the doorknob, turned it, winced when it clicked, and pushed the door open. A slight creak, but a radio playing inside the house masked the sound. He slipped into an empty brick hallway. The heat closed in and suffocated him.

The hallway and a warped wood floor stretched the length of the house and he could see the back door from where he stood.

With his back pressed against the wall, Vic pulled his trusty Sig from its holster and shuffled toward a doorway a few feet down the hall to the left. He spun into the darkened room; weapon ready. Nothing. Nobody home.

Clear.

*Deep breath. Move on.* He stepped into the hall and followed the sound of the radio. Just ahead, a second doorway sat on the right. The music must be coming from inside that room. Blood pumped into his brain and his temples throbbed with anticipation.

He glanced toward the rear door leading out to the porch. Where was Monk? He should have handled the guard by now.

*Can't wait. Move on.*

With silent steps, he crossed to the opposite wall and moved toward the second doorway. As he slid along the wall, a male voice speaking—what, Farsi?—wafted in the air. Something about moving the next day. Not if he could help it.

Vic reached the doorway and stopped. He pressed his shoulder against the door frame and spun into the room, gun aimed.

Before he could focus, the barrel of a rifle came crashing down from inside the wall, slamming into his wrist. Pain blasted through his hand and up his arm. He dropped his gun and it skittered along the floor, several feet away, unfired.

*Fuck.*

He grabbed his wrist and looked up just in time to see Sirhan spring out from behind the wall, AK-47 in hand. The bastard must have known he had a visitor, used the radio as bait and then waited alongside the wall. This evil piece of shit wasn't stupid.

Sirhan, now facing Vic, tried to swing his rifle up and get off a shot. Vic lunged, caught the end of the barrel with his right hand, grabbed the butt of the gun with his left, planted his legs and twisted the rifle hard, hoping to dislodge it from

Sirhan's grip. The wiry bastard held tight and Vic wrenched the man off his feet, whipping him in a circle. Sirhan landed on the floor flat on his back, still holding the weapon.

Vic straddled his chest and clung to the rifle, pressing it toward Sirhan's face, but the smaller man possessed shocking strength and pushed back. Vic, grinding his teeth, pushed harder.

*Crush.*

*His.*

*Skull.*

For one brief instant, Sirhan let go of the rifle with his right hand and snapped off a vicious punch to Vic's face, sending him reeling. Warm blood oozed from his lip. The little fucker packed a wicked right hook.

Sirhan scrambled backward on his elbows, grabbed the rifle and struggled to one knee.

*Shit.*

Vic lunged forward and kicked the rifle out of Sirhan's hands, into a far corner of the room.

A choking fury rose inside Vic. He should go for his Sig. He was closer to it now than Sirhan. He came to kill the son of a bitch, but suddenly he didn't want it to be so quick. Not after the terror he'd inflicted on Gina and the kids.

Not after Tiny.

No, Vic wanted to put his hands on this evil monster and feel his life depart.

He took a step back and allowed Sirhan to rise to his feet. They must be alone in the cabin. Otherwise additional guards would have already been to Sirhan's side. "Get up, you piece of shit."

For a second, Sirhan stared at Vic, baffled. His eyes shifted to the Sig. *Not a chance, asshole.* Then the psychotic prick smiled and rose to his feet, his fists clenched.

"Surprised?" Vic asked, raising his fists. "Surprised I'd give your weak ass a fighting chance?"

Vic sure was, but he needed to pound out the anger consuming him.

They squared off in a fighter's stance, circling slowly. A smile spread across Sirhan's lips and darkness settled into his glazed eyes. Insanity at its worst. He grinned, and harsh grunts came from deep within his throat.

They moved to the center of the room and Vic gave a sideways glance into the quiet hallway.

He shot forward, snapped a hard right to Sirhan's head, and pain fired through his banged-up wrist. His opponent slipped the punch and darted to his left...laughing.

*Laughing.*

Fucker.

Vic gave a nod, surprised at the man's quickness. He caught a glimpse of something over Sirhan's shoulder out in the hall, a shadow maybe. Sirhan capitalized on his distraction and hammered him with a kick to the chest. Vic's lungs strained from abuse and he staggered back, hands up, protecting his face.

Sirhan charged forward and threw a punch, but Vic ducked his head right, and the blow grazed his left cheek and ear.

Sirhan pivoted and drove a knee deep into his lower stomach.

*Whoosh.* The air left his body and Vic, off balance, doubled over, pain biting into his gut. He hunkered back, lowering his arms to protect his stomach. Recover. A few seconds...just a few seconds.

Sirhan charged again, leaping into the air, the soles of his boots aimed directly at Vic's face.

*No way, asshole.*

He drew a deep powerful breath, held it and, squelching the pain in his stomach, sidestepped. As Sirhan flew past, Vic lifted an elbow, spun, and slammed it to the back of his neck.

Sirhan hit the floor and Vic pounced. They rolled in a tangle of flailing arms and kicking legs until they came to a stop. Vic on top, raining down punches, watching the blood spew from Sirhan's face.

Another roll had Sirhan on top, sending down his own fisted missiles.

*Legs. Use the legs.*

With the crazed man straddling him, Vic lifted his legs, wrapped them around Sirhan's neck and, with everything thing he had, yanked them back toward the floor.

Sirhan screamed, rocketing onto the wooden floor where he lay in a boneless heap. Then, like a jack-in-the-box, he sprang to his feet.

The resilient little bastard wouldn't give up and clearly knew his way around a street fight. Vic shot up, his breath heaving, and they faced off again.

Sirhan tackled Vic at the waist. They went down hard and pain exploded through his tailbone.

Vic grunted. Crap. That hurt.

Sirhan struggled to his feet. *And here we go again.* Vic rolled to his side, forced himself up and lunged forward, grabbing Sirhan at the throat with both hands and squeezing.

He had him this time. Every ounce of rage he harbored poured through his hands as he squeezed.

Sirhan's dark eyes filled with hate and he narrowed them for a second before he slammed an elbow across Vic's forehead. Twice.

The room spun in a dizzying circle and he crashed to the

floor, his head throbbing and stomach churning. Vomit rose into his throat and he swallowed it back.

*Dammit.*

He had to kill this fucker before he ran out of what little energy he had left.

A warm stream of blood ran down his face and Vic reached up, touched two deep lacerations on his head.

He swiped at his forehead, blinked through blood-gummed eyelashes, but all he could see was Sirhan's shapeless form moving toward him.

Nuh-uh. No way.

Vic struggled to one knee, tried to raise his hands, but another blow to his jaw sent him sprawling. Down, flat on his back, the room around him darkened for a second, and his head lolled sideways as the pain dragged him to a state of oblivion.

He shook his head to clear the fog.

*No—fuck no.* The room flashed back. The blood from his forehead ran down behind each ear and his vision cleared. He rolled left just as Sirhan came crashing down with a boot. He raised his other boot, but Vic caught him at the toe and ankle and twisted hard.

Sirhan hit the floor face-first and his nose splattered like an overripe tomato. Vic spun to his feet and started forward.

Movement. Left.

Sirhan's mistress bolted through the open doorway, shrieking at him, her eyes filled with madness. Arm raised high and screaming, she gripped a large knife as she charged Vic.

What. The. Fuck.

No way he wanted to kill a woman, but he wasn't about to be butchered either.

He held his breath, braced himself for the next round.

His fatigued arms hung loose at his sides and he tried to raise them. No juice. Damn, they wanted to fall off. And forget about the wrist.

Forcing his body to move, he sidestepped her charge, caught her arm, spun her around and pulled her into his chest. He wrenched the knife from her hand as she screamed obscenities at him.

"Crazy bitch," he muttered as she tried to reach back and scratch his face and eyes.

He shot a glance at Sirhan and found him standing across the room, the Sig in hand. The crafty asshole held the gun out, wiping a thick smear of blood across his cheek and into his hair.

The prick was going to kill him with his own gun.

## 29

*Man Law: Never give the enemy an easy kill.*

VIC RAISED THE KNIFE TO THE WOMAN'S THROAT. "DROP THE gun, or she dies."

Through a blood-splattered face, Sirhan smiled.

Pure insanity.

He raised the gun higher and squeezed off a round. The bullet tore into the top of the woman's head and she collapsed in Vic's arms like a puppet with its strings cut.

Sirhan smiled again. "You think I cared about that whore?"

Not liking the odds of a knife against a gun, Vic adjusted the woman's body, trying to prop it up as a shield.

Sirhan laughed.

The burning wrath flying through Vic should have incinerated him. He loathed this maniac in a way he never thought possible.

Then at the doorway, Monk spun into the room, gun raised.

"To your right," Vic yelled.

Too late.

Sirhan whipped toward Monk, pointed his gun, and fired. Monk howled, grabbed his stomach and fell to the floor.

"Vic...Vic," he growled, writhing on the floor. He bit his lower lip and grimaced before sliding his gun across the floor.

*Grab the gun.*

In one quick motion, Vic dropped the woman and dove to the floor, slamming his forearm against the hard wood. His already banged-up wrist gave way as bullets whizzed above him. Shit. Broken. He rolled to the gun, grabbed it with his good hand and came to his knees firing.

*Blam. Blam. Blam.*

Sirhan's head jerked when the first bullet caught him under the chin. The second disappeared into his ruined nose. The third bullet blew the top of his head off.

He fell like a bag of shit.

Vic dropped to his elbows, shook off the aches plaguing him and said a silent thanks for practicing shooting with his non-dominant hand. He stole a look at his friend and charged to his side. Blood soaked Monk's shirt, converting it to a darker shade of tan.

*Not again. Fuck. Not again.*

He tore at the shirt to inspect the wound and Monk winced. "Ah, crap, that hurts. The son of a bitch better be dead."

"You bet. One-way ticket to hell."

Vic scanned Monk's bare stomach. Just above his waist and to the right was a clean bullet hole.

"Listen," he said, "I need to roll you to your side. See if the bullet exited."

Monk nodded. Vic stripped off his undershirt and wadded a corner into a knot. "Bite on this."

He opened his mouth and Vic placed the knot of fabric between his teeth. Monk clamped down and closed his eyes.

As gently as possible Vic rolled him over and Monk howled from pain.

"Sorry," he said, "but it's a clean exit wound. Not bleeding."

Meaning, no major organs hit. *Thank you.* The tension in his shoulders shattered. Monk probably felt like shit, but he'd be all right.

He tugged his shirt from Monk's mouth. "You'll live, asshole."

"Gee, thanks."

"Yeah, well, at least the little bastard didn't try to kill you with your own gun."

Monk forced a smile and closed his eyes. "It hurts too much to even laugh."

Vic squeezed his shoulder and waited for him to open his eyes. "Here's the deal. I'll get you to the car, but it'll hurt like hell."

"That's okay. I'll kill you for it later. With your own gun."

Vic grunted. "Everybody's a comedian. Let's get the hell out of here."

"*THE BODIES ARE PILING UP.*"

*Vic closed his eyes. He couldn't look at Tiny's head. Not with chunks of brain matter hanging from his open skull, the other half matted and sticky with oozing blood.*

*Tiny swiped at the red liquid dripping down his neck. "Damn blood won't stop."*

Vic flinched. His subconscious screamed at him to wake up, but sleep held him hostage in that half asleep, half-awake state where the images are abundant and all too real.

Dreaming.

He had to be dreaming.

"Tiny?" He heard himself say.

*"Yeah, it's me. I'm still here, but the bodies are piling up. Just look at 'em."*

*Tiny motioned toward the stack of bodies behind him. Stacks and stacks of bloody bodies, some with bullet holes, some with slashed throats and all with their eyes open. Sirhan sat on top, laughing.*

*"Who's next?" Tiny jerked his thumb to where Gina, the kids, Mike and Roxann stood. "Will it be one of them?"*

Vic clawed his way from the dream and came awake with a gasping breath.

Holy shit.

His gaze darted around the plane's cabin, took in the dark leather seats and beige walls. His heart pumped like it would beat itself to death. The corporate jet. Vic had fallen asleep on the flight home.

"What?" Monk unbuckled his seat belt and, trying to protect his taped-up midsection, rose from the seat.

Vic shifted, raised his right arm to wipe the sweat from his face and clunked himself with the temporary cast on his wrist. *Ow.* If his face weren't so banged up, it wouldn't have hurt.

Fucking nightmares. Fucking Sirhan. Suddenly, the torment of the last weeks balled itself into a flaming mess in the pit of his stomach and every moment of anxiety he'd corralled burst free. Gina, Lily, Tiny, Baldridge, Conlin. Sirhan.

One by one, he could feel each compartmentalized piece snickering at him as his emotional armor fell apart.

"Nightmare?"

Vic, still seated, opened his mouth to speak, but a screaming roar came out.

What the hell? The sound of his own yelling careened in his head, but he couldn't stop. *Make it stop.*

He pushed out of his seat to work off the anger, but his knees buckled and he crumbled back into the seat. Crap. Total fucking meltdown.

"Goddammit!"

He stared at the seat in front of him, tried to focus on the brown leather, but the rage kept coming. Taunting him. He tensed his forearms and released. Nothing. Shit. *Move.* He had to move or he'd tear something apart.

"Vic," Monk yelled. The sound of his voice penetrated, but nothing registered except the swirling, scorching anger. Vic lifted his leg and rammed his foot into the seat in front him. The seat broke free and flew against the wall.

He inhaled through his nose and focused on getting his quaking body under control. *Relax. Get it together. Concentrate.*

Staring up at the ceiling, he ignored the caged-in sensation overtaking him. Trapped. In this fucking plane. He needed to get out. Get out and fucking pummel something. Crazy, ballistic fury spewed and his eyes bulged with pain. Ah, shit. He opened his mouth, sucked in air and a wheezing sound filled him. *Dammit.* Nothing. His chest so tight and squeezing, squeezing, squeezing. Goddammit, he couldn't get any air.

"Vic," Monk yelled louder, but he knew if he came too close, he'd get an ass whooping.

The cockpit door opened and one of the pilots stuck his head out. "What's wrong?"

Monk blocked the pilot before he came out. "We're fine. I'll take care of it."

As fast as his injury would allow, he hustled back and stood over Vic, snapping his fingers in front of his face. "Are you awake? Look at me."

Awake? Yes. *I might be dying. Fucking elephant on my chest.* Vic gave his head a solid shake and stared at the wall. He gripped the arm of his seat until stinging pain shot up his fingers. *Alive. Good.* He inhaled and his battered lungs did their job. *Air. Not dying.* He let his heaving, spent body sink back into the chair.

"Are you all right?"

*No.* "Meltdown."

"Yeah. A grand one." Monk patted his shoulder. "Take it easy. I'll get you a drink."

Monk winced from moving too fast and slowly walked to the galley.

On his way back, the plane lurched, and Monk handed him the bottle of water before sliding into his seat to buckle up.

Vic glanced down at his dangling seat belt and did the same. They'd just killed people and they were buckling up for safety. Ironic, but he wasn't sure why. Maybe someday he'd laugh about it.

"We're almost home," Monk said. "Maybe another hour."

Outside, the dark sky called to him and he stared out for a second. Goddamn blackness. Drowning in it. He checked his watch. Twenty-three hundred hours.

"We did the right thing," Monk said. "The world will literally be a better place without Sirhan and his pack."

And who was Monk trying to convince? Vic wasn't sure. He hated the entire sordid thing. The smell of blood, the death. His stomach pitched, and he swallowed. He couldn't stand it anymore. Too much had happened over these weeks.

"I'm done."

"What?"

"I can't do this anymore. I can't watch people die. The nightmares, the living on the edge and getting banged up all the time. I'm done."

"You need a break."

Vic closed his eyes. "Yeah. A permanent one."

"You're serious?"

"Bet your ass. I've got a shot at a life here and I'm not blowing it."

"Gina?"

"Yep."

"Well, o-*kay*." Monk sounded skeptical.

"You lost a marriage to this life. When you think back, was it worth it?"

"Hell, no. Which is why I don't think back."

Vic sat forward. "I don't want to feel that way, and I can't let her go before I even know what'll happen."

Monk shot him a grin. "A sane man wouldn't, but no one ever accused you of being sane."

He held up his middle finger and Monk laughed.

"She's good for you," he said. "Steady. Not a lot of drama. She does what needs to be done and doesn't make a fuss. You're not good with fuss."

Vic snorted. "No shit there."

But was it too late? Would she even take the chance? Could he convince her he could stick?

He had to. He just lived through hell so they'd have a fighting chance. He couldn't let her call it quits. No way.

If it took the rest of his days, he'd prove to her he could make changes.

## 30

*Man Law: Never let a good woman get away.*

GINA STOOD AT THE BASE OF HER BATTERED OAK STAIRS practicing her deep breathing. In the next hour she could treat herself to a lakefront bike ride—alone—and think some things through.

First, she had to get these kids moving and out of the damned house. "Matthew, just put your shoes on. Uncle Michael will be here in five minutes and I'm not in the mood for his yelling.

"Bad enough I'm yelling," she muttered to herself and went back to the dining room table to help Lily clean up her puzzle.

A knock on the back door. Could be Billy. Her dearest brother refused to do away with the round-the-clock security until Vic gave the all clear. Not only did the man break her heart, she had to wait for his approval to lead a normal life. And who knew when that would be? She clamped her teeth together.

She went to the door, pushed the curtain to the side and jumped backward. Her head reeled as every emotion took hold.

Vic.

Home.

Safe.

A sudden rush of relief flooded her. She bent over, braced her hands on her legs and let the joy settle in. She'd allow herself this one minute of happiness before the overwhelming sadness of Tiny's death landed on her again.

She stood tall, tugged at the bottom of her shirt and opened the door. The man looked like a truck had run him down. The worst of it was his face. Two large and stitched gashes on his forehead, a fading bruise on his jaw and his bottom lip appeared to have been split. His short hair had grown a half inch since she'd seen him last, and dark shadows lay under his eyes.

"Hi." She waved him in. "You're a mess."

He half smiled, and his gaze drilled into hers as he crossed the threshold. She inclined her head toward the cast on his right arm. "What happened?"

"I broke my wrist."

"Rough trip, I guess."

She really didn't want to know the details. Or did she? He wouldn't tell her, anyway.

He smiled, but not his normal high-wattage one. Even his smile was worn out.

"I didn't see you in the office today," she said.

"Mike and I had some business out of the building, and then I had a doctor's appointment." He held up his broken wrist. "They put the cast on."

"Vic!" Lily rushed from the dining room doorway; her eyes filled with a light Gina hadn't seen in the past twelve days.

She hurled herself at him and he backed against the counter to absorb the brunt of the attack. He caught her but winced at the effort. That had to hurt.

A breath of air seeped from Gina, taking with it the initial happiness that came with seeing him. A couple of weeks ago this little scene could have been the start of something special. Now she didn't know what it was. She smiled in spite of herself. Her little girl wore a grin, and sometimes that was all she needed.

"How are you, sweet pea?" Vic hugged Lily tight.

"I'm good. I missed you. Did you get my messages?"

Gina straightened. Lily had called him? She had no idea.

"I did," Vic said, "but I was out of the country. I got back late last night, so I couldn't come see you."

"That's okay. I'm just glad you're back. Uncle Michael is taking us for pizza. Do you want to come? What happened to your face?"

Gina grabbed Lily from behind. "Honey, let's not bombard Vic with questions. Let him breathe."

Their eyes connected again and held. Something about him had changed. His eyes seemed different. Not as intense. Maybe Tiny's death had broken him. Of course, she'd never know, because Vic didn't talk about his feelings.

"She's okay," he said, hugging Lily again. "I had a little accident, but I'm fine."

The front door slammed.

"I'm here," Michael yelled. "And I'm double parked. Let's get it in gear."

"Ooh, gotta go." Lily wiggled out of Vic's grasp.

He grinned. "Abandoned again."

Gina rolled her eyes. "Don't even."

"Can I sit?"

He wanted to stay. He hadn't come by just to see Lily. Should she even let herself start to think there might be hope?

"Sure, let me get the kids out the door and I'll be back. Do you need Michael for anything?"

"No. He's pissed at me."

She glanced back at him. "What for this time?"

"I'll tell you when you get back."

Maybe, Gina thought as she walked back to the kitchen after seeing the kids off, he finally wanted to talk. Just because they couldn't be a couple didn't mean she couldn't be his friend. They had a bond now. Surely, they could figure out a way to move forward.

Sliding into the chair next to him, she examined his wounds. Disaster. "How are you?"

He braced his chin in his good hand. "I had a meltdown on the plane."

She sat back. "*You* had a meltdown?"

"Yep. Total annihilation. I broke Mike's plane. That's why he's pissed at me."

"What happened?"

"I wrecked one of the seats. Knocked the sucker right off its base."

Reaching for his hand right now would not be a smart move. They both knew what happened when they touched each other, and raging-hot sex, at this point, would do them no good. Touching him had to be off-limits. She wanted to, though. Admitting weakness must be destroying him, and she couldn't offer comfort in the way she would have liked.

Yep, they were back to being stuck, just like before they'd gotten involved.

"Anyway, we're going to pull the security. It's over now."

Over. Just like that? "You're sure?"

He held his hands toward his battered face. "Totally. Sirhan won't be bothering us again."

Screw not touching him. She reached for his hand and let its warmth work through her, processing the idea that Vic had probably killed Sirhan. She forced the thought away. "Thank you."

He jerked his head and tapped his other hand on the table. "Will you take a ride with me?"

A ride? Not a good idea. Unless...

"Is it going to change something?" she asked.

*Let him say yes. Please.*

He stared at her a minute.

"I'm not pressuring you," she said, "but you know how I feel. I don't think it's a good idea for us to spend time together right now. We need to figure out how to be just friends."

He shrugged. "It might change something. It would be up to you."

A tingle of hope wormed its way around her heart. "I'm confused."

"Take a ride with me and maybe it'll make sense."


"WHAT DO YOU THINK?" VIC ASKED.

He'd parked on the shoulder of the quiet country road, and they stood before rows of thick green corn stalks. Soon the stalks would be as tall as Gina. The evening sun cast shadows across the property and the wind rustled the leaves on the plants.

She scanned the area. "Uh, it's a cornfield."

He wiped a sweaty hand across his T-shirt. Nervous.

Comical given the life he'd led. All in all, his future sprawled in front of him and, now that he'd made the decision, he hoped Gina would want to be part of it.

"It's my new office."

She snorted. "You're going to be a farmer?"

*There's a scary fucking thought.* He laughed. "Hell no. I haven't gone completely off the rails. We're building a training center so we can teach people to do what we do."

After studying the field, she faced him. "Who's we?"

"Mike and me. We went to the bank today and signed the papers. We're fifty-fifty partners. It's my baby, though. All he wants to do is count the money."

She reached out and grabbed his hand. "I don't understand what you're doing. This is sudden. Have you thought it through?"

She had no idea how much he'd thought about it. He'd never discussed it with her, so how could she know? And wasn't that what she'd been begging him for? To talk to her?

"You think it's a reaction to Tiny dying?"

"I do."

"It's not. Mike and I have been talking about this for over a year, but we didn't have the acreage we needed. Mike met with the owner of this property last year and told him we wanted it. The guy came to him a few weeks ago and he made the deal."

She drew back an inch. "I didn't know that."

Weighty sadness dropped on him and he breathed in. "Maybe Tiny dying pushed me to finalize everything, but I'd been thinking about it. A lot."

He surveyed the ground, thought about what he needed to say before looking back at her.

"I know I screw up. I know I'm a challenge. I *know* I'll never talk as much as you want me to, but I'll stay put. All this crap with Sirhan brought things into perspective. Having you and the kids in my life is more important than playing cowboy. I know that. I knew it before I left for Pakistan, but I had to end it. I wanted us to have an honest shot at making this work, and the constant pressure of Sirhan being out there would have been a problem. It's not an issue anymore."

She blinked a couple of times, put her hands over her face and slid them down her cheeks. "Are you sure you can do this? I need you to be sure. I can't go on a roller coaster with you. You're either here or you're not."

He'd expected that. Even prepared for it, but suddenly everything he'd rehearsed seemed inadequate. He peered out over the thousand acres of property he now owned, and his stomach pitched. He owned property. And it wasn't for his mother. Look out, world, he was settling down.

He turned to Gina, waited for her gaze to lock with his before he spoke. "Right now, I figure I'm sixty-five, maybe seventy percent man. With your help, I think we can get me the rest of the way. I'm not perfect and I've got a ton of baggage, but I love you. I love your kids. Even the one that's a pain in the ass. And I'd like to be around for them. I'll never be their dad, but maybe I can help. That alone tells me I'm ready for this." He waved a hand toward the field. "All of it. It just took me a little while to figure it out."

Her eyebrows hit her hairline, but she had an ear-to-ear smile. A good sign. All this talking must have sent her into a state of euphoria.

He ran a hand over her soft curls. "The thing I know for sure right now is I want to be around for the next fifty years, and when I die, I want to die in your arms, not with some lunatic staring me down."

She stepped forward, slipped those arms he wanted to

die in around him, and his heart hammered. Nothing beat the feel of her body wrapped around him. He breathed in the scent of her lemon shampoo and kissed the top of her head.

With her cheek against his chest, she ran her hands over his back. Up and down, up and down, up and down. Was this a yes or a no? The longer she stayed quiet, the more he feared a no. This could be the equivalent of hanging naked from a fucking flagpole.

"Gina, please say something. Tell me to go screw myself if you have to, but say something."

"Okay." She smiled up at him. "I love you. And the only person I want you screwing is me."

Relief swarmed and the tension eased from his body. He plastered her face with sloppy kisses because he suddenly understood contentment. And maybe even liked it. "When I'm with you it feels like home, and that hasn't happened since I left my aunt's house eighteen years ago. Thank you."

She pulled him close. "I missed you. I wasn't sure I'd recover from you."

He laughed. "You still may not, but if anyone can handle me, it's you. You always give me another try."

"Well," she sighed, "who am I to reject someone with so much potential?"

"Oh please." He gave her a light shove and they both laughed. "Speaking of potential, my mother is coming to visit."

Her mouth flopped open and he laughed. "Yes, I said my mother. Since you two are such good friends, you get to help me entertain her. I don't even know what she likes to do."

Gina slapped her hands against her cheeks, but amusement lit her eyes. "Who are you and what have you done with the man I love?"

"Listen, honey. You created this monster and you're stuck with it."

"I'll help you with your mother. On one condition."

Ugh. Conditions. Everything had a cost. He'd have to suck it up.

"What is it?"

"You have to promise to spend some time alone with her, talk."

"But—"

She held up a hand. "And I mean really talk to her. Tell her you're angry and let her explain. Then you need to let it go. You're a grown man and you're capable of a lot more than you let yourself believe."

Well, okay, then. She told him. "Yeah, well..." was the only lame-ass answer he could come up with. Shit. He'd become a wuss. Next she'd have him vacuuming. He shuddered.

Gina laughed and the sound echoed in his head. He slung an arm over her shoulder and they stood staring at the setting sun and one hell of a huge cornfield. His cornfield. No. Their cornfield. He'd build them a life with this property. A good life, where he could come home every night, have dinner with the family and listen to the kids fight or whine about homework. Maybe he'd miss playing cowboy, but the love of a good woman couldn't be beat. He knew that now.

"We've got a future in this field, babe," he said.

She tucked her hand in the back pocket of his shorts. "A big one."

He nodded and puckered his lips. "Say, how do you feel about babies?"

She slid into the wide-eyed oh-no look. "As long as they're someone else's, I love them."

"Hmmm," he said. "We'll have to work on that response."

## 31

*Man Law: Never avoid competition.*

NOVEMBER

"THIS IS JUST TOO MUCH," GINA SAID FROM HER SPOT ALONG the wall of St. Theresa's Catholic School gym.

Daddies and daughters wandered between different events, waiting for the assigned group to compete while moms and family members watched from the sidelines. Of course, Michael, being Michael, couldn't resist getting in the middle of it and promptly made his way to the center of the gym for a strategy session with Vic and Lily. Matthew stood next to them, throwing his two cents in.

"I think they're getting a little carried away," Roxann said.

Gina laughed. "No, really?"

Poor Lily stood between the two men, her head swinging

back and forth as they engaged in a heated debate. When Lily held up her finger and tried to butt in, Vic put his hand on her shoulder but kept jabbering with Michael. She turned toward Gina and shrugged.

Matthew didn't fare much better, because when he said something, Vic and Michael each put a hand on his chest and shoved him away. Matt laughed and strolled off. Male bonding was a complex and nutty thing.

"This has been going on at my house all week," Gina said. "They've been running a mini boot camp in my driveway."

"Lily doesn't seem to mind."

"She loves it. She came to breakfast this morning and announced she'd—" Gina made air quotes, "—'pound Misty Franklin into the ground.' Where do you think that came from?"

Roxann covered her mouth to hide a laugh. "I'm sorry. You're right. Maybe he's gone too far, but it is funny."

"Someday I'll laugh."

She huffed and, seeing movement next to her, shifted to see Dora Franklin making her way over. Her insides sunk to the floor.

"Oh, crap. Here comes Dora. I can only imagine the shots she'll take at me."

Roxann casually glanced over Gina's shoulder. "The one with the baggy jeans and tunic?"

"Yep. That's her. She used to tell everyone I dressed like a tramp. That's changed since you got a hold of my wardrobe, but still, it wasn't right."

"Hello, Gina," Dora said, her chirpy fake-nice voice grinding Gina's nerves.

She smiled big. "Hi, Dora. How are you?"

The woman's bright orange hair and blue eye shadow could have lit up Times Square. Good Lord.

"Well, your *boyfriend* seems to be enjoying the day."

Ugh. Shot number one. Gina held up her left hand so the flaming bitch could take a gander at the boulder on her finger.

"Fiancé. I wouldn't let him do this with Lily if he were only my boyfriend."

"I see," Dora said, again with the fake smile.

And... *Did this bitch just tilt her head and check out Vic's ass?* Well, who could blame her, but to be so blatant about it?

Besides, Gina couldn't picture old Dora and her four-hundred-pound husband having any good, healthy sex. Sex would probably give the man a heart attack.

"Vic does have a competitive nature, but this is nothing," she said. "You should see what the man can do in the bedroom." She raised both hands and fanned herself. "Whew! It's a wonder my body hasn't burst into flames by now. That's how hot it gets."

Roxann bit down on her bottom lip.

Dora cleared her throat.

"Yep," she said, "I hit the jackpot with him. I mean, just look at him. Hot, hot, hot."

A burst of laughter finally erupted from Roxann, and Gina shrugged. "I can't help it if the man is insatiable. And that big, beautiful body is all mine."

Dora sucked in a breath, spun on her heel and stormed off.

"You are rotten," Roxann said. "Not that she didn't deserve it."

"That'll give her something to gossip about."

Gina focused on Vic, bent over tying a bandanna around his and Lily's legs for the three-legged race.

Lily swung her head toward Gina with a big toothy smile. A few of her curls had come loose from her hair band, and she tucked them behind her ear. She had one hand on Vic's shoulder for balance, and the sight of her happy baby smacked Gina in the chest. Lily's dream of competing in the Daddy-Daughter Olympics had come true.

They moved up to the starting tape, Lily's gaze firmly planted on the finish line. Gina swallowed hard. The girl would be crushed if they didn't win. When the whistle blew, Lily and Vic took off in perfect step. They sailed ahead of the pack, but Lily kept her eyes focused ahead. When they reached the finish line, Lily glanced back to see Misty and her dad barely halfway there. She raised her arms in victory and let out a whoop. Vic cracked up and loosened the bandanna binding them together. The two of them did a double high five along with some weird butt wiggle they'd come up with as a celebration dance.

A tingle shot up Gina's arms.

"Now, this is embarrassing," she said, but couldn't help giggling.

Her baby would have a daddy she'd remember.

Daddy-Daughter Olympics. Who would have thought it would be such a great day?

And that *Vic* would be the daddy?

God help her.

Want more of the Private Protectors series? Read on to enjoy an excerpt from *Negotiating Point*.

# NEGOTIATING POINT

BY ADRIENNE GIORDANO

Enjoy an excerpt from *Negotiating Point*, book three in the
Private Protectors Series:

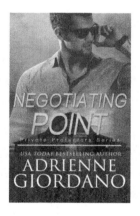

Chapter One

At ten-twenty, Gavin stepped into Mike Taylor's office and
found his boss sitting at his pristine, glass-topped desk, his
sleeves rolled to his elbows and his dark hair sticking up in
the back.

He checked his watch. Yep. Ten-twenty.

*I'm screwed.*

The man's appearance was typically as neat as his office. His hair sticking up? This early? In Mike's OCD world? Unacceptable.

Whatever Gavin had been summoned for had to be a disaster. Stabbing pin pricks crawled up his neck. He shifted his gaze left. Vic Andrews, Taylor Security's executive vice president, leaned against the windowsill with his arms crossed, eyes narrowed and a general I'm-pissed-off-at-the-world aura.

*Screwed.*

Gavin stepped forward. "What's up?"

Mike held his hands prayerlike in front of him, his fingers mashed together until his veins popped.

*Screwed in a big way.*

Vic boosted off the windowsill. "Roxann has been kidnapped."

*Bam!* Forget the warm-up. Gavin threw his shoulders back and those pin pricks turned to dagger stabs. Had he heard right? He shifted to Mike. "Your Roxann?"

Mike nodded.

"Have they made contact? Ransom?"

"Not yet. I got a call a few minutes ago. They said no cops and to expect communication in the next hour."

"Where'd they grab her?"

Mike looked down, shook his head and scrubbed his hands over his face. "I don't know. We left together this morning. She was heading to the lake house to get ready for the Fourth of July party on Saturday. I've got Gizmo tracing her car."

That wouldn't do them any good. Even the most inexperienced kidnapper would know a high-end Mercedes would have factory-installed tracking. Couple that with the car being owned by the man who ran not only Chicago's, but one of the nation's most elite private security companies and it was a no-brainer they'd be able to locate the car. The kidnappers probably abandoned it somewhere. Mike knew that and Gavin wouldn't voice it.

"Are you considering calling the FBI?"

Vic moved to the side of the desk. "No feds."

Gavin ignored him. "Mike?"

"No FBI."

*Lost that round.*

"The FBI," Mike continued, "has to play by the rules. We don't. I want my wife back without having to deal with red tape."

"Damn straight," Vic added. "We got everything we need. We find her and we get her. End of story."

Gavin finally looked at him. "End of story? What's wrong with you? You and your merry men charging in there with your flash bangs and weapons will escalate the situation."

"Screw that," Vic said. "These assholes won't know what hit them. Once we find her, we'll be in there so fast they won't have time to draw on us. Besides, what the hell do we need the FBI for when we have you?"

Gavin breathed deep. A sound argument considering, prior to six months ago, he'd spent the last twelve years as an FBI hostage negotiator. "Has it occurred to you that we are not in some war-torn country? You're talking about a takedown on U.S. soil. In case you weren't aware, if someone gets shot, there are laws against that sort of thing."

Mike put both hands up. "Enough." He dragged his gaze from Vic to Gavin. "Look, Gavin, all due respect, I'm not calling the feds."

"Thank you," Vic said.

"But we're not going tactical either. *Yet.* Gavin will negotiate her release."

There it was. The assignment of his career.

"Mike," Vic said, "why waste time trying to head-shrink our way out of this?"

Jab number one. Gavin folded his arms, let the anger inside flash and burn before reacting. Considering Vic was married to Mike's sister and his own emotions were likely in play, he'd give him a pass on the head-shrinker comment. "We're not *head-shrinking*. We don't know who these people are or what they want. Let's figure that out and then make a plan."

# ALSO BY ADRIENNE GIORDANO

## PRIVATE PROTECTORS SERIES

Risking Trust

Man Law

Negotiating Point

A Just Deception

Relentless Pursuit

Opposing Forces

## THE LUCIE RIZZO MYSTERY SERIES

Dog Collar Crime

Knocked Off

Limbo (novella)

Boosted

Whacked

Cooked

Incognito

The Lucie Rizzo Mystery Series Box Set 1

The Lucie Rizzo Mystery Series Box Set 2

The Lucie Rizzo Mystery Series Box Set 3

## THE ROSE TRUDEAU MYSTERY SERIES

Into The Fire

## HARLEQUIN INTRIGUES

The Prosecutor

The Defender

The Marshal

The Detective

The Rebel

## JUSTIFIABLE CAUSE SERIES

The Chase

The Evasion

The Capture

## CASINO FORTUNA SERIES

Deadly Odds

## JUSTICE SERIES w/MISTY EVANS

Stealing Justice

Cheating Justice

Holiday Justice

Exposing Justice

Undercover Justice

Protecting Justice

Missing Justice

Defending Justice

## SCHOCK SISTERS MYSTERY SERIES w/MISTY EVANS

1st Shock

2nd Strike

3rd Tango

## STEELE RIDGE SERIES w/KELSEY BROWNING

**& TRACEY DEVLYN**

Steele Ridge: The Beginning

Going Hard (Kelsey Browning)

Living Fast (Adrienne Giordano)

Loving Deep (Tracey Devlyn)

Breaking Free (Adrienne Giordano)

Roaming Wild (Tracey Devlyn)

Stripping Bare (Kelsey Browning)

Enduring Love (Browning, Devlyn, Giordano)

Vowing Love (Adrienne Giordano)

**STEELE RIDGE SERIES: The Kingstons w/KELSEY BROWNING**

**& TRACEY DEVLYN**

Craving HEAT (Adrienne Giordano)

Tasting FIRE (Kelsey Browning)

Searing NEED (Tracey Devlyn)

Striking EDGE (Kelsey Browning)

Burning ACHE (Adrienne Giordano)

# ACKNOWLEDGMENTS

First off, a big whopping thank-you to my husband for his love and support while I chased my dream. The journey hasn't been easy, but we got there together. I love you. To my mom for being an outstanding example of everything a mother should be and for always believing my time would come. And for the rest of my family, thank you for always giving me a place to land when my brain needs a break.

John and Mara Leach, my dynamic duo, you have been with me from word one. John humored me when I wanted to bend the law in ways it shouldn't go and Mara always proofread the results. Thank you for traveling this wonderful road with me. To my amazing friend, Theresa Stevens, there are no words for your generosity. You continually push me to do more with my writing and I am so very grateful for your presence in my life. To my critique partners, Tracey Devlyn, Kelsey Browning and Lucie J. Charles, who talk me through the chaos in my head, I don't know what I'd do without you, and I hope I never have to find out. Milton Grasle, thank you for always being available to brainstorm my action scenes. You help me give them the extra zing that I'd never figure out on my own.

I also owe a thank-you to the members of the Lethal Ladies critique group for the early help on this story and the title idea.

Gina Bernal and the team at Carina Press, thank you for giving my challenging hero a home. I am grateful for the opportunity.

Finally, to my son, who makes me laugh on a daily basis and inspires me to do more. Thank you for the hugs during the tough times and the endless joy you bring to my life. I love you.

# A NOTE TO READERS

Dear reader,

Thank you for reading *Man Law*. I hope you enjoyed it. If you did, please help others find it by sharing it with friends on social media and writing a review.

Sharing the book with your friends and leaving a review helps other readers decide to take the plunge into the world of the Private Protectors. I would appreciate it if you would consider taking a moment to tell your friends how much you enjoyed the story. Even a few words is a huge help. Thank you!

Happy reading!
*Adrienne*

# ABOUT THE AUTHOR

Adrienne Giordano is a *USA Today* bestselling author of over forty romantic suspense and mystery novels. She is a Jersey girl at heart, but now lives in the Midwest with her ultimate supporter of a husband, sports-obsessed son and Elliot, a snuggle-happy rescue. Having grown up near the ocean, Adrienne enjoys paddle-boarding, a nice float in a kayak and lounging on the beach with a good book.

For more information on Adrienne's books, please visit www.AdrienneGiordano.com. Adrienne can also be found on Facebook at http://www.facebook.com/AdrienneGiordanoAuthor, Twitter at http://twitter.com/AdriennGiordano and Goodreads at http://www.goodreads.com/AdrienneGiordano.

Don't miss a new release! Sign up for Adrienne's new release newsletter!

Made in United States
Orlando, FL
26 August 2022

21558030R00192